TH

Paul Grzegorzek joined the ... as a riot medic and metho... demonstrations and enact... ...moved on to plain clothes work on undercover drug operations around the city. While in the police he met Peter James, and became an advisor on the Roy Grace novels. After six years in the police, Paul moved into the defence industry where he became the security manager for government defence projects across the globe. He lives in Brighton with his wife and young son.

@PaulGlaznost

Also by Paul Grzegorzek

The Follow
When Good Men Do Nothing
But for the Grace of God
Flare
Subversive

PAUL GRZEGORZEK
THE FOLLOW

KILLER READS

A division of HarperCollins*Publishers*
www.harpercollins.co.uk

KillerReads
an imprint of HarperCollins*Publishers* Ltd
1 London Bridge Street
London SE1 9GF

www.harpercollins.co.uk

This paperback edition 2019

First published in Great Britain by Endeavour Press 2011

A catalogue record for this book
is available from the British Library

ISBN: 978-0-00-832998-3 (PB)

This novel is entirely a work of fiction.
The names, characters and incidents portrayed in it are
the work of the author's imagination. Any resemblance to
actual persons, living or dead, events or localities is
entirely coincidental.

Set in Minion by
Palimpsest Book Production Limited, Falkirk, Stirlingshire

Printed and bound by CPI Group (UK) Ltd, Croydon, CR0 4YY

MIX
Paper from
responsible sources
FSC
www.fsc.org   FSC C007454

In loving memory of Inspector Andy Parr and WPC 'Aunty' Sue Elliott. Lost but not forgotten.

1

I'd been a copper for eight years the day I became an accessory to murder. But before I tell you about that, I need to go back to the beginning, back to that day in the summer of 2008 that Quentin Davey walked out of court with a grin on his face and the blood of one of my colleagues still on his hands.

The day started much as any other as I left my house on Wordsworth Street in Hove and drove to work, enjoying the morning sun streaming across the seafront. Early summer is my favourite time of year in Brighton, it makes it feel alive with the promise of things yet to come. I hummed along to the Snow Patrol track my MP3 player had selected, my Audi darting through the traffic as if it wasn't there. In no time at all I was in the underground car park of John Street police station, trading jokes with people who were leaving from the night shift, their white shirts crumpled and their faces sagging as they finally shucked off their paperwork for another twelve hours.

I bounded up the stairs and through the locker rooms, then up two more flights of stairs to the first floor reserved for the CID teams and headed through into the DIU office.

The Divisional Intelligence Unit, in my opinion, is where the real heart of policing in Brighton sits. Intelligence from everywhere across the division, from coppers and the public, comes through the office and is sorted for relevance before being passed on to the Intelligence Development Officers: us, the IDOs. Everything involving the police is reduced to a three-letter code.

I strolled into the office, past the picture of our five-a-side team from last year that was still pinned up on the door, and the tension hit me like a slap in the face. The room holds about thirty people, officers and researchers with not a uniform in sight. We're the ones who sneak around town and chase drug dealers, car thieves, rapists and burglars, and it's hard to do that if they can see you coming, so the office was full of jeans and T-shirts, much to the annoyance of everyone else in the building. That morning all of them were muted as if waiting for something bad to happen.

The tension was for a very good reason, a reason that I had been trying hard not to think about. Six weeks earlier, I'd been on a surveillance job with a few others from the office, trying to catch a big-time heroin dealer called Quentin Davey, who lived in Hollingdean.

What we didn't know at the time was that he had just blagged a load of heroin on tick, and that, if he didn't get the money sorted out, he was in big trouble. So when we jumped him, instead of putting his hands up or running away, he pulled a knife and stabbed Jimmy Holdsworth, my partner of three years, piercing a lung and putting him on life support for two weeks before he began to recover.

Of course we'd taken Davey down, but it looked like Jimmy wasn't going to get a payout, as he hadn't been wearing a stab vest – everyone knows you can't wear one on surveillance. Nothing screams copper like a covert vest; you look like the Michelin Man and move about as fast too.

So that day was the day of the court case and I was the star witness, having been inches away when it happened. Every time I thought about it I got butterflies in my stomach and goose-bumps, so I was doing my best not to.

I smiled at our researcher, Sally, as I sank into my chair in the drugs pod. The room is split up into various different pods, or work areas, demarcated by brown felt dividers that stand to about chest height. I glanced around my littered desk, covered in reports both new and old, all filed with the care that only eighteen-hour days can produce. It was a pigsty.

The divider wall next to my computer was covered with pieces of paper, some tacked over others, showing the faces of local criminals, pictures of me and the lads on skiing and fishing holidays and a picture of a huge bride being fed cake by an equally large husband on their wedding day, with the legend 'nom nom nom' printed underneath. I had that up there so that I would see it every time I fancied a doughnut.

I'd been fighting to keep my chest from sagging into my stomach for a while, and it was a battle I was finally winning.

'Anything relevant?' I asked Sally as I waited for my computer to boot up.

She smiled at me as she turned her chair, displaying a heart-shaped face framed by golden curls and eyes that I regularly wanted to fall into. She should have been a model, not a police researcher.

'Not really, Gareth, just a few serials about that BMW in Whitehawk again, and one about dealers in East Street by the taxi rank; they're probably coming over from the YMCA.'

Nothing new there then. Despite the fact that the YMCAs were set up to help people living on the streets, they had quickly become hotbeds of crime, mainly heroin and crack dealing and petty thefts, and you could guarantee that wherever a YMCA opened, the crime rate would rise. They seemed to be filled with people too stupid to realize that you didn't shit on your own doorstep. Not that all of the occupants were like that, some of them were genuinely just down on their luck, but sadly they were tarred with the same brush as the majority.

The hamster that ran my computer finally woke up and started

3

turning the wheel, allowing me to check my emails and update the intelligence sheets before the morning meeting.

The rest of the drugs pod was on a job in Hove, but I was exempt that day because I was giving evidence in court, so I got to do all their reports as well as mine. Not that it was a problem, since the previous day had been a series of dead ends and poor leads that amounted to almost no paperwork for once.

Paperwork is the bane of any copper's existence. The poor bastards downstairs on uniform (and I mean no disrespect, I was one for years) are supposed to run about eight crime reports at a time per officer, as well as respond to calls and make enquiries, assisting the CID teams and generally doing all the other work that no one else has time to do. Most officers I know have somewhere over twenty reports each and are snowed under with paperwork. The truth is, you won't get in trouble for not answering a 999 call, but you can lose your job for not doing your paperwork properly, so officers will turn their radios down and sit in the corner of the office, frantically trying to finish their reports before a sergeant finds them and turfs them out to pick up yet more jobs.

I felt more than lucky that I had managed to find a way into DIU. I had come somewhat of an unusual route, having gone onto Local Support Team, the LST, which specializes in warrants, riots, protests, bashing in doors and violent prisoners. Dealing with the latter, not bashing them in, I should add. After I'd been on the unit for a few months, our remit had changed and we had become half- plain clothes, half-uniform, so you could come in in the morning, do a drugs warrant in uniform, then change into plain clothes and go out hunting scallies in the town centre. I'd quickly discovered that I had an aptitude for the surveillance work, and when I got an attachment to DIU I'd just kind of stayed for a few years, and had no intention of leaving.

I really feel like I have my finger on the pulse of the city, and I probably know as much about what's happening in it as anyone else in the world. It's a funny feeling, but one that I've grown to love.

My inbox was full of pointless emails from other units with three-letter names and none of them applied to me. At least I'd hoped not, because as per usual I deleted them without really looking. If they had been important they'd have emailed me again.

Sally leaned over with a cup of tea as a waft of her perfume tickled my nose.

'Thanks, Sally. How was the film last night?' I vaguely remembered that she had been going out with one of the string of boyfriends that treated her like shit, despite our regular advice about the type of man she should go for.

'Yeah, it was okay, but Darren made me pay for the film *and* dinner again. He's such a jerk!'

Another voice floated over the partition, and I swung round to see Kevin Sands, one of the three detective sergeants that run the office, leaning casually against a nearby pillar.

'Sally, I've told you before, all you have to do is dump him, and I'll kick Mrs Sands out. You can have her half of the bed.'

From anyone else it would be harassment, but Kev has the ability to be rude, sexist, and generally as non-PC as you can get, yet make it clear that he doesn't mean any of it. He had spent more than thirty years in the force and came back on the 'thirty plus' deal, which meant that he could do another five years. He's one of the funniest men I have ever met. Not only does he have a mind that's more devious than a politician's, he has comic timing that Bill Bailey would kill for.

Sally laughed at him and went back to her desk while Sands took the empty chair at the desk behind mine.

'You all ready for court this morning, Gareth?' he asked, trying unsuccessfully to press the height lever on my chair with his foot.

I nodded. 'I think so. What's not to be ready for? I saw him stab Jimmy; if I'd been any closer I would have been the one that got stabbed.' Just the memory of it made me angry, seeing again the look of pleasure on Davey's face as he jammed the knife into Jimmy's chest.

It's a common misconception that most stabbings are done with combat knives. Nine out of ten are done with kitchen knives that you can pick up in almost any store for a few quid. Every other car I've stopped in my career has one tucked somewhere, whether it be in a tool box or hidden under the driver's seat. But they rarely get turned on us.

'Come on now,' Kev said, obviously seeing my faraway look. 'You know the drill; just concentrate on the questions they ask you and don't babble. Answer "yes" or "no" if you can, and don't try to explain unless you think they're trying to lead you. Not that I'm trying to teach you to suck eggs.'

I smiled, appreciating the pep talk. I'd been to court dozens of times but each time I still got stage fright, especially in crown. Not only did you have a judge, the defendant and the lawyers to deal with, but you also had twelve members of the public staring at you, trying to decide if they believed you or not.

One of the first things I had learned about court was that your evidence didn't matter if you didn't come across well. If you could convince the jury that you were solid, dependable and honest, they would believe you if you told them that the sky was green. If they thought you were bent, however, the case was lost no matter how compelling the evidence. You may think that's an exaggeration, but trust me it isn't. I've seen watertight cases lost because an officer got a bad bout of nerves and mumbled their evidence like they didn't know what they were saying.

'Oi, wake up,' Kev said, leaning forward and pinching the fleshy bit of my arm above the triceps hard enough to make me yelp.

'Ouch, that's assault!' I complained as he got up and ambled out of the pod, studiously ignoring me. I shook my head and turned back to finish the reports, hurrying as I glanced at the clock and saw that I had to be in court in little less than an hour.

2

Hove Crown Court looks more like a library than a courthouse from the outside, with dark brown brick and dirty white walls. It's situated on the corner of Holland Road, with no parking for anyone other than workers, and it sits several streets away from any of the bus routes. It is as convenient and well thought out as the rest of the justice system.

I paced up and down in the police waiting room trying not to annoy DI Jones, the officer in charge of the case. Normally, the OIC was a detective constable but, since it was a police officer who had been stabbed, they'd bumped it all the way up to an inspector.

She looked very smart in a no-nonsense trouser suit, with her hair scraped back into a tight bun and just a hint of make-up to hide the strain of a four-week court case. She sighed as I walked past her for the eighth time in the tiny room.

'Gareth, can you please sit down?' she asked, looking threateningly at me over her glasses.

'Sorry, ma'am, I'm just nervous. I want him to go down and I'm a bit wound up.'

'We all want him to go down, Gareth. But right now I'm trying to read through the file and you're putting me off.'

I stopped pacing and stood in front of the mirror, checking

myself for the twentieth time since I'd been in the room. I'm not used to wearing a suit and it had felt strange to be looking smart. I'd chosen a grey double-breasted affair with a lavender shirt and tie, and was extremely grateful that I'd remembered to shave that morning. Usually I don't, due to the fact that a few days' stubble makes you look less like a police officer when you're on the streets. I hadn't, however, managed to get my hair cut and my brown locks were getting long enough that they were starting to curl over my ears.

The door opened and a court usher stepped in, the black gown looking strange over the security-style uniform she wore underneath.

'PC Bell?'

'Here,' I said, sounding like a naughty schoolboy as the nerves made my palms sweat and my stomach flip over.

'They're ready for you now. Would you like to swear or affirm?'

'Affirm, please.' Not that I have a problem with swearing on the Bible, but not being religious, it had felt to me like I would be lying from the outset, which isn't a good frame of mind in court.

She led me across the corridor and into the court, situated right at the back of the building on the top floor. As I entered, I headed towards the stand, nodding at both the judge and jury as I went in.

Once I had been safely escorted to my position, the usher placed a card in my hand and I read the words with barely a quiver in my voice. 'I do solemnly, sincerely and truly declare and affirm that the evidence I shall give shall be the truth, the whole truth and nothing but the truth.'

As I introduced myself, I let my eyes drift around the courtroom, taking in the jury, all trying to look thoughtful and solemn, the barristers in their ridiculous gowns and wigs, and Quentin Davey himself, secure behind a Perspex screen.

Davey was staring at me intently, with a half-smile that I didn't like playing around his lips. Although not an imposing man at five feet six inches, four inches shorter than me and only half my build, there was an air about him that had made the hackles rise on the back of my neck. He has a blatant disregard for anyone or anything else, and that shows in almost everything he does.

I once jumped one of his runners, Peter Finn, a heroin user trusted just enough to sell small amounts of the drug for Davey, and had arrested Finn and seized the five bags of heroin he had left on him. For the loss of the £50 the drugs would have made, Davey had thrown an entire kettle of boiling water into Finn's face, disfiguring him for life. Try as we might to get Finn to prosecute, some kind of twisted loyalty, or maybe just fear, had held him and he still works for Davey even to this day.

The man that would scar someone for life and stab a copper was staring at me and trying not to laugh. He had to have something up his sleeve that I hadn't thought of, but what?

'PC Bell, did you get enough sleep last night?' The judge's voice brought my head round with an almost audible snap.

'I'm sorry, Your Honour, I was just looking at the man who stabbed my partner.' When lost, confused or cornered, go for the throat.

The defence barrister shot out of his seat like a cork out of a bottle. 'Objection!' he called, putting one hand to the wig that had nearly slipped off during his heroic launch.

'Sustained,' said the judge, one that unfortunately I didn't recognize. 'PC Bell, I don't want you leading the jury with unsolicited statements, am I clear?'

'Yes, Your Honour.' I did my best to sound repentant, but I could see a few members of the jury giving me looks of approval. *Strike one.*

After my little outburst, I was first given to the prosecution barrister, who very neatly led me through my statement asking no awkward questions, but instead asking me regularly how I felt as I first subdued Jimmy's assailant and then applied the first aid that had saved my colleague's life. I spoke vividly of the minutes I waited for the ambulance, my hands covered in Jimmy's blood as I held a credit card to the outside of his chest to prevent the lung from collapsing as it filled with fluid.

I told the jury about the looks and threats that Davey had thrown at us as I laboured to save Jimmy's life, about his laughter rolling over me as I was busy keeping my friend alive.

I told them about the blood that had flowed down Hollingdean Road like a flood, staining the pavement while the ambulance crew worked on Jimmy, trying to stop the bleeding before they moved him. I knew as I glanced at the jury that I had them. I could feel tears in my eyes as I finished, and my fingers were white as they gripped the edge of the box. I glared at Davey as if daring him to challenge anything I'd said but he just looked right back at me, his thin face still struggling not to break into a grin.

Soon enough it was the defence barrister's turn to question me, and he began without preamble. 'PC Bell, am I right in thinking that it was you who seized the knife in question, after PC Holdsworth had been removed in the ambulance?'

'That's correct.' I didn't like his tone; he sounded like he was about to unleash something nasty at me.

'And did you follow the correct procedure when you seized this knife?'

'Yes, I did. I placed it in a knife tube, sealed the tube and wrote out an exhibit label, which I then applied to the tube. I then placed it all in a clear plastic bag which I sealed with a cable tie.'

'So, PC Bell, would you say that you are confident that the tube has not been opened since you sealed it?'

I thought for a second, realizing that the only option the barrister had was to discredit the evidence; the rest of the case was too strong to touch. 'I haven't had hands on the tube since it went into the store at John Street. I would have no way of knowing, but I presume that if someone had opened it then they would have followed the correct procedure.'

Let him work his way around that and still find a way to blame me for whatever was coming.

'Your Honour, I would like to produce exhibit GB/250308/1355, which should be a black-handled kitchen knife, stained with the blood of PC Holdsworth.'

The judge motioned with a lazy hand, indicating his approval.

The defence barrister, with slow, deliberate movements accepted the exhibit from the court usher with both hands, holding up the clear plastic bag for the jury to see. Inside the bag sat a knife tube, a plastic cylinder of two halves that screwed together to make varying lengths of tube for holding sharp objects.

'So, PC Bell, you are saying that this is the knife that you claim my client used to stab PC Holdsworth, is that correct?'

A cold feeling blossomed in the pit of my stomach, trying to claw its way up into my throat and stop me from speaking. What the hell was he playing at, I wondered? Of course it was the knife.

'Uh, yes.'

The barrister slowly undid the plastic bag, then pulled out the knife tube. From that distance I could see the knife within, but not make out any details. I wondered whether it was my imagination or it looked different somehow.

He unscrewed the knife tube, stripping off the tape that sealed it first then tipping the knife onto the desk in front of him. Instead of the clatter I was expecting, there was a dull thud, as if the knife was made of rubber.

Which, somehow, it was.

He held the knife up, wiggling the rubber blade from side to side with one finger, while I stood there with my jaw hanging open almost to my chest.

'So, PC Bell, you are saying that my client stabbed PC Holdsworth with a rubber knife, which you then seized and exhibited falsely as a real knife? Would you like to tell us what really happened that day, officer?'

I could only stand there stunned, unable to work out what

11

had happened. Then it clicked. Davey must have someone inside the police station on his payroll; it was the only thing that made sense. I looked over at him, seeing him almost doubled up with repressed laughter, and something inside me snapped. I swung back to glare at the barrister, standing there triumphantly waving a rubber knife at the now thoroughly confused jury.

'Davey stabbed my partner, then I took the knife off him. I administered first aid to Jimmy, then I seized the knife, the real knife, not the one your client paid someone off to swap. I should arrest you both right now for perverting the course of justice.'

My voice rose at the end, and I spat the words at him as if they were sharp things that would cut and tear at him. I stepped towards him, intent on carrying out my threat, and I'd made it halfway across the court when the insistent hammering of the judge's gavel brought me back to myself and I remembered where I was.

'PC Bell!' he shouted, spit flying from the corners of his mouth. 'You will not treat my courtroom like a police station. There are rules here and you will follow them. You are dismissed from court while we adjourn to sort this mess out. The *police's* mess, I might add.'

I froze, my fists still clenching as I saw the barrister throw a quick, knowing look at Davey. He must have been in on it. Somehow, God only knows how, they had managed to find someone in the nick who was dirty enough that they would screw with the evidence in a case that involved another copper being stabbed. Just thinking about it made me want to throw my head back and scream in anger.

Game, set and match to Davey and his empire.

I turned and strode from the court before I could do anything they'd regret, kicking open the door to the police waiting room.

DI Jones had been in the back of the court but was now standing in the corner of the room on her mobile, a look of sick fear mixed with anger on her face. As I slammed into the room she snapped her mobile shut and glared at me, as if it was somehow all my fault.

'We're going back to John Street; the chief super wants to see us. What kind of *wanker* would do something like that to the evidence?'

The look she gave me clearly said that she thought I might be that kind of wanker, and I felt my hackles rise in response to the implied accusation. 'Don't look at me. I've been working with Jimmy for years. I don't think we'll help each other by throwing shit and arguing, so let's get back and see what Pearson has to say, huh?'

Jones picked up her bag and strode past me without another word, leaving me to follow in her wake as her heels clicked angrily down the stairs towards the exit.

3

Thirty minutes later, I found myself sitting on one of the far-from-comfortable chairs that occupy a little alcove near the chief superintendent's office on the second floor of John Street police station. My only companions were a photocopier the size of a car and a ball of cold fear and anger in my guts which dwarfed the machine a hundredfold.

DI Jones had been in the office with the chief super, Derek Pearson, for about ten minutes, and I could hear raised voices through the wall, albeit not well enough to make out what was being said.

I tried to look relaxed and casual as people walked past, but I could tell from the looks I was getting that the rumour mill had once again beaten any other form of communication and everyone already knew what had happened.

I loosened my tie and top button, then did it up again as the smell of my own nervous sweat hit me. It was a copper's worst nightmare. Not only did it look like a criminal who had stabbed one of us was about to go free, but evidence had gone missing in a high-profile case. It would be all over the news by evening, and the force would be looking for a scapegoat. It was either me or Christine Jones and, knowing the system, I felt that as the OIC she was more likely to get the chop. Not that it made me feel any better; I wanted blood for this and, by hook or by crook, I was going to get it.

A few minutes later, the door opened and DI Jones came out looking flushed and angry. She didn't speak to me as she walked past, looking down instead at the faded blue carpet and avoiding my eye.

Pearson's PA, Sarah, came out from her adjoining office and fixed me with a sympathetic smile. 'Gareth, he's ready to see you now. Don't worry, it'll be fine.'

I smiled back, a weak attempt, and entered the room with a heavy feeling in my heart.

Derek Pearson is a tall man in his mid-fifties, with dark hair going grey and the build of a scrapper. As with all officers, he had spent his time on the street before rising through the ranks and, as far as senior officers go, he's one of the good guys. Usually.

That day, however, he had a face like thunder and his hands were folded carefully in his lap as he sat behind the desk in his otherwise bare office; a sure sign that he was angry and wanted to hit something. 'Gareth, sit.'

I sat.

'What do you think happened today?' His voice was low and even, and I had the strong feeling that if I were to say the wrong thing, he would explode, his tightly controlled temper unleashed.

'I think that Davey found someone in the nick that he could get leverage on or pay off, sir.' I was proud of how calm I sounded.

'And do you have any idea who that might have been?'

I shook my head. 'Haven't a clue, sir, but I can assure you I intend to find out. Jimmy is still weeks away from even leaving the hospital, and I can't let it stand without justice being done.'

Pearson stared at me over his desk for so long that I began to get nervous, before he finally spoke. 'I'm sorry, Gareth, but I'm going to have to put you on restricted duties. PSD will probably want to suspend and interview you, maybe even have you arrested,

15

but I personally don't think that you have anything to do with this and you'll have my support. That's all.'

I stood and left the room, my anger and fear surrounding me like a swarm of biting insects, all attacking me at once. Professional Standards has a horrendous track record of ruining officers' lives and reputations and then discovering that the charges they're trying to bring are false. They are every honest copper's nightmare; they never seem to find the bent ones, few though they are.

Restricted duties meant that I wasn't allowed any contact with the public, so I would have to stay in the office for however long it took, stewing slowly in my own juices as Davey sat around drinking, laughing at us and selling drugs.

As soon as I walked into DIU, Kevin waved me over and ushered me into the inspector's office, which was empty owing to the fact that our guv'nor was off long-term sick with stress. He thought *his* job was stressful; he should have been where I was standing.

Kev sat down in the chair, leaving me to perch on the edge of a filing cabinet. 'Talk to me.'

I shrugged. 'What can I say? Someone found their way into the evidence and planted a rubber knife. God only knows what they did with the real one.'

He stared off into space as he asked, 'Do you think it was someone from this office?'

I shook my head. 'No way. No one in here would do that to Jimmy. I'd bet my job on it. My guess is that it was one of the temps they've been using in the store.'

The property store – G83 as it is known to us – is one of the dullest places in the building to work, and owing to the heavy lifting, long hours and lack of daylight, we have a hell of a time retaining store clerks, so over the previous eighteen months or so we had had a string of temps come in to do the job. It made it confusing as they all seemed to use a different

16

system and, personally, I had already wondered how good a security check they were given before they were allowed to work in the building.

'That's not a bad thought; I'll pass it on. You know you're on restricted duties?'

I nodded. 'Word travels fast, huh?'

Kev smiled and shook his head. 'Not really. Pearson came down to see me, and I told him that if you were suspended you'd probably end up chasing after Davey on your own. He agreed, and decided to restrict you instead.'

'No way!' I exploded. 'He told me it was *his* decision to just put me on restricted duties and that he was on my side! Just goes to show who you can really trust, doesn't it?'

Kev just looked at me, smiling the smile that told me that he agreed, but wouldn't say so openly.

'I'm sure the chief super would never take someone else's idea and pass it off as his own, Gareth. Who would ever dream of a senior officer doing that?'

It's well known that if someone wants a promotion, they either steal a lower rank's idea or invent a new form that makes life for the lower ranks even more complicated.

I shook my head in disgust and headed back into the office, throwing myself into my chair hard enough that it almost tipped over.

Sally turned to look at me, sympathy written all over her face. 'Are you okay, Gareth?' she asked, and for once I had no wish to drown in her eyes.

'Not really. Someone screwed around with the evidence, I'm stuck in front of this damn desk for God knows how long, and Davey is probably in a bar somewhere drinking champagne and laughing at us right now.' I tried hard not to sound like a whining teenager but I could hear it in my voice.

'Has anyone told Jimmy yet?' she asked as she turned back to her computer.

'I hope not. I'll grab a car and go and tell him. I'm sure they won't mind me going up to the hospital.'

I jumped out of my chair, glad to be getting out of the office. Kev threw me a set of keys when I checked in with him, and within ten minutes I was walking into the ward at the Royal Sussex, where Jimmy was being looked after.

His little curtained off cubicle was awash with flowers, grapes and books of crossword puzzles, all sent by concerned colleagues and friends, and somehow they made Jimmy himself look smaller, as if he were shrinking under the weight of the gifts. His usually tanned complexion was pale and he had lost a good stone and a half since he had been in hospital. Where once he was all gym muscle and sense of humour, he was pale and skinny, a shadow of his former robust self.

'How's the knife magnet?' I asked, sitting on the edge of the bed near his feet.

'Almost ready to go home apparently,' he said listlessly, not bothering to put on a brave face; we know each other too well. 'How did the court case go?' A hint of hunger entered his voice as he asked, a need for closure on what was probably the worst experience of his life.

I couldn't meet his eyes as I explained the whole debacle, but I could still see his face drop as he realized that any hope of that closure was gone forever. Even with our statements and Davey being at the scene, the loss of evidence effectively stopped us from ever prosecuting him for what he did to Jimmy.

'Any chance you can pop round to his house and cut his balls off?' Jimmy asked, sensing my distress and trying to make me smile. That's typical of Jimmy. He's always the one to bring people out of bad moods with a joke or some idiot act that makes everyone laugh. On the morning that my marriage had finally fallen apart, he had strapped one of our removable blue lights to the top of his helmet and walked into a briefing for a murder inquiry. I laughed so much that I nearly choked and he got stuck on for inappropriate behaviour, but it had helped and I'd been pulled out of the depressive mood I'd been in.

I smiled at him and picked a grape off its stem, throwing it at his face with pinpoint accuracy. 'Don't be a knob. I wish I could, but they'd know it was me and then I'd be in a cell next to one of his friends, I have no doubt.'

He nodded and lay back, rubbing at the cannula embedded in the back of his left hand. 'It's a shame we can't destroy his business then. Can you imagine what would happen if he started having trouble with his suppliers? They'd do the job for us!'

I started to laugh, then stopped as the idea ran through my mind, gathering speed as it went. We had details of his whole operation: who was working for him, where they dealt, who bought from them. In fact, there was so much information that we simply couldn't deal with it all and we left many of his dealers in place purely so that we knew who to watch.

If someone were to use that information to make life difficult for Davey, it might indeed have the effect Jimmy had just mentioned. Suppliers were notoriously hard on people who had difficulty paying, so maybe it was time to get a little old school and let them solve our problem for us.

As usual Jimmy knew what I was thinking before I did and he threw me a warning look. 'Don't even think about it, fella. If you start screwing around using police intelligence, they'll fucking crucify you. And besides, he's not worth it. His time will come.'

I nodded distractedly, still thinking about how best to get hold of the information without it being traced back to me. All the Sussex computer systems have a keystroke program built in so that they can trace who is doing what and when. The only way around it is to find someone who hasn't shut their computer down and use it, while making sure that you haven't used your swipe card to get into that office, effectively making you invisible to the system.

'Oi, Muppet!' Jimmy's call made me look up and realize that I had been staring into space. 'If you even think about doing anything like that, I'm gonna smack you in the face. Just as soon as I can get out of bed, that is.'

I looked at him with my best innocent smile. 'Who, me? Wouldn't dream of it, mate. I'm in enough trouble as it is, what with the knife going walkies. It's typical of Davey that he couldn't make the knife just disappear, he had to make us look extra stupid in court, the bastard. Rubber knife my arse. You know we're never going to live this down, don't you?'

He nodded, tiring fast from the effort of conversation.

'There's no point getting so worked up over it, he's just one of a hundred dealers in the city. I mean, I know he stabbed me and I'd love to see him swing for it, but his time will come, you know it will. And he didn't stab me because of me, if you know what I mean, it was just because I was stopping him from getting away. It could have been any one of us, and I just haven't got the energy to take it personally. Neither should you.'

I nodded, struggling to put what I was feeling into words.

'It just seems to me that no matter what we do, no matter how hard we try, they keep getting away with it. Drugs took my brother away from me; they nearly took you away from me; and I don't intend to keep watching it happen with my hands shoved in my pockets.'

Jimmy shook his head. 'Easy mate. You can't go taking out all your crap on people like Davey or you'll end up doing something stupid, and then you'll be for it.'

'We'll just have to agree to disagree there, but don't worry, I promise I won't go doing anything stupid. Not too stupid, anyway.' I gave him my best winning smile, and he did his best to match it before glancing around hopefully as if he had just remembered something.

'Look fella, you'd better chip off. I'm getting a sponge bath in a minute and I'm hoping it's gonna be that fit Filipino nurse that's around somewhere!'

I rose, being careful not to jostle him too much. 'All right, mate, well you take care. I'll let you know if anything comes up, okay?'

He nodded and waved, as I walked out through the ward, pausing next to a hugely overweight male nurse who barely squeezed into his blue uniform. As I got close, I could smell his sweat, strong enough to make me want to gag.

'Uh, excuse me, mate, the chap in bed four is expecting a sponge bath. You couldn't pop over and do it for him, could you? He was injured in the line of duty.'

I flashed the nurse my badge and he smiled and nodded as I left the ward, wishing I could see the look on Jimmy's face when bath time came.

4

The trip back to the office should have taken me only a few minutes but I drove out and over the back of Whitehawk instead, needing to clear my head. I couldn't shake the idea Jimmy had given me about ruining Davey's empire, and I wanted either to be rid of it or to have a plan by the time I got back. I was mindful of my promise to not do anything stupid, but I couldn't help but wonder if a few friendly warnings would make things a little warmer for Davey and let him know that we weren't ready to give up.

I was just driving down Elm Grove towards The Level when my radio blurted an assistance call. On the old radios we had been reduced to shouting for help, but on the new Nokia handsets there's a little red button on top that, when pressed (occasionally by my armpit, much to comms' annoyance) produces the horrendous blatting sound that I now heard.

It also opened the radio mic so that I could hear an officer shouting in the background and the sounds of heavy breathing and fighting. One of the better features of the system is that it sends a GPS signal back to comms so they know exactly where the officer needs help. As soon as the air cleared, an operator came on the line.

'*Charlie Lima 92 needs assistance, Vogue Gyratory. Units to acknowledge.*'

I flicked the switch nestled between the front seats, just behind the handbrake. Blue lights flashed and sirens screamed out from the grille. The Gyratory was only a few hundred yards away and as I shot down the hill, weaving through the traffic like a madman, I managed to find the pressel with my left hand, joining in the chorus of officers booking on to assist.

'Charlie Papa 281, I've got a short ETA. Any update?'

I let go of the button just before swearing loudly at a man in a Clio who didn't seem to know how to react to me driving at him at 70 miles per hour in a 30 area. When he finally finished panicking and drove up a kerb, I shot past and gave my attention back to the radio.

'... Stop check on a vehicle, black Ford Mondeo near the Gyratory, four up, markers on the vehicle for drugs and bilkings.'

The usual then. People who sell drugs seem to object to simple things, like paying for petrol, and you can almost guarantee that if a car is associated with drugs, it will also be known for bilking – driving off from a petrol station.

I made a sharp turn into a side road that I knew joined the Lewes Road about halfway along and tore down the hill, wincing as I wrecked the suspension on the speed bumps. I barely paused at the bottom, swinging right and accelerating towards the BP garage at the Gyratory. The line of stationary cars told me exactly where my colleagues were and I drove down the wrong side of the road until I was level with the aforementioned black Mondeo.

As I got out, I could see Sergeant Mike Barker from LST – CL92 – rolling around on the ground with a wiry chap in his early twenties. He was being assisted by Adam Werther, another LST officer, and it didn't surprise me at all that it was my old team rolling around with drug dealers once again. A third officer, Nigel Coleshill, was keeping the other two occupants of the car contained by way of pointing his pepper spray at them through the open passenger window. All the officers were in plain clothes and a large crowd was gathering as they struggled with the man

23

on the floor. He was bucking and writhing, forcing Adam to put his hand around the man's throat to prevent him from swallowing whatever he was clenching his teeth to keep hidden.

I ran over, throwing myself on the guy's back with both knees landing first in the hope that I would wind him and make him spit out his mouthful. He groaned but didn't unclench his teeth, so I grabbed both of his legs to stop him from squirming and lay back on them so that he couldn't gain the leverage to rise to his feet.

'It's always you, isn't it, Barker-boy?' I called over my wriggling charge. 'What's he got in his mouth?'

Barker's face was a study of concentration as he fought to keep control of the arm he had. Believe it or not, it's incredibly difficult to restrain someone safely when they want to fight, no matter how many of you there are.

Next time you see four coppers lying on someone, just remember they're doing it so that they don't hurt him. It would be so much easier if we could hit them a few times, and sometimes you have to, but generally it's safer and less damaging to them if we use locks and pressure points. I wish criminals felt the same about us, then maybe we wouldn't go home with as many lumps and bruises as we do.

'He threw a bag of heroin wraps into the front of the car when we stopped it, and Adam saw him put something in his mouth. He thinks it was crack,' he gasped, fighting for breath. It's also extremely tiring fighting someone for more than about twenty seconds, and don't let anyone tell you otherwise.

'Open your mouth, unclench your teeth!' Adam shouted as I opened my mouth to speak again, much to the apparent amusement of our audience, some of whom now had mobile phones out to record our brutality.

A pair of booted feet appeared by my head and I jerked out of the way of a potential kick before I realized that they belonged to another officer, Steve Warnham. As per usual he had neglected to put on his stab vest and his white shirt was so bright in the sunlight that I had to squint to look at him.

'Hi Steve, do you think you could move the crowds back a bit? I don't fancy getting a boot in the face.'

He nodded and began ushering the crowd back as more sirens approached. I like Steve, he's solid and dependable and has years of experience which gives him a calm manner that few argue with. Other officers began arriving, accompanied by the double blip of sirens shutting off as the numerous cars disgorged their uniformed loads. Another officer, a young chap whose name I could never remember, took over my leg hold, allowing me to sit up and move towards the head, dusting my back off as I went.

Werther still had his hand on the man's throat and I could see the muscles working against it as he tried frantically to swallow. Werther couldn't do a lot else, what with his other hand keeping an arm locked up, so I placed a hand on one side of the man's head and stuck the knuckle of my index finger into the nerve point under the ear, the mandibular angle, right where the neck and the jaw meet. I held it there for a second before pressing, and leaned in so that only he could hear me.

'I want you to listen to me very carefully,' I whispered, just loud enough for him to hear. 'I'm going to dig my knuckle into your nerve point unless you open your mouth, and it's going to be the most painful thing you've ever felt. It's going to feel like I'm sticking a hot needle into your neck.'

Now please don't think I was being cruel. It's been proven that if you set people up for pain before using a nerve point, the anticipation makes it hurt far more and you get the result you want with less chance of harm to the person. That was the safest and easiest way to get him to open his mouth and not swallow the package, which I could just make out as a white lump behind his teeth.

The man looked at me and then tried to turn his head away, which I took to mean that he wasn't playing ball, so I dug the

25

knuckle in hard, shouting, 'Open your mouth, open your mouth NOW!'

I held it there for a few seconds, and his body went rigid as the pain shot through him. I've had it done to me in training and it really is horrible; it feels like your head is going to explode, so I felt more than a little sympathy for him as I did it, despite knowing that I was hurting him far less than I would have if I'd been hitting him.

His teeth remained firmly closed, so I released the pressure. There's no point keeping it on if it doesn't work, that's torture, and I think the human rights people have an article or two that deal with that.

Steve Warnham, still dealing with the crowd but close enough to overhear what was happening, turned at that point and called out in a voice pitched to carry to everyone watching: 'Please sir, open your mouth; we're concerned that you may have heroin or crack cocaine in your mouth and if you swallow it you could put yourself in danger. We can't allow that to happen for your own safety!'

Someone give that man a fucking medal, I thought, as I saw the crowd nodding and muttering to each other.

Adam was still shouting at the guy to open his mouth, fool-ishly trying to reach into it armed only with a pair of purple rubber gloves. Our prisoner unclenched his teeth just long enough to bite Werther hard on the finger, then clamped them together again and tried to laugh.

I drove my knuckle back into the pressure point, hoping to surprise him into opening his mouth again – but it didn't work, as he went rigid once more against the pain but somehow held on. I released the pressure, getting frustrated but knowing that if I kept going, I would only be doing so in revenge for Werther's finger.

His body relaxed as I let go, but Adam had pulled his hand away from its place on the throat to nurse his bleeding finger, and the guy swallowed whatever was in his mouth, then began shouting about police brutality in a coarse south London accent.

Now that the excitement was over, I pulled a pair of handcuffs from my covert rig and slapped them on his wrists while Barker arrested him for the drugs in the car and assaulting Adam. A pair of uniforms hauled him upright and into the back of a waiting police van; just one of about seven marked units that had come in response to the call.

Barker motioned me over to a nearby wall once his charge was safely locked in the van, and I followed, glad to be moving away from the view of the crowd. You never know who's watching and it isn't unknown for some of our 'customers' to try and take phone pictures of plain-clothed officers so that they can pass them on to anyone interested.

'There was another one who got away,' he began, massaging the wrist that had been keeping a lock on the prisoner. 'He was a white male, about twenty-five, with a horizontal stripy top. I think it was George Ludlow.'

My ears pricked up at this little titbit of information. Ludlow had started off as a smalltime user, but recently had started working for Davey. 'Oh really? Which way did he go?' I asked, now eager to go out and search.

'He ran off towards Bear Road, but I was too busy to see where he went after that.'

'I'm not bloody surprised; he was a handful. Any idea who gnasher is?' I nodded in the direction of the van.

'Nope, never seen him before, which is unusual. Adam thinks he might have nicked him on the seafront a couple of years ago but he's not sure.'

That didn't surprise me. Then, there seemed to be a pecking order with drug dealing in Brighton. Either you were local and you did what you liked, you were from Liverpool and you stabbed local people until they let you do what you liked, or you were from London and you started dealing shit on the beach in the evenings until you got caught. If you managed to keep your mouth shut, you progressed to being driven around the city by a user who was paid in heroin, delivering to phone boxes and alleyways across Brighton. That way you could just claim that you were getting a lift and knew nothing about the drugs in the car. Sadly, the British justice system tended to believe this little lie on a regular basis and people got away with it in droves.

I turned my attention back to Barker, who was trying to light a cigarette with shaking fingers. I aided him by plucking the cigarette out of his mouth and placing it in my own.

He scowled and drew another from the crumpled packet. 'Help yourself.'

'Thanks, I did.' I lit them both, then headed back to my car with a final wave, palming the cigarette so that no one would see and complain.

I remembered to turn the flashers off before I pulled away and then drove in the direction that Ludlow had been seen fleeing. He lived on The Avenue in Moulsecoomb, and I figured if I knew him like I thought I did, he would run straight back home to his constantly pregnant girlfriend. I was fairly sure they wouldn't mind me stopping in for a little cup of tea and a chat and, if they did, well I'd just have to find a reason to arrest him.

5

Ludlow is a chubby Brightonian born and bred – if you factored in the possibility of chimp DNA. He's about five foot ten with heavy jowls that he doesn't need to shave and a mess of ginger curls that make him stand out like a sore thumb wherever he is. Not surprising really that one glimpse had allowed Barker to recognize him as he ran away.

As I drove along the Lewes Road towards The Avenue, I spotted my quarry staggering past the university building on the far side of the road. He looked exhausted, his large gut heaving and his cheeks redder than his hair. Obviously being a dealer didn't allow much time for the gym. I pulled into the road that he would be crossing shortly and got out of the car, making sure that my baton and spray were within easy reach. Wearing a covert harness is all well and good but I frequently forget which armpit is sheltering which piece of kit and I really didn't want to pull out my radio instead of my baton if he got feisty.

I leaned casually against a wall, flicking my cigarette butt into the road, missing the drain I'd been aiming for by several inches. Walking over and scuffing it into the drain was the perfect excuse I needed to bump into Ludlow and, as he apologized and went to walk around me, it was the work of seconds to throw my arm around his throat and put him in a chokehold.

'Police, keep your hands out in front of you,' I growled into his ear.

He immediately tried to use his weight to throw me off balance, but I sawed my arm sideways across his Adam's apple. His hands flew up to grab my arm as I cut off the circulation and breathing, fingers scrabbling at me in panic. He began to make pathetic retching sounds and I released the pressure just enough that he could breathe again, but not enough for him to try and slip away.

'Now we're going to walk back to the wall, and then you're going to sit down like a good boy so that we can have a little chat, okay?'

He nodded, and I walked him out of public view down an alleyway between two houses. Once safely hidden, I released him, and he moved away from me faster than you'd expect.

'You can't do that to me. That's illegal. You could have killed me!' he whined, rubbing the vivid red marks on his neck.

'Tough shit. You shouldn't have run away from the car. Give me one good reason why I shouldn't nick you for possession.'

He looked around as if trying to find a way to escape, and I saw that he was shaking in fear. 'You can't nick me! I've got a kid on the way and if I go away again I won't get to see it. I'm on licence; if I get nicked I go down.' A look of animal cunning crossed his face, clear for all to see. I can only assume he was a terrible poker player. 'Besides, I wasn't even there, you can't prove nothing!'

'That's a double negative, George, it means I can prove something. Anyway, we've got a full description of a fat ginger tosser in a stripy top running away from the scene. You see any other fat ginger tossers round here, George?'

He looked down at his top, as if only noticing for the first time that horizontal hoops in fact *didn't* make you look slimmer. 'Look, you can't talk to me like that. I'm gonna make a complaint. What's your number?'

I almost said 999, but managed not to at the last second. Riling him even more wasn't going to get what I wanted, despite the fact that I wasn't quite sure what that was, yet. 'Listen George, I won't nick you. I wouldn't want your kid to grow up without seeing its father once before social services take him away. That would just be cruel.'

He nodded as if I wasn't being sarcastic. Bless him.

'All I need is a little bit of information, George. Then, you can go back to your missus and no one needs to know about our little conversation. I'll tell my lot that I couldn't find anyone matching your description and you get away scot free. Fair?'

He considered it for a minute, eyeing me as if I was about to bite him.

'What d'you wanna know?'

'Davey,' I began, but stopped when he backed away, shaking his head.

'No fucking way I'm gonna say shit about Davey, no way!'

I sighed again and reached under my jacket for my handcuffs before suddenly remembering that they were on a prisoner on his way to custody. I kept my hand there anyway and said the immortal words: 'George, I'm arresting you on suspicion of possession of class A drugs. It is necessary to arrest you to ensure a prompt and thorough investigation. You do not have to say anything, but it may harm your defence if you do not mention when questioned, something which you later rely on in court. Anything you do say may be given in evidence.' I smiled and stepped towards him, watching his face carefully as he weighed up the options. Finally, he put his hands up and slumped against the wall.

'You promise no one's gonna know?'

'Scouts honour.'

'Go on then. Ask. I don't know much though. He don't tell me much.'

I thought carefully. What *did* I want to know? And how would I use it if I found out anything useful? Suddenly a question sprang to mind.

'How do you re-supply?'

'I call a number and a car drops it off to me.'

'The same car each time or different ones?'

'Different, depends who's on.'

'Okay, when are you next going to re-supply?'

'Tonight at about six.'

I thought furiously, wondering where exactly I was going with this. Was I really considering doing this on my own, without authority? The answer was yes. I was. I was supposed to be on restricted duties and there was no way that they would let me anywhere near Davey's operation until I was back out on the streets officially. It would be a PR nightmare otherwise. After what had happened in court, it would be seen as harassment if Davey happened to be in the car making the drop. I doubted he would be but, like any good boss, occasionally he went along with the workers to make sure that everything was going well, and to remind the people in the lower echelons who the boss really was. But then, if all I was going to do was have a little chat with them, what harm could that really do?

'Just a couple more questions. How many people are usually in the car?'

'Only two. More than that and the pigs notice.'

'What, like we did down the road? So where are you going to re-supply tonight?'

He shook his head. 'I can't tell you that. If you turn up after what happened today, they'll know I talked and they'll fucking kill me. No way.'

I realized that I'd overplayed my hand and tried to reassure him. 'I'm not going to turn up, mate, I just wanted to make sure you were telling me the truth, that's all. Don't worry about it. I'll let you get on home now. Remember, not a word about this conversation from either of us, okay?'

He looked at me suspiciously, then lumbered off down the

alleyway at what he laughingly thought was a run. My gran could have caught him and she's been dead for years.

I waited until he was long gone, which took some time, before heading back to the car. I had a plan in mind, but I knew that first I would need to explain to Kev how I had been caught up in a drug bust while I was supposed to be at the hospital visiting Jimmy. Although he's as relaxed as supervision can get without falling over backwards, there are some things that even he has a hard time believing, and I knew if I wanted to have my little chinwag with the dealers that night then I needed to look whiter than white.

6

I dropped the car back without getting grilled for my part in the earlier arrest, Kev understanding that you don't ignore an assistance shout, no matter what.

I faffed around the office for the rest of the day getting no real work done, and studiously avoiding looking at any kind of intelligence that related to Davey or his business. I didn't want anyone thinking that I was going to go out looking for revenge, and I was fairly sure that at least one person in the office would have been tasked to keep an eye on me.

I was more than a little nervous about my plan for that evening, especially on the back of the evidence being swapped. It would take very little for someone to decide that it was me who had done the fiddling and haul me in for questioning. If anyone saw or even suspected that I was going to have a chat with some of Davey's boys, I would be for it.

Four o'clock rolled around with agonizing slowness and the moment the hands hit the right position I barrelled out of the office and down into the car park.

Fifteen minutes later I was home and getting changed, selecting my wardrobe with care. I chose a pair of faded blue jeans, an old beige jacket that I never wore but was currently vaguely in fashion and a plain blue T-shirt.

I drove across town to The Avenue, the day still warm enough that I began to wish I hadn't worn the jacket. Late afternoon sunlight streamed in through the windscreen, a golden glow suffusing the air and making me feel as if I were trapped in amber. All too soon I was parked up outside Moulsecoomb Library, facing the end of The Avenue with a clear view of Ludlow's house. When I say Ludlow's, I mean the council's, as God forbid should a drug dealer pay unsubsidized rent, that just wouldn't be on. Instead, our taxes go towards paying for their umpteen kids and their bloated wives, getting fat off the fruits of our labour while hubby is out peddling death to desperate addicts. And my friends wonder why I'm so cynical.

As I sat there waiting patiently and trying to look as if I belonged, the nerves hit me again, far stronger than they had that morning at court. My palms were sweaty enough that I couldn't have turned the wheel had I needed to and I had a lump in my throat the size of a melon. Part of me – a small part I might add – was telling me that I wasn't going to achieve anything by doing this. I had a sudden fear that they would just laugh at me and tell me to piss off and that I should just drive back home and get on with my evening. I buried the nagging voice, concentrating instead on what I could say that would make them worried enough to stop dealing without actually threatening them. I couldn't think of anything, but I've always done my best work on the fly and I was fairly confident that I would find something at the right moment.

Besides, if it all went wrong, I figured, I could book myself on duty. That's the great thing about being a police officer. If you see something illegal while you're off duty, you can deal with it and, technically, it puts you on duty. I'll give you an example:

Say I'm down the pub with some mates and I bang into some

bloke and spill his pint, so he takes a swing at me. At that point, I'm still off duty. If I swing back at him, I'm still off duty. But if I decide to arrest him instead, or if I identify myself as a police officer, I'm instantly on duty and covered by all the insurance and regulations that come with it.

So if it all went bent that night, I knew I would just tell the powers that be that I was out for a walk when I saw a suspicious vehicle and went to stop check it. They might not like it, but it was all legal and they wouldn't be able to touch me. Hopefully.

An hour or so later, just as I was beginning to think about going home and eating something to calm my rumbling stomach, a green Nissan estate pulled up outside Ludlow's house and beeped the horn. Subtle. I wrote down the registration, or the *index* as we call it in the police, for later use and sat up slightly straighter as tubby George waddled out of the house and up to the car, whereupon the passenger handed over a large package and took a roll of notes in exchange.

You might think that it's a little unbelievable, being that blatant, but doing it in plain sight like that makes them more invisible than meeting in remote locations or taking Ludlow around the block in the car. Just another shady deal in Moulsecoomb.

The car pulled away, and I knew that the only way out of the estate was back past my position or down one of two side roads that I also had covered from where I sat. In a few moments my quarry drove back past me, heading north on the Lewes Road. I pulled out and followed, leaving two cars for cover between myself and the target vehicle.

I also drove in the other lane of the dual carriageway so that they wouldn't see me unless they looked back and left, which drivers rarely do, even paranoid ones. I could see that there were two people in the car, both in the front, both male. Another bout of nerves hit me as I began to wonder if I was lying to myself and really I was looking for a fight to salve my wounded ego.

We carried on heading north for a few minutes, and I was nearly caught out as they did a sharp left turn into Wild Park and followed the gravel track that leads to the café. It was closed that time of night, so I could only assume that they were meeting someone else or picking up drugs from a stash point. I drove past and pulled up in a lay-by slightly further up the road before doubling back on foot with a choke chain held loosely in one hand.

I kept the chain in the car for emergencies, as it made a brutal weapon in close quarters but was totally legal to own and carry. It was also the perfect surveillance tool. How many people do you see walking in parks every day with a lead but no sign of a dog? Dozens, I'll bet.

I ambled up the path, occasionally calling to my non-existent hound, and got up to the Nissan without so much as a raised eyebrow from the occupants. It was parked at the side of the café, well hidden from the main road with the engine off and both the windows wound down, while the occupants enjoyed what smelled like very good quality weed. As I drew nearer, I could see that the passenger was a man whom I knew well but who didn't know me.

That's the joy of my particular job: you know all the faces, places and cars, and no one recognizes you in turn unless you blow out on a surveillance job, and then you're screwed. I've only done it once, but every time afterwards that my mark saw me in town he had shouted, 'Copper!' at the top of his voice so that everyone else would spot me. Sadly for him, he died of a heroin overdose a few weeks later, so it stopped being a problem. Had he not, I would have had to leave the unit and go back to uniform, or even change division.

So this particular chap, one Dave Budd by name, had been one of my nominal targets a few months before, which meant I knew more about him than his mother did, despite the fact we'd never met face to face.

He was known for drugs, violence, weapons and was on the sex offenders register for life after he sexually assaulted his five-year-old niece at a christening party last year. The driver was his brother, Billy, and if anything his record was worse. He was a distraction burglar, fooling old people into opening their doors so that he could check their meters and then robbing them blind.

On the odd occasion that they became suspicious, he would tie them up and beat them until they gave up their valuables. Somehow, he had only been given minor prison sentences so far, and the only reason we could think of was that he was a grass. Judges will sometimes shorten sentences if the defendant gives up useful information; although in Billy's case it would have been more appropriate to ignore the information and throw him in the darkest hole we could find for as long as possible. He is also the father of the girl that Dave had assaulted, yet didn't seem to care, which is apparent by their relaxed attitude to each other.

Both brothers are in their late thirties and hard to tell apart. They both have the same lank brown hair and squirrel-like faces, and are both five foot nine or so and wiry rather than skinny. The easiest way to tell them apart is that Billy's nose has been broken so many times that it sticks out in several directions at once and he tends to grow a beard, if you can call it that. Other than that, they could be twins.

I got right up to the car, leaning into the driver's window and smiling before Billy turned to look at me.

''Scuse me, lads,' I asked in a cheerful tone, 'you haven't seen a springer spaniel come past, have you?'

Billy breathed a lungful of smoke into my face, and the smell of grass mixed with the odour of rotten teeth was almost enough to make me gag. 'Police dog, is it, officer?'

So much for anonymity. I tried to bluff it instinctively, despite the fact I was about to show out anyway. 'I'm sorry? What the hell are you talking about?'

He laughed at my miserable attempt at dissembling. 'I saw you in the court this morning, mate, running out with your tail between your legs. Didn't know pigs' tails could do that!'

He and his brother both laughed, confident that I would be helpless to do anything.

As they laughed, something inside me settled, my nervousness washed away and was replaced by a cold anger that drove out all other feeling. 'Step out of the fucking car, Billy, and don't do anything stupid. We need to have a word.'

'Why, you going to hit me with a rubber baton?' he asked, sliding his right hand down the side of his seat surreptitiously.

'No, mate, this is a personal call. I'm not carrying. I just want a chat.' I opened my jacket to show that I was unarmed, and he didn't seem to register the lead in my hand. 'Keep your hands where I can see them and get out of the car.'

I moved back to give myself what we call a reactionary gap, so was fairly unsurprised when he hurled the door open and dove at me with a knife clenched in his right fist. I'd moved back quickly enough to avoid the door and, as he came out knife first, I kicked the opening door as hard as I could, slamming it shut on his arm. He howled in pain and dropped the knife, his arm hanging at an angle that told me it was broken.

I didn't have time to care, as his brother leapt out of the car and skidded across the bonnet towards me holding a steering lock in his hand. I stepped back again and waited until he swung the weapon at me, ducking the blow aimed at my head and whipping the chain I held across his leg, hitting the nerve point on the outside of the thigh. He dropped as if stunned, and I stamped on his wrist hard enough that I heard the bones grinding together. He screamed in pain and let go of the steering lock, which I kicked away before taking the other foot off his wrist.

Both of them were crying in pain, and Billy was fumbling for his phone with his left hand. I reached down and took it from him, then moved to the car and took the keys out of the ignition as a precaution.

Ignoring their cries, I raised my voice to be heard. 'Right, gentlemen, now that I have your attention I would very much like to know where the drugs are.'

Billy glared up at me, his face a mask of pain. 'You're fucking going down for this you wanker, you're fucking dead!'

I smiled and shook my head. 'No, mate, I'm not. I've got a dozen witnesses that clearly put me at a police leaving do tonight, and you know how we all stick together.'

It was a barefaced lie but I suspected that they were too preoccupied to tell. Hopefully, they also couldn't see the horror I was feeling at what I'd just done. This was supposed to be a warning chat, not a brutal attack that left them broken and bloody. I'd slipped across the line without thinking, and the realization was making me shake more than the adrenaline ever could. I took a deep breath and forced my voice to come out steadily. 'So you can either tell me where the drugs are or I can shove this chain up your nose and pull out the pathetic thing you call a brain. Your choice.'

Billy began to shake as shock set in, his arm already turning a dark purple and swelling badly. 'Get me a fucking ambulance, I'm dying!' he blubbed, clutching the injured arm.

'Tell me where the drugs are and you can have your phone back,' I countered. I needed something to show for this, otherwise I would be arrested without hesitation and my career would be in tatters.

'Under the car, they're under the fucking car, okay?'

I nodded and bent down to check under the car just in time to avoid being brained by Dave, who had recovered enough to retrieve the steering lock and swing it at the place my head had been a moment before. I back-kicked him, landing my foot right in his nuts, and he folded like a deckchair, collapsing with an *oof!* and a clatter before curling into a ball with both hands clutching his groin.

Once I was sure he was down and staying there, I rolled onto my side and looked under the car. Sure enough, there was a box welded onto the chassis with a combination lock on it. They were becoming more and more popular, as not many officers would look under a car on a stop check or even if the vehicle was taken away to be examined.

'Code?' I snapped at Billy, who was watching me with hatred stamped all over his skinny face.

'Three one five,' he replied, and I clicked the rollers into position. The side fell open instantly and I whistled as I pulled out a couple of bags of heroin about the size of a hen's egg each. 'Looks like you boys were planning to be busy for the next few days. Instead, you'll have to spend them in a cell. Hard life.'

Billy looked down at me, confusion on his face. 'I thought you said you was off duty. So how you gonna explain this? You've fucked yourself, mate!' He managed to grin through the pain. The fear that flashed through me must have hit my face as I realized that he was right.

Even if I did book myself back on duty, I could never explain why I was in the park with a dog lead, no dog, and just happened to stumble across two of Davey's lads. After the events of that morning in court, inference would be drawn, no matter what I said, and I would likely be out of a job and up on charges of GBH. I thought furiously for a second, trying to find a way out of the mess I had just created and finally an idea sprang to mind, stupid and dangerous as it was.

Scrambling to my feet, I carefully wiped my fingerprints off the phone and keys before handing them back. I held up the packages of drugs. 'I'm going to hold on to this for insurance purposes. If there's one sniff of you talking to the police, it appears in the front office with your prints all over it.' So saying, I took hold of Billy's injured arm and pressed his thumb firmly onto the plastic wrapping of one of the bags, ignoring the yelp of pain he produced.

'Tell Davey that this stops or he's going to find that every copper in Brighton will be looking for an excuse to take him down. Not that they don't have one already.'

I put the packages in my pocket and scrambled up the road-side and into the bushes, heading back towards my car. Bad enough that I'd parked my own car nearby, but if anyone saw me walking back to it from here, I was as good as done for. Nausea hit me as I lost sight of the Nissan, and I paused for a moment, taking deep breaths to stop myself from throwing up and leaving chunks of my DNA spattered all over the grass. How could I have been so stupid? I pushed the thought to the back of my mind and focused on getting away clean. I would worry about the consequences later.

I waited in the bushes until the road was quiet, then darted to the car and pulled away quickly, turning left up Coldean Lane and losing myself on the A27 before turning off into Hove. My thoughts were churning, almost making me crash several times, but I managed to keep control. After what felt like a year of constant glances over my shoulder for blue lights, I finally parked up a few streets away from my house as the realization hit me.

What the fuck had I done? I'd assaulted two people, one of them a clear GBH, and stolen illegal drugs to the street value of, well, I wasn't sure but it was one hell of a lot when I'd only been expecting a few wraps. I may as well hand in my warrant card now and get it over with. A feeling of sick exhaustion swept over me as I wondered what I was going to do with the packages. I pulled them out of my jacket and looked at them, trying to gauge their worth. If it was uncut heroin, it would probably be worth about ten grand, less if it had been cut already. I didn't want to keep it, that would mean a jail sentence if I was caught, but I couldn't just throw it away. It was my only leverage over the Budds after my ruthless attack on them.

An idea came to me and I almost ran from my car to the house and went straight through to the kitchen. I looked out the back at the garden next door, wild and unkempt where mine was neat and uncluttered. The house next door had been empty for weeks, and by the number of 'to let' signs clustered sadly by the front gate, I guessed that it wasn't likely to be occupied any time soon.

I opened the back door and stepped out into my yard, looking around to make sure that none of the overlooking windows had people in them. Once I was sure it was clear, I rolled over the top of the flint stone wall into next door's garden. The grass on the lawn came up to my knees and there was a buddleia that was threatening to dwarf the small shed in the back corner. I moved to the shed, struggling against the grass that pulled at my feet as if trying to stop me from intruding further into its domain. I eventually reached the shed, a small wooden affair perched on cracked and broken paving slabs.

With a little effort, I managed to lift one of the slabs and scoop out enough earth to hide the drugs, settling the stone back on top and scuffing the grass around the edges until I couldn't see the result of my labours anymore. Satisfied, I climbed back over the wall and had just finished washing my hands when the door-bell rang.

I hadn't been expecting anybody and I began to get nervous as I went to the front door. If this was a salesman, he was going to get a bloody good earful. I opened the door to a man and a woman in smart clothes standing on the top step. Everything about them said police and I took a step back in alarm.

'Can I help you?' I asked suspiciously.

The man stepped forward, holding up a Sussex Police warrant card. 'Gareth?' he asked, and the pit in my stomach yawned wide enough to swallow a battleship.

'Yes,' I answered, trying to stop my knees from shaking.

'I'm sorry, there's no easy way to say this. My name's DC Steve Barnett from PSD Ops. I'm arresting you on suspicion of perverting the course of justice. We need you to come with us.'

7

They took me to Worthing custody instead of Brighton: a small mercy as I know far fewer people on West Downs division. The woman, Andrea Brown, was driving while Barnett sat in the back with me as if I was a common criminal.

They hadn't searched me or cuffed me, but Barnett was clearly ready for me to try something, sitting half turned towards me with his hands within striking distance just in case. For the first ten minutes or so they had tried to make light conversation, but my fear was making me snappy, so they gave up and we carried on in silence.

I'm honestly not sure that I can describe how I felt at that moment. Everything inside me felt tight, as if my body was squeezing in on itself, and I couldn't stop shaking from the shock. I felt angry, sad, scared, betrayed and exhausted all at the same time and thoughts kept popping unwarranted into my head. Did they know about the Budds and this was just a cover to get me in and throw questions at me with no evidence, what we called a fishing trip? Had someone pointed the finger at me about the knife going walkies? Or worse still, did Davey have someone inside PSD that had authorized my arrest as a final coup de grâce? It didn't bear thinking about, unlikely as it was.

About a hundred years later, we pulled into the long drive that led to Centenary House in Worthing, the police station and custody centre. We parked by the doors, and Barnett let me out of the child-locked door and into the custody centre. Brown followed close behind me in case I had any last-minute ideas about making a break for freedom, and I felt a chill as the heavy metal door slid closed behind me, cutting off the real world.

My usual luck held. Standing on the bridge was DC Helen Watkins, who had been on my intake when I joined. Great. Not only did she have the biggest mouth in the force but we hadn't got on from the moment we met and our relationship at that point could have been described as antagonistic at best. One look was all she needed to work out what was happening, and I saw the corners of her mouth quirk up in a poorly suppressed smile as she turned away and left the bridge. I guessed that in less than an hour, the whole force would know what had happened to me.

The bridge is a raised platform behind which sit three sergeants, separated from the prisoners they're booking in by three feet of fake marble cladding. The floor nonslip, dirty green and the walls painted off-white, broken up by the occasional green-framed window. All in all, it's just like any other custody centre in Sussex, bleak and depressing.

I was ushered in front of the only free sergeant, a man in his mid-forties with brown hair and the gut that inevitably comes with long hours behind a desk. Barnett gave the circumstances of arrest to the serious-looking man behind the desk, who eyed me with undisguised sympathy.

'Gareth, do you understand why you've been arrested?'

I nodded, not trusting myself to speak.

'Okay, you know your rights. Do you want a solicitor or anyone told that you're here?'

I thought for a moment. 'Yeah, can you tell the Federation? Hopefully they'll get me a solicitor.'

He nodded and made some notes on my custody record. The Federation are the closest thing we're allowed to a union as police

45

officers, for all the good it does us. Normally, they're about as much use as a chocolate teapot, but I paid £17 a month in case of situations like that and I was determined to get my money's worth.

Barnett spoke to me while the sergeant was busy. 'Look, we're pretty much ready to go; you'll be in and out in an hour.'

I raised one eyebrow but didn't deign to comment. It doesn't do any good to get too friendly with PSD; they see it as a sign of guilt.

The sergeant turned back to me, a thick wodge of paper in his hand. 'We're putting you on a paper custody record mate,' he told me, 'so you won't show up on the system if anyone looks, okay?'

I nodded, grateful that the whole force wouldn't be able to read what was happening to me like they would on an electronic record. I was taken down to a cell and searched rather than it being done in full view of the crowd that had gathered, presumably tipped off by Helen. My belt and shoes were taken, as was everything in my pockets. I was given a blanket and a cup of coffee before the door slammed shut, cutting me off even further from the outside world and leaving me alone with nothing but my fear for company.

I hate police cells, I always have. They're small, grey, miserable and there's a camera high up in the corner watching your every move, even when you have a shit. I slumped on the raised platform they laughingly called a bed, feeling the cold of the fake marble through the thin plastic mattress. I drew the blanket up to my neck in a useless effort to still the trembling that still affected me.

The minutes turned into hours and stretched away in a timeless blur. There was nothing to keep me occupied except my own dark thoughts and I went through almost every sour emotion you can think of, from rage, to fear, to despair. I knew that I hadn't done anything wrong, at least not that they'd arrested me for, but being nicked is one of the worst things a police officer can face. No matter how innocent or guilty you are, rumours will spring up and a reputation that can take years to build is shattered in an instant.

Not only that, but PSD actually have targets to meet. They have to arrest, suspend and charge a certain number of officers per month or explain why they haven't. Personally I think it's disgusting, the same as giving targets to uniformed officers. How do you quantify the three hours spent with an elderly woman who's been burgled, waiting for her family to show up? It doesn't tick any boxes but I think it's just as important as chasing down criminals, if not more so.

The same goes for PSD. What if there aren't any coppers breaking the law? Well, they just arrest them anyway on any kind of flimsy evidence, in the hope that they'll get lucky and find something to stick you with. I knew that if they'd had any idea what I'd just done they'd be dancing with glee, and their figures would soar. To be honest, I couldn't help but think that I deserved it. Coppers should keep the peace, not break it. I'd crossed a line and I was scared that I wouldn't be able to cross back over and carry on being one of the good guys.

I closed my eyes, seeking refuge in sleep that refused to come. Too many things were running through my head, keeping me awake and worried. A couple of times I got so scared that I nearly threw up, but managed to stop myself before I actually started retching.

Some indefinable time later the hatch to my cell slid open and a round, bearded face appeared at the slot. I heard the keypad outside being pressed and then the door clunked open, spilling bright light in from the corridor and making me realize that at some point they had dimmed the lights in my cell.

A portly inspector in a pristine uniform waddled into the cell, a smile fighting its way through the beard. 'Gareth? I'm Inspector Reg Turner. You've been here for six hours, so I have to do a review. Do you need anything?'

Six hours? I figured I must have fallen asleep at some point, as they should have offered me food before then, despite the fact that I wasn't in the least bit hungry.

'I could do with some water; my mouth is dry as a bone.'

He nodded. 'I'll get you some. I don't know why they're taking so long; apparently they're searching your house with the specialist search unit, so they should have been done hours ago. Unless you live in a mansion?'

I couldn't raise a smile at his attempt at humour, much as I wanted to. 'No, it's only a two-bedroom. I could search it in an hour by myself; my ex-wife took most of the furnishings. And the bitch took the cat.'

He made an *ah* noise, as if trying to sympathize. I didn't want his sympathy, I wanted to go home.

'Your solicitor has been informed of what's happening but they're not going to come until the morning now. My advice is to get your head down and get some rest. Do you want any food?'

I shook my head. 'No, just some sleep and the codes to all the doors.'

He laughed politely and swung the door shut as he left. So much for solidarity; it could have been my imagination but he seemed like he couldn't get away quickly enough. Muttering to myself, I settled down and drifted into an uneasy sleep.

8

I was woken by the sound of a custody assistant opening the hatch in my cell door and, for a moment, I thought I was dreaming. Then I remembered where I was and the fear squeezed my heart again in greeting.

'Do you want breakfast?' a male voice asked through the hatch.

'Uh yeah, is it a buffet or do I pay by the plate?'

'Funny man. You want cornflakes or all-day breakfast?'

I should have known better than to order the breakfast. When it arrived, it was a microwaved mess consisting of potato wedges and baked beans and tasting like cardboard. Still, it was hot and filling, even if it did have all the nutritional content of sandpaper.

I did the best I could to wash away the stink of sleeping in my clothes, using the tiny sink that sat just above my toilet. It wasn't the smallest en suite I'd ever had, but it came close.

I was just sticking a wet hand down my trousers to wash away the worst of the sweat when the hatch opened. I pulled my hand out guiltily, despite the fact that I'd only been washing. Masturbation is one of the most common pastimes for people in the cells and I didn't want to be thought of as following *that* particular herd.

A very tired-looking Steve Barnett looked at me through the

gap, and the door opened to reveal an equally tired-looking Angela Brown standing next to him.

'Morning, Gareth, your solicitor is here. We've given disclosure and now she wants to speak to you.'

I nodded and walked out into the corridor, letting them lead me to a private consultation room. Inside the room was a woman in her early forties with dark curly hair and a serious manner. She was wearing a knee-length skirt with a matching jacket and cream blouse and her manner shouted competence at me as she shooed the other officers out. That done, she stuck out a hand and introduced herself as Kerry Nielson.

I took the proffered hand, shaking it firmly. 'So,' I said, sitting down opposite the chair she took for herself, 'on a scale of one to ten, how shafted am I?'

She looked down at her notes, studying them intently. I could only assume that they were from the disclosure, which is where the police tell the solicitor most of the evidence they have, while holding a little back to 'test for truth'.

'Well I really don't think that they have a lot to go on; it's pretty shaky stuff. The reason you've been arrested is that on record you're the last person to have touched the knife which has now gone missing, making you the most likely person to have swapped the evidence.'

I shook my head. 'Look, I would have had to have done that at scene, still covered in Jimmy's blood and in front of five other officers. Don't you think someone would have noticed?'

She looked at me across the table. 'Yes, Gareth, I do. So do they, probably, but from what I'm picking up they need to show that they're doing something and the first logical step was to arrest you.'

I rose and began to pace the room. 'Okay, the first thing I want to make clear is that I didn't tamper with the evidence. Jimmy is my friend and my partner and there's no way I would ever do something to stop the son of a bitch that did this to him from going down.'

'I believe you, really I do, but we have to prepare for what they're going to ask you in interview.'

I stopped pacing to look at her. 'All I can do is tell the truth. If that isn't good enough I don't know what is.'

She smiled at me reassuringly. 'I'm sure that will be fine, but just so I don't have any surprises I need you to go through what happened that day, okay?'

I nodded and sat down, letting her grill me for about twenty minutes about the day Jimmy was stabbed. I was impressed with her manner as her sharp mind drove me to remember details that I'd almost forgotten. Once we had been through it all a good three times, she judged us ready for interview and we left the room to see my captors waiting impatiently in the corridor.

'Ready? Good.' Barnett could hardly wait to open the interview room door and gesture us inside.

The room was set up with the huge tape machine against the far wall and a table by the near wall surrounded by four chairs. Barnett sat and tried to make pleasant conversation, while Brown filled out tape labels with my custody number and got their file ready.

A few minutes later, Brown had everything prepared and pressed the button on the large tape machine. It buzzed annoyingly for a few seconds, and then the tapes began rolling. Brown began speaking, her clear voice echoing in the small room.

'It is 08.37 hours on Wednesday, the 14th of May 2008. We are in an interview room at Worthing custody centre. I am DC Angela Brown, DB429, and the other officer present is …'

Barnett chimed in, looking bored. 'DC Steve Barnett, CB776.'

Brown took the lead back. 'Thank you. Also present is …'

'Kerry Nielsen, solicitor for PC Bell.'

'Thank you. Can you tell me your full name and date of birth, please?' This to me, who was beginning to feel slightly left out.

'PC Gareth Bell, CB925; 7th September 1976.'

I probably shouldn't have added my rank and warrant number, but I was still a copper and I wanted that made clear.

'Thank you, Gareth. Do you agree that there is no one else present in the room?'

'Yes.'

'Okay, I'm going to caution you now. You do not have to say anything, but it may harm your defence if you do not mention, when questioned, something which you later rely on in court. Anything you do say may be given in evidence. Do you understand the caution?'

'I should damn well hope so,' I blurted before remembering I was on tape.

Angela smiled at me in understanding.

'Okay, the reason you have been arrested is that yesterday, in court, during the trial of Quentin Davey, it was shown that evidence vital to the case had been removed and replaced with something else. Namely, exhibit GB/250308/1355, a black-handled knife which had either been removed or was never placed in the tube, and instead a rubber knife was found there. The records show that you were the last person that touched the unsealed tube. What can you tell me about that?'

Just thinking about it made me angry and my carefully planned answers evaporated as my emotions took over. 'It's a travesty, that's what it is! That piece of crap stabbed my mate in front of me and somehow he paid someone off to swap the evidence over. I had no idea that it had happened. Do you really think that I would stand up in court against him if I'd tampered with the evidence? And how am I supposed to have done that if there were five other officers watching me when I put the knife in the tube?'

Angela looked slightly put out by my outburst. 'That's what

we're trying to find out, Gareth. So you're saying that when you seized the knife, you put it in the tube and sealed it, is that correct?'

'Yes, of course it is!'

'Okay, I'm just trying to get things straight in my own head, there's no need to get angry.'

'No need to get angry? *No need to get angry?* You've arrested me and accused me of tampering with the evidence that would have convicted the bastard who stabbed Jimmy! How am I supposed to feel? He's my best mate, I've known him for years and we're completely loyal to each other. Not that I'd expect you worms from PSD to understand that, always looking for excuses to shop in another officer. Listen carefully, I'm not going to repeat myself. *I had nothing to do with the evidence going missing.* If I find out who did, I'm going to drag them in here by the hair and hand them to you. Other than that, I have nothing more to say.'

I crossed my arms and sat back. Who the hell did they think they were to imply that I'd had anything to do with something that would hurt Jimmy? I glared at my interviewers across the table, daring them to challenge me.

Angela tried to sound calming, despite the colour in her cheeks and the annoyance showing clearly in her eyes. 'So you're saying that you won't answer anymore questions on this matter, is that correct?'

I just stared, knowing full well how frustrating it was as the interviewing officer to have nothing but silence on the tape.

Barnett leaned forward, taking his hand from the pepper spray it had strayed to during my outburst. 'Come on, Gareth, we're only trying to find out what happened. You can't blame us for that. We're trying to help Jimmy.'

I stared at the wall behind his head as I counted silently to ten. They tried a few more times, but I was having none of it, and at 08.43 hours they wrapped up the interview. Six minutes was probably the shortest PSD interview ever, but I didn't feel particularly special as I was led back to the consultation room and left there with my solicitor.

When we were alone I looked at Kerry, trying to gauge her mood.

'Uh, look, I'm sorry about that but this is bullshit and they know it. They're just wasting time in the hopes of an easy outcome while the person that did it is laughing at us.'

She sighed and shuffled her notes. 'We all know that but I really don't think you helped yourself in there. You don't respond well to pressure, do you?'

'Actually, I do. It's just bullshit that makes me lose my rag.'

'I see. Well, all we can do is wait and see what happens. I can only assume that you'll be suspended pending further investigation. With something this serious at least we can hope for a short bail date.'

I didn't really listen to anything past the word 'suspended'. My stomach tied itself up in knots again as I thought about the grief that Davey had wrought. Every time I thought the slimy little bastard had gone too far, he somehow managed to go still further. He couldn't have had a better result if he'd planned it this way.

A few minutes later I was hauled in front of the custody sergeant again. This time he had a bail notice for me. I was to return to Worthing custody at 11.00 a.m. the Wednesday after next. Kerry had been right about the short date, usually bail was for a month or more while they, or should I say we, tried to put together a convincing case. Kerry said goodbye to me at the doors and after taking my mobile number she drove off, leaving me with my arresting officers.

'You're okay getting back to Hove I take it, mate?' Barnett asked, his voice sweet as he turned and closed the door, shutting me outside with no hint of remorse.

Cursing under my breath, I began the long walk back to the train station, adding Barnett to the mental list I keep of people who will get their comeuppance come judgement day.

9

Two hours later I was sitting at home in my front room, enjoying the space that I hadn't refilled since my ex-wife, Lucy, had taken all of the furniture, apart from the sofa and my widescreen TV. I flicked idly through the channels, unable to concentrate on anything in particular as I tried to ignore the frustration that was nagging at me.

They had taken my warrant card before they chucked me out of custody and I felt more than a little naked without it. It had been a constant companion for eight years, a shield that I could use to help people without being dragged through the court system myself. Some use it had turned out to be.

My phone rang for the fourth time since I'd been back and I didn't even bother to take it out of my pocket, knowing it would be Kev Sands trying to make sure I was okay. I couldn't face talking to him right then; I felt like I might dissolve into tears if anyone showed me the slightest sympathy.

Eventually the ringing stopped, and I got up to go into the kitchen, tripping over the worn patch in the grey carpet that I kept meaning to get around to replacing. One day. I'd intended to make a cup of tea but one look at the mess I'd left the kitchen in put me off. I'd been working so much recently that I had been literally dumping stuff on the worktops and running and it looked like a group of students had moved in. Dishes and takeaway boxes littered the worktops and the sink was piled high with dirty crockery. Just looking at it depressed me even more. I grabbed my jacket from the end of the banister and headed out, not sure where I was going but needing to get away.

I got into the car and drove on autopilot, fairly unsurprised when I ended up sitting outside my dad's bungalow on Farm Hill in Woodingdean, where he's lived alone since my mother died of cancer ten years ago. It's a pleasant street, set back from the main road and dotted with a mixture of houses and bungalows that stretch up the hill towards the fields that separate the village from the A27.

I got out of the car and crunched up the gravel driveway, hearing Lily – my dad's German shepherd – begin barking as I intruded on her territory. I walked up the side of the bungalow, past the half-finished shed that has been in that state since before I joined the job, and was greeted at the back gate by a whirling dervish of black-and-tan fur. Lily's lips were pulled back to show her impressive teeth as she barked and snarled, but we knew each other of old and I knew that she was just showing off. As soon as I was through the gate, she turned the snarls into little yaps as she jumped up, trying to growl and lick my face at the same time.

True to form, my dad was ignoring the noise, trusting Lily to get rid of anyone who wasn't welcome, no matter how many times I told him to listen to her just in case. I tried the back door handle and found it unlocked. Sometimes I wished that he would get burgled, just so that he'd take a little more care in future.

I kicked Lily's football up the lawn, and she chased after it, grinding the leather with her back teeth as I walked into the kitchen. It was cleaner than mine and I set about figuring out the coffee machine as my dad finally came in from the front room to see who had invaded.

'Shouldn't you be at work?' he asked, sounding old and tired.

'Now there's a story. Let me make coffee and I'll tell you about it,' I replied, turning to look at him over my shoulder.

He looked as tired as he sounded and had dark circles under his eyes, presumably from lack of sleep. He isn't a tall man, only five foot six if he stretches, but he's stocky, with a belly that has always inspired me to fight my genetics, most of which I have inherited from him. His shock of white hair was sticking out in all directions, the same as it always does, and several days' worth of snowy stubble made him look older than his sixty years.

'If you keep growing that beard, you'll end up looking like Papa Smurf!' I warned him, as the coffee machine finally yielded to my ministrations and began to make the right noises. 'You having trouble sleeping still?'

He nodded, moving to the cupboards and getting out a couple of battered but serviceable ceramic mugs. 'Yeah, I've been having the nightmares again.'

'About Mum?' She passed away while holding his hand, lying in a hospital bed with dozens of tubes coming out of her and he hasn't been the same man since. When she died, something indefinable but vital went out of him at the same time. Then my brother Jake, already hooked on heroin, had disappeared without a trace, and it was a wonder the man hadn't fallen apart completely.

'Yeah. Anyway don't worry about me, I'll be fine. What's your news?'

More and more, my father had begun to live vicariously through me. He still worked when he felt like it, but he had made an absolute mint in the first dotcom explosion and he probably had more money squirreled away than I would earn in ten years. He's always wanted to be a copper though, ever since he was a lad, and I had honestly thought he would cry with joy the day I passed out of Ashford Training School.

I sighed, dreading telling him my news, not wanting to

57

disappoint him. 'I think you'd better sit down before I tell you this one, Dad, it's a biggie.'

He looked at me over the top of his glasses, a warning expression on his face. 'You can stop treating me like I'm made of glass; I can read the papers as well as the next man. Probably better, seeing as the next man is you.'

I ignored his jibe, swallowing the echo of guilt I felt from having dropped out of my English degree so many years before. Although it has never bothered Dad, I felt like I had let Mum down. She had been so proud when her little boy got into university. Suddenly the words he had used actually registered with my brain. 'Read the papers? Oh shit!'

He passed a folded copy of *The Argus* over to me while he took over coffee duty. The headline read, in massive letters:

POLICE OFFICER ARRESTED IN SHOCK ATTEMPTED MURDER EVIDENCE SWITCH!

It went on to explain in the article about the court case and the fact that one of the officers 'who couldn't be named for legal reasons' had been arrested and bailed pending further enquiries. All the other officers in the case were named, and the lack of mine in print was a glaring indication of who they were talking about, to me at least. So much for keeping this one quiet.

'You could have phoned to see if I was okay,' I accused my dad, feeling hurt.

'I did bloody phone you, twice! If you ever looked at the damn thing then maybe you'd know I called!' he threw back at me as he delivered a steaming mug of coffee that suddenly I didn't fancy, my stomach heaving as I read the rest of the article.

In a nutshell, it said that the police had screwed up in a case where a police officer had been stabbed and that, because of an evidence blunder, a notorious criminal had walked free.

It's a good job most of the local criminals can't read much

more than the health warning on a cigarette packet; there'd be an open season on police otherwise.

I walked through into the lounge and sat down on the creaky old leather sofa, looking around the room and enjoying the sense of familiarity that took some of the sting out of my situation. The room hasn't changed for years, the leather sofa accompanied by an ancientlooking leather recliner stacked up with cushions just the way Dad likes them. Dark wooden bookshelves line every available wall and at one end stands a dining table with four chairs around it, used only at Christmas and for the occasional poker nights.

A word of warning here, never, ever, play poker with my dad if you don't want to go home broke. I swear he has a sixth sense when it comes to cards.

At the other end of the room stands a TV that dwarfs the small table it sits on. Last year on his birthday I bought him a widescreen plasma, which I suspect still sits in its box somewhere in the loft. He doesn't believe in getting rid of things until they wear out and even then only when they can't be fixed anymore. The whole room smells slightly of dog and books, which is actually quite a pleasant combination if you've grown up with it, which I had.

My dad came into the room juggling a plate of ginger creams, a bowl of peanuts and his mug of coffee. I waited until he got comfortable before I started talking.

'So, I assume you can guess that I got arrested last night?'

He nodded, slurping his coffee noisily.

'Well, they think I might have had something to do with the knife being replaced. I hope that I don't need to tell you that I had nothing to do with it?'

The look he gave me told me everything I needed to know on that front.

'Okay,' I continued hastily, 'well I told them where to stick it, basically, but I've been suspended and bailed out until the middle of the week after next. I'm not fucking happy.'

59

I try not to swear in front of my dad; he doesn't mind but old habits die hard. Up until the age of eighteen I would get a smack round the head for anything worse than 'bloody'.

He finished the ginger cream he was eating and stared off into space thoughtfully before looking back at me. 'Is there any way that they can link you to anything that's happened? I assume that this Davey chap was the one who managed to get the evidence lost?'

I nodded. 'Yeah, he's the one who must have done it. He was laughing at me in court before it came out but I'm the last person logged to have touched the knife.'

'What about fingerprints, wouldn't they have dusted the rubber knife?'

I'd already thought about that and came to a conclusion about it on the walk to the train station after my interview. 'Well, PSD didn't mention it, so I can only assume that they checked it for prints and didn't find any. They probably neglected to disclose that so that there was more chance of me making an admission.'

Dad shook his head angrily. 'They really are bastards, aren't they? What did your sergeant, Kevin isn't it, have to say about all of this?'

I finished my coffee just in time to avoid getting it spilled as Lily streaked into the room and threw herself on my lap. 'I think he's on my side,' I said, fending the dog off, 'but he has to try and stay as neutral as possible. The only link he has to the case is that he's our supervisor. He wasn't there that day until after the evidence had been bagged and Jimmy was en route to the hospital, so he's in the clear, but if shit sticks to us it'll stick to him as well by association, if he isn't careful.'

Lily finally got the message and went off to hunt biscuits, leaving me brushing what looked like half her coat off my lap. Dad took pity and threw her one, which disappeared in a single gulp.

'Well,' he said, glancing at a picture of the family that hangs on the wall between bookcases, 'I'm only glad your mother isn't here or she'd be off down the PSD office dragging them around by the ear and shouting at them for being idiots!'

I smiled, knowing that he wasn't far off the mark. 'Yeah, well, in some ways I wish she was.'

We both lapsed into the awkward silence that springs up between us whenever Mum is mentioned. I'd been at university through the worst of it and carry a sense of guilt at not having been there that has never really faded, despite my dad's best efforts to reassure me.

'So what are you going to do?' he asked, breaking the spell.

I sighed and shook my head. 'I don't know, Dad, I really don't. All I can do is wait and see what happens, but I just feel so *useless*. I should be out hounding Davey's every step but instead I'm sitting around feeling sorry for myself. What would you do?'

'Just sit it out, son. Keep your nose clean. Don't give them an excuse to turn it into a witch-hunt.'

I nodded, knowing he was right, not daring to tell him about my encounter with the Budds. No matter how much he loved me, he would never approve, and the less he knew, the less he had to lie about if anyone came asking.

'You're right. I suppose I'd better get back and get in touch with Kev; he'll want to make sure I'm okay. Thanks for the coffee, I'll call you later.'

He waved as I left, stooping to fuss Lily on the way out.

Back at the car, I put the key in the lock, and then paused as my peripheral vision caught something that my copper's nose told me was out of place. I glanced around, trying to look casual, and saw a silver Clio parked about fifty yards up the road, right on the bend, with a person sitting in it reading a newspaper. It struck me as strange behaviour for a side street, and I automatically looked around for anything else out of place, only to see the curtains twitch on a house across the road as my eyes swept across it.

So PSD were having me followed. It didn't surprise me; if they thought I had something to do with the evidence, it made sense that they would have a surveillance team on me, hoping that I would run to Davey.

Being an SV officer, and pretty good at it, I knew they should have been better than that. The first thing they teach you on the surveillance course is not to stand out. Had the person up the road in the car been on the phone or just sitting there with the engine running it wouldn't have looked out of place, but reading a newspaper just screamed that they were prepared for a long wait. Add to that the fact that I would never have noticed the officer in the house opposite if they hadn't jerked back when I looked in their direction, and you had an SV team that were either poorly trained or wanted me to know they were there.

Shaking my head, I gave the guy hidden behind the curtains a cheery wave as I drove away slowly, making sure that they didn't lose me. If they wanted to know what I was up to I was equally keen to show them that I had nothing to hide. So long as they didn't start looking in next door's garden.

10

My situation hadn't improved by the next day, and I was still followed everywhere I went. That morning I had taken my gaggle of followers on a walk over the downs and returned home feeling marginally better than I had since I'd been arrested. I parked up just around the corner from the house and was more than a little surprised to see a uniformed police officer standing on my front step as I trudged up the road.

I didn't recognize him but, as he looked about twelve, I assumed that he was from the tutor unit. He looked at me with worry written all over his face as I approached and came up the steps towards him. He put out a hand that hovered hesitantly in front of my chest.

'Uh, I'm sorry, sir, you can't come in. This is a crime scene.'

I looked at him in amazement. 'Crime scene? This is my bloody house!'

His cherubic face took on a look of anger as I swore. 'Sir, I'm warning you under Section Five of the Public Order Act, if you swear again I will be forced to arrest you!'

I looked around ostentatiously. 'Do you see anyone here who is likely to be harassed, alarmed or distressed by my swearing?' I asked, seeing the doubt blossom on his face as I quoted the act right back at him. 'I don't – and, as you can't be the one to feel any of that, I suggest you stop being a pillock and get someone who knows their job.'

I wasn't making a friend here, I knew, but I wasn't going to stand around and be dictated to by a kid who hadn't even hand-cuffed someone on his own yet. We were saved by an officer I knew sticking his head out of the door, presumably to see what the commotion was about. Andy Coucher is a top-rate officer and, about a year before, had moved on to the tutor unit to pass on some of his hard-gained street knowledge.

'Ah, PC Bell, you horrible excuse for a police officer! When was the last time you washed up?'

I felt my face go red as I realized that they would have seen the state of my kitchen. I still hadn't got around to cleaning it up; it just didn't seem important somehow. 'Uh, I've had family staying,' I lied, 'and I've been doing eighteen-hour shifts the last week. I was going to wash up; it's not normally like that!'

I saw the grin that crept over the probationer's face as his tormentor was publicly embarrassed and I wished I could slide through the floor.

'Look, can I come inside? And apart from my kitchen what the bloody hell are you doing here?'

Andy looked a bit awkward. 'Burglary, mate, someone saw a couple of guys break into the house and called us. They were gone by the time we arrived.'

I shouldered my way into the house before he had finished speaking, concerned about my passport and driving licence, both of which were in the concealed cupboard under the stairs along with the bag containing my riot gear and spare pepper spray – which I wasn't supposed to have. After a few moments of frantic searching, I sighed with relief as I found both of the items right where they should have been, hidden under the carpet next to my untouched PSU bag.

Andy had followed me in and I turned to him, hearing people upstairs. 'How many of you are here?'

'Me, Bobby on the front door and two other probationers upstairs. We're a little short on tutors at the moment, so we're tripling up.'

'Who called it in?' I asked, surprised that someone had actually noticed. Almost ninety per cent of burglaries were committed during the day, and they were rarely discovered until the owners came home.

Andy looked a little uncomfortable as he answered. 'That's the funny thing, the serial was restricted. Not even the comms supervisor could read more than the first line; it came from HQ.'

Serials, the jobs that come in via the phone, can be restricted from view by anyone but authorized viewers and this is most commonly done when they contain sensitive information or involve a police officer. For a serial to be restricted so that not even the comms supervisor could read it could only mean one thing: PSD must have called it in, which meant that they must have either been sitting outside and let it happen or have installed technical equipment, bugs and cameras, in the house. I felt my anger stir again and took several deep breaths so that I wouldn't blurt anything out in front of Andy.

'Did you get a description?' I asked when I was calm enough to speak.

He took his flat cap off and scratched his head, looking puzzled. 'That's another funny thing; the descriptions were excellent.' He consulted his notebook, pulled from the pocket on the front of his stab vest.

'Two white males, mid-twenties. Male One had light brown hair, short, and had two earrings in his left ear. He was wearing a brown leather jacket with black elbow patches and blue jeans. Six foot one, stocky build.'

'Male Two was five eleven, with a green parka jacket, a black roll-neck jumper, black jeans and white trainers with blue flashes on them, and had a skinhead.'

He was right; most members of the public wouldn't have got

half of that, so for that level of detail it had to have been someone trained to remember everything. Namely a police officer.

'Thanks, Andy, have you got a point of entry?'

He nodded. 'Yeah, the front door. They slipped the Yale with a piece of plastic, we reckon. There's no sign of forced entry.'

I cursed, realizing that I had left in such a hurry that morning that I hadn't used the mortise lock.

Yale locks are easy to slip if you have a piece of curved plastic, like half a Coke bottle, and the knowledge of where to put it. It's fast and simple, and there was little chance of them having left anything for forensics.

I looked up at Andy, hoping that he would give me a break as I asked, 'Look mate, I've had one hell of a week. You know I got arrested the other day?'

He nodded.

'Well the last thing I want is more coppers wandering around the house, no offence. Is there any chance you can just leave me an MG11 and I'll drop it into the nick when it's done?'

MG11s are statement forms, and while I normally did mine on the computer, I would gladly scrawl a quick aggrieved statement out by hand if it gave me a bit of peace.

'Sure mate,' he pulled a crumpled MG11 out of his trouser pocket, 'got one right here. Just leave it at the front desk when you're done.' He called up the stairs and a pair of yet more fresh-faced probationers, a man and a woman, came down. They gave me matching sympathetic smiles as they headed out of the door, closely followed by Coucher.

Alone at last, I threw my coat over the end of the banister and went into the front room, looking around carefully for anywhere they could have hidden cameras. The only things in the room big enough to hide anything are the sofa and the TV, and if they had unscrewed the plate on the back of the latter, I'd have gone spare as it was still under warranty.

Throwing caution to the wind, I pulled my mobile phone out and began running it over the sofa, about a centimetre away from the fabric. The speaker on the phone should feedback from any microphones they had left, making that blipping noise you hear from speakers when your phone checks for a signal. After about thirty seconds, I was rewarded with the noise I was only half expecting and pulled up the sofa cover on the right arm to see a tiny black dot about the size of a coat button wedged in-between two parts of the cushion.

So I'd been right, they had bugged me. Nice to see how much I was trusted after my eight years of slogging it out with the underbelly of humanity. Knowing that where there was a bug there would probably be a camera, I looked around the room again but couldn't see anything that gave the location away. Feeling more betrayed than angry, I leaned down close to the bug and spoke into it in a conspiratorial whisper.

'This is Broadsword calling Danny Boy, Broadsword calling Danny Boy, will you please come and take this shit out of my house? I've played ball with you, and this is enough for me to take out a grievance against PSD for harassment. You've got ten minutes before I phone the Federation, or the newspapers, whichever one I can find the number for first.'

They would know as well as I did that I could never phone the papers and expect to keep my job, but I was getting past caring and I hoped that they knew that. I pulled the bug from its hiding place and set it on the arm cover, then went into the kitchen to start the horrifying job of washing up while I waited for PSD's next move.

I didn't have long to wait; within twenty minutes there was a knock on my door and I opened it to find Steve Barnett and a tall, greying man that I didn't recognize standing on the step. Barnett was looking at me with resignation written all over his face as if he had given up trying to catch me out but wasn't happy about it.

'Gareth, this is DS Peel, he's the sergeant in charge of your case. Can we come in?'

I nodded at Peel and stepped back to allow them entry, waving them into the front room. They sat on the sofa, studiously ignoring the bug I had placed in plain sight while I leaned against the bare wall.

'So, I assume that you were the ones who called in my burglary? I suppose I should be grateful that Sussex Police cares enough to be keeping an eye on my house while I'm out.' I didn't do a very good job of disguising the sarcasm in my voice.

Peel looked annoyed, his pinched face becoming even thinner as he pursed his lips. '*PC* Bell,' he said, emphasizing my lower rank, 'PSD has a job to do, whether you like it or not. We have a duty to try and get to the bottom of what happened with the evidence in PC Holdsworth's case.'

'And you think that the best way to do that is to arrest his best friend and the person who saved his life? Good set of FLOPSIES gentlemen!'

It sounds like I was being rude, but I wasn't: FLOPSIES – Forensics, Linked series, Other, Property, Suspects, Intelligence, Eye witnesses and Strategy – it's the rules we follow with every investigation and helps to avoid confusion.

Peel squirmed uncomfortably on the sofa. I wasn't surprised; the springs had gone almost a year before, which was probably the only reason Lucy had left it behind.

'It does seem that we were a little hasty, but you must admit it does look suspicious.'

Had I just heard PSD apologize, or as close as they get? 'Can you say that again for the benefit of the tape, please, DS Peel? Are you saying that you now don't believe that I had anything to do with the evidence going missing?'

He ignored my flippancy, finally finding a place on the sofa that, by the look on his face, was no more comfortable than his original position. 'New evidence has come to light. We checked the tape on

68

the outside of the knife tube for prints and we came up with a partial match that doesn't tally with anyone in the police database or the barristers that have had access to the exhibits.'

The police database contains the prints of all officers on the force and every civilian that works directly for us. It's there so that SOCO can quickly run any prints found at a scene and eliminate the police officers first. Some of us apparently have sausages for fingers and it's not unusual for us to leave dirty great prints all over a crime scene that we think we're being oh so careful with, so they needed to come up with something that would stop SOCO putting our prints in for full analysis every time. It doesn't, however, hold the prints of temps, which made my theory about who had done it even more valid in my opinion.

'So you're telling me that you now think someone else fiddled with the evidence?' I asked, wanting to get a clear admission out of him.

'That's correct.'

'Right. Have you considered the fact that it may have been a temp that did it?' I asked, my need to catch them greater than my need to make PSD look stupid.

'Yes, we have. In fact that's what we're working on right now. Anyway, if you'll excuse us, we need to grab a few things and then we'll be going. Your warrant card is already on its way back to your sergeant; you can collect it in the morning when you go into work.'

If he expected me to thank him, he had another thing coming. I followed Barnett around the house as he collected his technical equipment, nearly losing my temper again as he pulled a tiny camera out from under the free-standing bath. It had been pointing straight at the toilet.

'Are you some kind of voyeur?' I asked as I followed him back down the stairs.

'Look, people feel their most secure on the bog, we have to put cameras there,' he retorted, not looking at me.

'Yeah yeah, whatever. Just remind me not to look at your holiday snaps.'

He ignored me as he collected Peel from the front room and they left the house. Just as I was about to close the door, Barnett's shoulders slumped and he turned back towards me, his right hand held out.

'Look, no hard feelings, huh?' He raised the hand slightly so that I couldn't miss the peace offering.

'Of course not!' I said, smiling sweetly as I closed the door in his face.

70

11

I walked into the office to a round of applause. People stood at their desks and clapped as I walked by, and I felt my face go red. I've never been great at accepting anything like praise even if, like then, it was only people showing their pleasure at having me back in the office. I made my way into the drugs pod, squeezing Sally's shoulder as she smiled at me.

Ian Rudd was there, one of the officers on the team, as was Simon Tate, the nominal team leader by dint of years in the job, both wearing the trademark short-sleeved shirts that were so useful for hiding covert kit. Both of them shook my hand and I sat at my desk to find that some wit in the office had made me a card that simply said on the front:

SHAME YOU CAME BACK, I WANTED YOUR CHAIR!

Everyone in the office had signed it and, after the embarrassment faded, I felt a warm glow when I realized how much support I had there. I shouldn't have been surprised; when you work as closely with people as we do, and for as long, you can't help but develop a bond that's something more than friendship – but strangely sometimes less as well.

I got straight to work, wanting to busy myself as my mind was

71

still churning over the burglary the previous day. I had a strong suspicion that the intruders had been working for Davey, probably looking for the heroin, but I knew I couldn't tell anybody or I may as well just have handed myself in.

'I've already done the meeting sheet,' Rudd said, swinging his chair round to face mine, 'so I think it's your turn to make the tea.'

I sighed; I'd rather be writing than making tea for thirty people but I couldn't really say no after he'd done my work. Rudd is one of those people who always looks annoyingly young; at twenty-seven he could still pass for eighteen. During his uniform days this had caused him no end of grief as people seldom like to be told what to do by people who appear younger than them, but as a surveillance officer it makes him invaluable.

He could easily pass as a student or a young office worker, and frequently he and Kev pretend to be grandfather and grandson, much to everyone else's amusement. He's slim, but I know that he's deceptively strong, as years ago we had been part of the same kung fu club and he has more stamina than the rest of the office put together. Last time we'd been on a run together, he had sped on into the distance and picked me up on the way back, which he kept reminding me about, much to my chagrin.

I picked up his mug and then Tate's, a serious-looking older officer in his early forties with a barrel chest and a calm manner. He is almost the exact opposite of Rudd, having short brown hair instead of the younger officer's wavy blond locks, and the only thing they really have in common is their confident manner.

I'd managed to get halfway around the office and the tray was piled high with cups when Kev came into the office almost at a run, a thing all but unheard of.

'I need six with kits and ready to go,' he called before he even made it to his desk.

I dumped the tray next to Kate, one of the researchers, with an apologetic look and ran back to my desk to get my covert radio kit. The kit is designed to be well hidden under clothing and take advantage of the natural curves of the body to look as though it isn't there. A multitude of wires then spread out across the body, ending with a pressel that can be placed somewhere unobtrusive, with the radio safely tucked out of sight.

The earpiece is so small that you can't actually see it, even if you know it's there, which is probably why the kits cost just shy of a grand each. Worth every penny though, in my opinion, as no one can tell you're wired unless they hear you talking.

Rudd and Tate were both getting their kits on, as were Julian 'Eddie' Edwards, Mike 'Tommo' Thompson and Ralph 'Ralphy' Smith. Everyone who works in any kind of surveillance ends up with a nickname – don't ask me why – and most were fortunate enough not to have one as bad as mine. I'd gained it on my first day in the office after screwing up embarrassingly on my first follow. I'd been forced to take it in good humour, despite the fact that I hated it from the second I heard it.

'Are we going to need fighting kit?' Tommo asked, holding up the covert harness that contained spray, baton and cuffs.

'Take it in a bag but keep it close. I'll brief in two minutes,' Kev replied, struggling into his own kit.

Before the two minutes were up, we were all squeezed into the inspector's office, with Kev once again in the only chair. The rest of us perched as best we could on the minimal furniture dotted around the room that suddenly smelled of sweat and the other odours that congregate wherever several men gather. Kev ostentatiously cleared his throat to get our attention and I listened closely, intrigued as to what could get him in such a state of excitement.

'We've got some intel on a robbery that's going to happen at a jeweller's in the South Lanes when they open at nine. It's only just come in, but we're expecting four of them, all Eastern European, with a vehicle as yet unidentified. Apparently they're going to hit Wester's on Union Street, just opposite the Font and

Firkin,' he said, naming a local pub that's known by anyone who has worked Brighton for more than a few months.

'We need to put someone in the shop, in the back room, so we need to leave in the next five minutes. Tommo, that's you if you don't mind. Ralphy, you're driving. I want the car on Ship Street just south of the entrance to Union Street. That's the most likely place for them to park, and I want the car identified as soon as it arrives. Rudd, you're with me. We'll be around the corner inside another jeweller's, waiting for the call from Ralphy or Tommo. That leaves Ding' (I really hate my nickname), 'and Eddie as pedestrians, with Tate in CCTV in case they get away, and doing the log, please.'

Every surveillance job has a log that goes with it, where the log keeper writes down anything relevant so that it can be referred to later. It's a godsend as, after a four-hour follow, it's easy to forget key parts that could be vital if the job goes to court.

Kev looked around the room at us, an uncharacteristically serious expression on his face. 'I want stab vests on, gentlemen. We don't think they're going to be armed but they may be.' He ignored our groans as we thought about all the rejigging of kit we would have to do to fit the cumbersome vests. It was just like Kev to let us get kitted up and then tell us about the vests; no doubt he thought it was hilarious.

'We'll have LST on standby in a van on Middle Street and, just in case, we've got a plain clothes firearms unit who will be parked up at Bartholomew Square. Questions?'

Tommo half raised a hand. 'Yeah, if I don't hear anything first, I take it I call as soon as they enter the shop?'

Kev nodded. 'Yes. We've warned the jeweller's and they've agreed to open anyway, with just one male member of staff. We should be right around the corner, so hopefully we can be inside before it gets nasty. Anything else?'

We all shook our heads and filed out, picking up our stab vests and strapping them on as we headed down to the car park. We headed out in two cars: me, Tommo and Eddie in one and the rest in the second that Ralphy was driving. We dropped Tommo at the entrance to The Lanes that opened onto North Street and then dumped the car in King's Place, leaving the logbook on the dash so that it wouldn't get a ticket. Eddie and I then ambled through The Lanes together, chatting about nothing much and trying to look for all the world as if we were window shopping. I'm not sure how convincing we were at eight thirty in the morning, but we did our best.

The brick-paved pedestrian area known as the South Lanes is a lovely part of Brighton, with interesting shops and cafés that sell all manner of items and old buildings that tower overhead, making you feel as if you're walking through a man-made ravine. They also act as a confusing warren of twisting paths and are ideal for criminals trying to make an escape, so the jewellers here are hit every couple of months or so, often without us ever finding the culprit.

I stopped outside a shop offering bongs and pipes, pointing out to Eddie the huge cannabis leaf stencilled on the window. 'Subtle. I bet they do a roaring trade with all the students.'

'Yeah, can you hear that buzzing?' he asked, indicating his hidden earpiece.

I shook my head. 'No, mate, clear as a bell here. Hang on. Eddie from Ding, test call?' I said, pressing the button hidden in my pocket.

'*Yeah, Lima Charlie,*' he replied via the radio, giving the loud and clear signal.

On the private channel we use for surveillance jobs, we tend to use nicknames and first names rather than the call signs that are reserved for use on the main divisional channels. It takes too long to use a call sign every time you want to get hold of someone, and there's a much more relaxed feel to the communication. Often we use a mobile phone as cover, having a made-up conversation and pressing the pressel only during certain parts, imparting information to the rest of the team. I had used this technique a few months before on a job when I had been sitting on a park bench and our target, a small-time dealer, decided that he would sit next to me and enjoy the sunshine. Before he could engage me in a conversation I had pulled out my phone and pretended to answer a call, giving Kev answers to the questions he was asking via the radio while the target hadn't even twitched.

That morning, however, it was far easier for me and Eddie to stick together. It seemed more rational to have two of us wandering around together than two apparently unrelated people window shopping at that hour of the day. I felt a little bulky and obvious with the stabbie on under my short-sleeved shirt, but hoped that the jacket I'd thrown over the top would stop anyone from noticing. We stopped at a nearby café and I bought us a couple of takeaway coffees, then we strolled around The Lanes enjoying the sounds of the city waking up.

The traffic noise was muted there, thanks to the tall buildings that threw the sound around in odd ways and there was a warmth to the air that promised to build into a scorching day. I was just beginning to relax and enjoy myself when the radio crackled to life in my ear, Ralphy's voice coming through loudly enough to make me start.

'Contact, contact, dark green Mercedes, index November 367, Delta Yankee Tango. Four up, three males and one female, all Eastern European-looking, well dressed. One of the males is driving and they're parked up right at the end of the street.'

I checked my watch and guessed that this would indeed be the target vehicle as it was five minutes to nine. Ralphy spoke again, hushing his voice despite the fact that they wouldn't be able to hear him.

'Three out, two males and the female, and heading into Union Street. The driver remains in the vehicle and the other three are away from my view eastbound.'

Kev's voice came over the radio the instant Ralphy stopped

talking, like the well-oiled machine that our team is.

'*Kev has control and they are towards Wester's, to the door, and the female is knocking while the males stay out of sight to either side. Tommo did you receive my last?*'

Three clicks came over the radio – the signal we use for yes when we can't talk; two clicks for no.

Kev picked it up and resumed the commentary.

'*Three clicks for yes, received. Standby, the door is open and one of the males is in with the female, the other male stands on the door facing out. All units wait for Tommo's call.*'

I glanced at Eddie and saw that he was as rigid with the tension as I was. This part of a job is the worst, wanting to get into the shop and stop them before anyone gets hurt but after they have done something criminal. It's a fine line and it's easy for something to go wrong.

Tommo's voice came over the radio in a frantic whisper, and before the words, '*Go, go, go!*' were fully out of his mouth, Eddie and I were racing around the corner towards the startled-looking brute that stood on the step of the jeweller's. He was wearing a smartlooking suit, dark grey with a black shirt, and had shoulders that looked twice as wide as I was tall. He had slicked back black hair and a swarthy complexion, and he turned as we ran down the street towards him.

Both Eddie and I automatically made it look as if we were running past, and I made a show of looking at my watch as we approached. 'Three minutes,' I called to Eddie, and saw the guard relax slightly as he dismissed us from his mind. We swung back sharply into his focus as I veered suddenly to the left, directly towards him, and his right hand shot inside his jacket.

Just as I went for the grab, Eddie leapt into the air towards him with his knee up, aiming for his solar plexus. Unfortunately, owing to the fact that the man was on a step, Eddie's knee caught the guy in the groin with his full weight behind it and he collapsed with a scream.

I leapt over his writhing form and slammed into the door hard enough to rattle the shop front, tumbling through as the lock burst under my weight. Eddie followed me through and I saw a young man, obviously the shopworker, being held up against the wall by another man in a suit with the same slicked back hair as the lookout. A blonde woman in grey slacks and a white blouse pulled jewellery from a display and shoved it into her large bag as her colleague subdued the young man.

As I came through the door, Eddie hot on my heels, I yelled, 'POLICE!' at the top of my lungs in case there was any misunderstanding. At my yell, Tommo appeared from a door in the corner and pounced on the man holding the terrified worker up against the wall. I ran to help him as the man turned and threw a punch at Tommo. The punch connected with his jaw but Tommo shook it off and grabbed the offending arm, twisting it into a lock so hard that I thought it would snap.

I grabbed the other arm and we put the guy into an armlock known as the flying angel, with both his arms outstretched behind him and his wrists bent sharply upwards. He tried to struggle but we both increased the pressure at the same time and he yelled in pain. The struggles stopped and I glanced over my shoulder to see Eddie scrapping with the woman, who was trying to rake his face with her nails and make it to the door at the same time. I didn't dare let go of my prisoner to help, but Rudd came through the door and solved the problem by grabbing the woman from behind and pinning her arms.

Kev then came in, and I could hear from what he was saying that he had switched radio channels.

'Yes, Charlie Papa 163, we need an ambulance to Wester's on Union Street. We have a male, about thirty years old, who has what looks to be a serious groin injury, but I'm not going to check it myself.'

I looked over at Eddie who was now wiping the blood from the scratches on his face, and he shrugged at me as if to say, Oh well.

I shook my head then concentrated on my prisoner again as he tried to wriggle free. So there I was on my first day back and one of the team had managed to hospitalize a prisoner already. It wasn't turning out to be the best week I'd ever had.

12

Having disposed of our prisoners to LST, we trooped back to the nick to debrief. The job had gone well apart from a suspected ruptured testicle, and the driver had also been caught trying to make off. I was worried about the injury Eddie had caused, not because the guy didn't deserve it – they deserved everything they got in my book – but because it's hard to make a case claiming reasonable force when you've effectively GBH'd someone.

My mind skipped back to the other day when I'd broken Billy Budd's arm and I forced it away quickly, determined not to even think about my secret activities in a room full of police.

Eddie's saving grace with this one was that apparently the man had a nasty-looking combat knife and a taser hidden under his jacket, so his instincts had been right, but I was sure that PSD would remind him that he hadn't known that when he struck the guy. Maybe if they spent a few days a month on the streets of fear, as we affectionately call them, they'd remember what it was like to have to make decisions on the spur of the moment that could affect whether you lived or died. Though I'd like to see the powers that be try and enforce that rule on them – there'd be a mass walkout.

The debrief was quick and to the point and all the bases were covered within ten minutes. We all checked and signed the log, and then everyone else went up to the bar on the fourth floor for tea while I stayed behind to chat to Kev.

'Nice work,' he said, putting his feet up on the desk and massaging the knee that has bothered him for years.

'Yeah, thanks. How much shit do you think Eddie's going to be in for hurting testicle boy?'

He shrugged. 'Hard to tell. He was armed with a taser, which as you know is classed as a firearm, so he should be okay. Although we're not exactly the PSD poster boys at the moment.'

I grunted, having been concerned about that already. 'What do you reckon, statement under caution?'

Kev nodded, and I felt a little more relieved. A statement under caution means that you write a normal statement but spend a little more time justifying exactly why you did what you did – after you write out a version of the police caution at the top which says that you are aware that if you don't get it right then you're deep in the shit. It is the easiest way for PSD to deal with something, and then it's touch and go as to whether the Independent Police Complaints Commission will get involved. Nowadays it seems that there are more people watching the watchers than ever and, if it carries on, there'll be one poor sod in a uniform with 30,000 evaluating his performance, and then the government will wonder why the crime rate is rocketing.

And while I'm ranting, did you know that almost all government crime statistics are a lie? They basically add and remove groups from the statistics depending on what they want to push through Parliament. If they want the public to think knife crime is down, they ignore all incidents that are committed by people under sixteen, which is a hell of a lot. If they want to scare the public into accepting some draconian measure, they simply add in the twelve to sixteen year olds, keeping the ten to twelves in reserve, just in case they need to add more weight at a later time.

If you don't believe me, ask any copper if he thinks violent crime is getting worse and whether the statistics truly reflect it.

Kev brought me out of my musing by throwing a balled-up piece of paper at me, hitting me in the chest. 'If you're going to be that much use all day, can I recommend that you get your statement done and go and visit Jimmy?' he asked, which I thought was a sterling idea.

I went back to my desk and cracked on with the statement. I don't know if it's the halffinished English degree or just my sense of the dramatic, but I've always enjoyed writing statements, and I like to get as much detail into them as possible. Any idiot can write, 'I saw X punch Y in the face, and Y fell over,' but to put the reader, often months later in court, at the time and place of the incident, you need to get a little more creative: 'I saw X draw back his right fist and swing it with full force at Y's head. The fist connected with a crack and I saw Y's head snap backwards as the blow landed. The punch was so powerful, in fact, that Y flew backwards and I heard a dull "thwack" as his head bounced on the pavement when he landed.'

Which do you think is more likely to get someone convicted? I know which one gets my vote.

So an hour later I was just finishing my statement, paying special attention to how I was in fear of our target reaching for a weapon, and that in my experience his body language told me that he was armed and ready to fight, when the others came back from their extended coffee break. They all sat down and began their statements. I left mine out on the desk after I had printed it so that it could be collected by whoever was collating the file.

An officer should never read someone else's statement before they have written theirs, as that means they have colluded on the evidence. If it was on the desk and I wasn't there, however, I couldn't be blamed if someone took a sneaky peek to make sure that our versions of events weren't wildly different.

* * *

I grabbed some keys off the board that hung behind the sergeant's desk and drove up to the hospital to see Jimmy. I'd totally forgotten about the fat nurse until Jimmy saw me and immediately put on an aggrieved expression.

'You fucking arsehole!' he greeted me, looking as if he wanted to get out of bed and thump me. 'I'd arranged to get that Filipino nurse and you ask Frankie bloody Howard to wash me instead! Do you know how bad he smells?'

I tried my best to look innocent. 'Me? I don't know what you're talking about, mate. I just asked on the way out that he made sure to take good care of you. It's hardly my fault if he wants to scrub your privates; you shouldn't be such a good-looking boy!'

I reached over to pinch his cheek, and he batted my hand away, trying to stop the grin from spoiling his annoyed expression. 'Yeah, whatever. So no problems with PSD now, all cleared up huh?'

I'd told him the whole story about the night before the moment my suspension was over; I'd been expressly forbidden any contact with him while I was off. Why, I'm not sure. You'd have to ask PSD. 'Yeah, although we may have got ourselves in a little trouble again this morning.'

I related the job to Jimmy and by the end of it he was shaking his head. 'I can't believe it. Your first day back and the team is hurting people. You know they'll probably find a way to make it your fault. Do you think he's going to be okay?'

I nodded, hoping that I was right. 'Yeah, I'm sure it's not that serious. If it was, Eddie would be under arrest by now, wouldn't he?'

He shrugged and the conversation tailed off as I tried to think of something to say that wouldn't reinforce Jimmy's inability to heal properly and get back to work.

'So ...' I began, and then stopped as a familiar figure walked past the end of the ward holding a bunch of flowers that still had the price tag on them. *What the hell was Dave Budd doing here*, I wondered.

'So?' Jimmy prompted.

'Hang on, I'll be right back. I've just seen something.'

Jimmy nodded, understanding, and I walked out of the ward and in the direction that Dave had taken.

The next ward over gave me the answer to my question.

In the bed nearest the door was Billy Budd, his right arm in plaster and a drip in his left. The arm above the cast was dark red and purple and looked infected. Dave was sitting on the end of the bed chatting to him and next to him stood a man in a brown leather jacket with black elbow patches.

The previous day's burglary jumped back into my mind and I realized that the intruders must indeed have worked for Davey. From the description Coucher had given me, one of them was talking with the guys I'd fought and stolen the drugs from. Shit.

The first thing that occurred to me was that Jimmy, or they, needed to be moved, but how the hell could I go about that without alerting anyone's suspicions?

An idea came to me and I approached the desk that sat at the junction between the two wards, catching the eye of the ward sister by flashing my badge.

'Uh, excuse me, can I have a quick word in private?' I asked.

The sister, a stressed-looking woman in her late forties, was small enough that she looked almost lost in her shapeless blue uniform but the look she gave me showed exactly what she thought of unsolicited visits by the police.

'As long as it's quick,' she said, leading me into a cramped office that held at least two more desks than could comfortably fit in the room.

'I'll get straight to the point,' I said, needing her goodwill. 'There's a chap called Billy Budd in the bed at the end of Catherine James ward. He's a drug dealer and he works for the guy who

84

stabbed Jimmy Holdsworth, who is currently in bed four over there. Is there any chance that one of them could be moved? I don't think that it's safe to have them so close, not with the sort of visitors that Billy is getting.'

I looked at her hopefully but the frown on her face just deepened.

'I'm sorry, but we just don't have the beds here. Also, we need them to be in the wards they're in or they would be elsewhere already. Sorry.'

Her sharp tone annoyed me; although I think she realized that I only had my friend's best interests at heart as she added, 'But we can put a member of security behind the desk if that would help?'

I shook my head. 'Sorry, Sister, but unless they're armed, they won't stop these people if they decide to have another pop at him; I'll have to find another way.'

I left the office before she could reply, not wanting to overplay my hand.

I walked back to Jimmy, trying to work out what to tell him that would make him take any warning I gave him seriously. As I reached the bed he looked up at me enquiringly.

'Well?'

I sat on the bed again, taking my time as I decided how much to tell him. Jimmy is the closest thing I have to a brother since Jake disappeared. If I can trust anyone it's Jimmy, but then, I was afraid of what he would think of me if I told him the whole truth. Finally I settled for something halfway between truth and fiction.

'Look, Jimmy, do you remember the Budds?'

He nodded, clearly unsure where this was going.

'Well, they work for Davey, and one of them is in the next ward with his arm in plaster. I've got no idea what happened to him but he's being visited by some pretty unsavoury types. I just want you to watch yourself, okay? The last thing I want is them seeing you like this and deciding that you're an easy target to vent their frustrations.'

I felt terrible as I saw the implications of what I was saying hit him. Jimmy is always the first into a scrap and always prides himself on being able to take on all comers. To suddenly be faced with a very real threat that proved just how weak he was must have been horrible for him. Maybe I wouldn't have felt quite so bad if it hadn't all been my fault.

He looked at me with genuine fear in his eyes. 'What do I do?'

I thought hard. 'Well, for one, keep your phone on and near you and put me on speed dial. I never turn my phone off, so I'll pick up instantly. Any trouble and I'll get the cavalry and come running.'

I glanced around to make sure no one was looking. 'Here, take this.' I pulled my pepper spray out of its holder and passed it to him quickly before anyone could see. 'I know you're off duty but you need something, just in case. For Christ's sake don't use it if the fat bloke tries to give you another sponge bath though, okay?'

He ignored the joke. 'What will you do for pepper spray?'

'Do you still keep yours in your top drawer?' I asked, knowing the answer already.

'Yeah, and the key is Blu-Tacked to the underside of my monitor. Just try not to spray anyone unless you have to or they'll ask some awkward questions.'

Each can of Captor has a unique number that we write down every time we change cans or spray someone. If there's a discrepancy, it can be a job-loser as the spray is classed as a firearm.

'Okay, I'll be careful. I promise you, Jimmy, this won't be forever. You'll be back home in no time and after a few weeks you'll be back out with us, causing all kinds of grief and then screwing up the paperwork, yeah?'

This time he did grin, and it was a relief to see. 'So, Ding, my old buddy, what are you lot intending to do about Davey?'

I shrugged. 'Dunno, I'm sure Kev has got a plan. Why, you got an idea?'

His face became animated as words spilled out of him almost too fast to follow.

'Well first things first; I reckon that you need to hit the little dealers, make them afraid to go out and deal. Then that'll force the bigger boys to come out and deal and you can start taking them out too. Eventually it'll get to the stage where no one will sell for Davey and he'll end up owing so much money that they'll take it out of his hide. Either that or he'll have to come out and deal himself and we catch him and put him away. Problem solved!'

What he was saying made sense, even though we'd tried it a few years earlier with little success. Dealers tend to work in pyramid theory with one guy at the top and a host of others below him. Those below in turn have their runners, and they have *their* runners, so getting the bigger fish near the top has always been a problem for the police. Quite simply there are always too many little fish willing to jump into the game at the bottom of the pyramid to make a quick buck and we rarely get any higher; but if we could make an entire level of the pyramid afraid to even leave the house we could take down the whole thing.

On the previous attempt to get at the big guy on top of the pyramid, we hadn't the resources back then and they kept pulling the few we did have off onto other jobs. Finally the whole operation had been swept under the carpet as an embarrassment. So I wondered, maybe if I took it to Kev and he pulled some strings, someone higher up would take it and run with it. Every copper in Brighton wanted Davey after what he'd done to Jimmy, from the tutor unit up to the chief super, so I thought there was a chance that we could actually make it work this time. I certainly couldn't think of any better ideas.

'I like it. You're not as stupid as you look, are you?'

Jimmy settled back into his pillows, one hand still wrapped

around the can of Captor half hidden under his blanket. 'What do you think I've been doing in here all this time, scratching my nuts and listening to the radio? I've thought up about a hundred different ways to take Davey down and this is the only one that stands a chance of working, unless you want to start throwing his goons in the sea with concrete socks?'

I smiled, and then it faltered as I thought again of Billy Budd lying in the next ward with injuries that I had given him. 'Okay, I'll take the idea to Kev and see what he says. Just remember, be careful and don't get caught with the spray. I want to try and keep my job as long as possible, right?'

He nodded and slid the canister under his pillows.

'Oh, and Ken says hurry up and get out of hospital so you can come back to kung fu; he misses the screams you make when the exercise gets too much for you!'

Jimmy and I had both been going to kung fu for about five years, although I had stayed throughout and Jimmy came and went depending on his love life. Being married to Lucy, I'd been only too happy to get out of the house twice a week, so I always won our little play fights.

Jimmy waved as I got up to leave. 'Yeah, yeah, tell him I want my money back cos it didn't stop the knife. I thought I was supposed to be invincible by now.'

We both laughed, and I left him to it, already working out in my head exactly what I would say to Kev to convince him to run with Jimmy's idea.

13

As soon as I got back to the nick I approached Kev, dragging him into the inspector's office and closing the door. I started without preamble.

'Jimmy's got an idea for taking Davey down.'

'Oh yeah, what's that?'

'Do you remember a couple of years ago when we were trying to take down those Liverpudlians who had all the local runners and we started taking out the bottom of the pyramid?'

Kev nodded. 'Yeah, and what a screw up that was. All we ended up doing was blowing out most of our officers, and then they took away half the team for that paedophile operation. Made us look like idiots.'

I shrugged. 'But the idea was sound. Do you think now that Jimmy's been stabbed, the powers that be might see their way clear to allowing us to try it again, this time on Davey and with as much manpower as we can get our grubby little hands on?'

Kev scratched his nose thoughtfully. 'It could work, I suppose, but we'd need to keep hitting it every day without letting up. We left it too long between hits last time and they had time to regroup and get more people out dealing.'

He began to look animated as he thought about it.

'We've got a much better chance of remanding people prior

to court nowadays, which means that we wouldn't keep blowing out and being spotted. If we can get some good PWI charges, I reckon the chief super would be more than happy to help.'

'Ding, you're a genius, leave it with me.' He got up and strode out of the office.

'Uh, Jimmy's the genius!' I called after him, receiving a distracted wave in response as he trundled towards the main door.

I shrugged and headed back to my desk to discuss the idea with the others, who were buried in piles of intelligence reports and surveillance requests as per usual.

I outlined the idea and they all agreed that it could work if we kept at it.

An operation like that, which would have us all out of the office for most of every day, is something that we long for. No one joins the job to do paperwork, but somehow it seems to keep most of us at our desks for ninety per cent of the time. This would be a chance to get out and do the job we'd joined to do.

'So, providing that Kev gets the okay, where do we start?' Rudd asked after we'd batted the idea around for a few minutes.

I shrugged. 'I suppose we look at the intelligence and see if we've got any regular dealing sites that we can link to Davey and his crew.'

Sally swung her chair back to her desk and rummaged through a pile of intelligence logs that were sitting next to her keyboard. She turned back holding a single sheet of paper which she waved at me.

'Actually, Gareth, I think you'll have more luck if you work on people that we know buy only from Davey. We know that there are a few, like John Melling, who are easy to follow. Have a look at this.'

She handed me the intelligence log that she was holding, and I grinned as I read the information on the sheet while a plan began to form in my mind.

* * *

Regency Square was quiet, the sun now hidden from view behind the tall buildings that lined three sides of the square. Although many of them are listed buildings, more than a few are DSS hotels filled with heroin and crack users, petty thieves and sex offenders. Strangely, most of the other buildings are also hotels, albeit somewhat nicer and, surprisingly, they have little or no trouble from their seedier cousins.

The central square is actually more of an oblong of grass on three slightly different levels as it slopes down the hill towards the sea. Underneath is a car park that's famed for being one of the least secure in Brighton. Our target, John Melling, a big blond chap who limps around town and is covered in needle sores, will regularly walk out of his DSS hotel (paid for by us, the taxpayers), head down into the car park and break into six or seven cars by smashing the windows, then stroll back into the hotel with whatever loot he has found just carried openly in his hands.

Somehow he keeps avoiding prison, which had ceased surprising me some years ago. In a way it is actually quite useful, as he is so unaware of being followed that you can walk ten feet behind him all the way to a dealer without him ever looking back, which is what we intended to do that evening.

I sat on a park bench at the top of the grass, nestling between a still-wet glob of spit on one side and an even wetter lump of seagull shit on the other. The only things there are more of than drug users in Brighton are seagulls.

Glancing at my watch, I saw that it was nearly eight o'clock, which meant that Melling would be out any time soon according to the information that Sally had found for us. We get intelligence from all manner of sources, from police officers to drug users themselves, and someone close to Melling had obviously decided to shop in his schedule for God only knows what reason. It was more than likely a personal feud; but we are never fussy where good intel is concerned.

Most heroin users work on a four-hour schedule: apparently

that's how long it takes for them to get a hit, for it to wear off, and then find money for the next hit; Melling is like clockwork. He gets up at eleven after a state-sponsored lie-in, eats a state-bought breakfast, and then ambles into town at twelve to buy his first £10 bag of the day. Then he takes it somewhere, leaves the needle for a child to find, trip over or stab themselves with and then he starts either stealing handbags from elderly ladies or he scours the town centre car parks to get enough money for his next hit. Then at about four he buys again, and so on.

Almost at the stroke of eight the door opened and he lumbered down the steps, heading up and towards Western Road, one of the local shopping areas and a major bus route.

'Contact, contact, I have the X-ray heading north on the east side of the square towards Preston Street,' I murmured into my radio, hearing clicks as the rest of the team acknowledged my call.

I followed at a distance; Melling might not be SV aware, but many are and you can never tell when individual users will form a gaggle, all heading for the same dealer. The other officers were dotted about nearby, and I felt sorry for those on the seafront who would be running towards Western Road by now so that they could get ahead of the target. Surveillance, especially with small teams, is bloody hard work and don't let anyone tell you any different.

My target took me up Preston Street and onto Western Road, pausing at the corner opposite Sainsbury's to chat to another user I recognized, Tracy Holden. Tracy is about as foul a creature as you can find anywhere, with only three teeth left and those black and reeking of decay if you dare get close enough. She was slim and suntanned with a slight bump that showed that she was pregnant for the third time in as many years. She had killed the first two at four and six months pregnant respectively by taking too much heroin – and I had suspected the third would go the same way.

She keeps her jacking-up kit inside her, so every time she gets arrested there's a farcical scene where two unhappy female officers with two sets of rubber gloves on each usher Tracy into a search room while we all wait outside with sympathetic looks, as they take from inside her the Coke can base, needles, spoon, lighter, and tin foil with just enough residue to keep her going.

John and Tracy broke off their conversation and John headed up the hill and into Hampton Place, while Tracy wandered off into town, presumably to steal handbags from cafés, which is her speciality.

I followed John, closing the gap slightly as he disappeared around the bend that took him towards the back of Waitrose. It was unusual that he hadn't made a call from a phone box yet, but more and more users have mobile phones so their human rights aren't infringed by having to use public phones for their drug arrangements.

Kev called over the radio, and I saw him walking down the hill towards the junction that John had taken, approaching from the other direction.

'Kev has control, and X-ray is into the Waitrose car park and towards the north-west corner. Target is believed to be a blue VW Golf, index unknown, two males sit within. Units at Montpelier to be ready to strike. Rudd acknowledge.'

'Yes, yes.'

'Thank you. Tate acknowledge.'

'Yes, yes.'

'Thank you. Gareth, with me. You make the approach to the vehicle; I will remain nearby to assist. Gareth acknowledge.'

'Yes, yes,' I said, feeling the adrenaline begin to build.

As I reached the corner, I paused for a second and then walked around it as naturally as possible, my eyes not looking at anything particular. I needn't have bothered, as Melling was walking straight towards the top end of the Waitrose car park with no thought to checking behind.

In the corner he was heading for, I saw the battered blue VW Golf and the pair of guys sitting in the front seat. Another user, one I didn't recognize – there are over 3,000 in Brighton at any one time – was just leaving the car and yet another user was approaching from the far side of the car park. I was amazed at how blatant they were being even for Brighton, but realized that with the commanding view the dealers had of the car park I would have to rely on the rest of the team getting to me fast if it went wrong.

Melling had served his purpose and I ignored him as he scored and then left via the far side of the car park. I waited until there was a gap in the near constant flow of users then shuffled towards the car as if I had injection sores.

I had chosen my clothing carefully, wearing old jeans that were a couple of sizes too big – thanks to my regular trips to the gym over the year – which, with just a dash of motor oil, looked as though they had been worn for a year. The outfit was finished off with a big grey duffle coat that was ripped up one side. I had got a great deal of ribbing during the briefing but I was hoping that it would pay off and let me get close to the car before they realized that something was wrong.

I reached the car and shuffled up to the passenger window as the other users had done, keeping my head tucked into my chest. I needed to get them out of the car somehow, or get myself around to the driver's side so that they wouldn't just drive off when we struck, but I wasn't sure how.

Then an idea came to me.

'Brown or white?' I recognized the voice. It was Paul Denton, a young Scouser who, according to the association chart, was in debt to Davey for several thousand pounds. I risked a quick glance at the driver and recognized him as Vincent Attlingworth, or Vinnie to his mates, another low-grade user, who makes his living driving dealers around town for cash and drugs.

'Brown, just one,' I said in my best rough Brighton accent.

It seemed to work, as Paul rustled around between his legs for a moment before holding a hand out for the cash. I kept my pressel down so that the rest of the team could hear what was happening and be ready to come to my aid judging by what they could hear.

My cunning plan revolved around an old lottery ticket that I had in the coat pocket. I was hoping that he would be working on autopilot and that I would be passed the drugs before he realized that it wasn't a £10 note in his hand.

I passed the ticket, and his right hand automatically passed me a small clear bag of brown powder which I shoved in my pocket and then began to walk away.

'Oi, OI!' he yelled as he realized what had happened, and I began to shuffle faster across the car park, hoping that they would run rather than drive after me.

I was right and Paul, closely followed by Vinnie, raced over to me, letting me know where they were by the sounds of their steps. Just as I thought the first one was about to reach me I spun around, dropping into a crouch with my right leg while sweeping my left out in an arc behind me.

It worked like a charm and Paul went sprawling over my extended leg, banging into the gravel face first. Vinnie tried to slow down, but he was already moving too fast as I used my bent knee to launch myself upwards, my hand already raised to grab his arm and twist it up behind his back. I managed to pull the move off and he screamed as I pushed him off balance, using the pressure on his shoulder to keep control. I could hear the sounds of running feet and knew that the rest of the team was coming to my aid, but as I looked up to see how close they were, a huge weight hit me in the back and I fell on top of Vinnie, making me release my grip and tumbling us both to the ground.

Paul had regained his feet and thrown himself on me, pummelling the back of my head with his fists. I tucked my head in and rolled over, dislodging him, but one of his fists caught me in the mouth and I felt my top lip split open. Now lying on my back, I raised my leg high and dropped my heel into his face as he tried to scramble away, feeling it connect with bone. He yelled in pain and I rolled back to my feet, wiping the blood away from my mouth with the back of my hand. It hurt like blazes and as the rest of the team caught up and jumped on the surprised pair, I moved away and nursed my lip.

Vinnie tried to run but only made it a few yards before Rudd rugby tackled him, skinning his knuckles as they fell to the ground. Paul disappeared under the combined weight of Tate and Kev and very quickly resurfaced wearing a pair of handcuffs and a hangdog expression.

I ran over to help Rudd with the violently struggling Vinnie and, between us, we managed to contain him by dint of placing him in a ground pin, which is a double armlock that involves both officers kneeling on the hollow between arm and back, while raising the arms straight up while the prisoner is face down. Much like the pressure points, we had all had it done to us in training, and I can personally vouch for just how painful it is if you struggle.

Kev looked around to check that we were all okay, frowning when he saw my lip. 'You okay, Gareth?' he asked.

I nodded, still keeping both hands on Vinnie's right arm. 'Yeah, fine. He just clipped me.'

'I'll do more than clip you next time, you wanker!' Paul called out to me.

I ignored him, as did the others while Kev began issuing orders.

'Tate, you sit young Paul over there by the wall and make sure his hands stay in front of him. Rudd, Gareth, you two stay like that for a minute while I make a call.'

So saying, he took his mobile out and called comms direct, asking for a van and extra officers for a search, rather than use his radio and give the opposition a chance to work out what sort of kit we were using. All it would take on any job, would be for one of them to work out that we had covert gear on and the game would be up. Up till then, and even now, all of them seemed to think that plain-clothed officers used those clear curly-wurly earpieces that you see so often in films and we didn't want to disabuse them of the notion.

I heard Kev ask for a drugs dog as well but guessed by the expression on his face that the news wasn't good.

'Problem?' I asked as he put his phone away.

'Yeah, bloody cutbacks. Only one drug dog on for the entire force and that's in Hastings on a warrant. Minimum of two hours before it gets here.' He pulled a face, not wanting to vent further in front of the prisoners.

I'm not sure how long we knelt there waiting for backup to arrive and help with searching and transporting prisoners, but my arms were beginning to shake and my legs had gone dead by the time a police Transit arrived. Four officers got out, and I recognized Andy Coucher, young Bobby, and the two other probationers from the other day.

I grinned at Bobby, who had the good grace to look embarrassed, and gratefully surrendered my hold to another probationer as Andy looked on. I stood shakily and stretched my legs, wincing as the returning blood brought pins and needles with it.

'Thanks,' I said gratefully, patting the probationer on the back, and limped over to help Kev search the car.

As I got to it he pointed to the front passenger seat where Paul had been sitting and I saw a coin bag that was about half full of little brown and white packages. I turned back to the prisoners and opened my mouth to say the words, but Kev nudged me and whispered, 'Let them do it, and then they get the paperwork.'

I nodded and grinned, wincing as my lip split again, and went to give Andy the good news.

14

The events of that evening had delayed the start of our monthly get-together outside of work. It had become a tradition and I have to admit it was nice to spend some time with the guys without being paid for it. I arrived at the Pitcher and Piano just after nine thirty and nodded to the doorman as I entered. He studiously ignored me, just like he does every time I go there, and I shook my head as I climbed the stairs up to the bar.

The Pitcher is a fairly new bar at the end of East Street just over the road from the beach and it's very nicely decked out. For some reason it's become a favourite for police officers despite the high prices and occasionally snotty door staff.

The last one to arrive, I slid onto the end of a bench seat that curved around a large table and nearly fell over backwards as the combined weight of the team's aftershave hit me in the nose.

'Jesus, have you lot been in a brothel?' I asked, waving my hand in front of my face for effect.

Tate laughed and pushed a weird-looking red cocktail in front of me. 'Blame Rudd, he seems to think that he smells alluring.'

We all laughed while Rudd stood and began making body-builder poses until one of the door staff drifted over and frowned at him.

'Wow, friendly here, aren't they?' I remarked as the suited gorilla moved away.

Kev shook his head. 'Didn't you know it's illegal to smile and work security at the same time?'

'Come on, they're not all bad,' Ralphy butted in from behind a glass so filled with fruit and umbrellas that he looked as if he were drinking a jungle. 'You find me one doorman that either doesn't want to be a copper, isn't taking steroids, or doesn't walk around like he's got a roll of carpet under each arm and I'll give you,' he paused and checked his pocket, 'thirty-seven pence.'

I felt myself beginning to relax as the friendly argument kicked off. 'Come on, Ralphy, what would you know about steroids?' I gestured towards his more than ample figure, knowing that he wasn't the least bit ashamed of it.

'I'll have you know that beneath this well-paid-for shell beats the heart of an athlete.'

'Does he want it back?' Kev asked.

'Come on, lads, less chatter more drinking,' said Eddie, draining half his pint in one swift motion. 'Who wants another one?'

I raised my red concoction. 'I'll have something that a human could drink, please, preferably with vodka in it.'

The bar specializes in cocktails, with over fifty on the menu, yet somehow they'd managed to order me one that tasted like machine oil and perfume.

Eddie took orders and wandered over to the bar with Tommo in tow, while the rest of us continued to talk rubbish.

I relaxed into the camaraderie, slipping it on like a comfortable shirt and enjoying the lack of work talk. Inevitably it would eventually turn to it, as alcohol helped us trade war stories, but for now it was just a few lads relaxing after a hard week at work.

Every so often, my mind would dart back to the Budds and the drugs I still had hidden, but I pushed the thoughts away and instead concentrated on getting thoroughly drunk.

By eleven I'd had enough that I was tempted to go out clubbing, but the others were more interested in the casino a few streets away.

'Come on, Ding, what else have you got to spend your overtime on?' Eddie cajoled me, and finally I gave in.

We have a deal on nights out; we all go to the same place, no matter what, or we go home. There's no splitting up until the very end of the night if you stay out. I suspect this is so that we can all keep an eye on each other, as the only thing more dangerous than a bored South African is a pissed copper, as my dad is fond of saying.

We staggered out of the bar holding each other up and moved in a herd towards the casino. Kev split from the group, despite our protests, insisting that he had to get home and tuck Mrs Sands in. We walked him to a taxi first, then ambled to the casino and waved our membership cards at the doorman who didn't even look at them before waving us through.

'Good evening, gentlemen,' he said in a thick Eastern European accent as we passed him and headed for the lift.

The gambling hall wasn't that busy, with maybe fifty people clustered around the tables playing the various games. Personally I'm a great fan of the £2 blackjack table, as you can play for hours without losing too much cash. I convinced Ralphy and Tommo to join me, while the others went to either the bar or the other games.

As soon as Ralphy sat down, he waved a waitress over and ordered his free sandwich and coffee, ignoring my laugh. 'Need fuel, Ding, or I can't concentrate on beating the house now, can I?'

I ignored the growling of my own stomach, not wanting to order food after laughing at Ralphy, so instead turned to the table and began to play.

After about twenty minutes and the same amount of money

leaving my pocket, Tommo nudged me and leaned over to speak quietly in my ear. 'Do you see that bloke over there by the toilets?'

I looked to where he nodded and saw a man in jeans and a T-shirt, with long hair that fell past his shoulders. 'Yeah, what about him?'

Tommo tapped the table to tell the dealer he was sticking and lowered his voice even further. 'Well, every so often the bloke with the shades on his head over by the roulette will take someone into the toilets, and then rock star over there stops anyone else from going in. Once the other chap comes out, whoever he's been in there with leaves the building. Want to guess what they're doing?'

I closed my eyes for a second. 'Tommo, we're not working. He's probably just selling a few grams of coke. Is it worth blowing out in front of a whole casino while you're pissed, just to bag a low-level dealer?'

He shook his head. 'Thing is, I don't think it's low level. One of the blokes that he went in with was Peter Connelly.'

My ears pricked up at this, and I turned to study the people involved more carefully. Connelly is a medium-sized cocaine dealer, usually selling a minimum of ten grams at a time, if our intelligence is accurate.

That meant that whoever he was buying off had to be a step up the chain.

'Look, we call it in, and then keep playing. I'm not getting involved when I'm this drunk.'

Tommo gripped my arm. 'You're not that drunk, I've seen you fight off three blokes drunker than this in Heist, remember?' He was referring to another night out where it had all gone wrong a few years before.

'Yeah, I remember, but I had no choice then.'

Tommo shook his head again. 'Look, I'm telling the others, and then we can make a group decision.'

Before I could stop him he was off his chair and heading over to Eddie, Rudd and Tate, who were all leaning on the bar trying to chat up the lone barmaid.

'Where's he gone?' asked Ralphy.

I told him what Tommo had pointed out and he threw his cards in and headed over to the others at the bar. Left with little choice, I followed him rather than be left alone. By the time we got there Tate and Tommo had already formed a plan of action.

'Right,' said Tate, looking around to make sure we couldn't be overheard. 'Tommo, you go for a piss. Stay there until the bloke with the shades goes in again and we'll come in a few seconds behind, after we've dealt with his hippy bouncer. Keep it nice and simple, no frills. Questions?'

I nodded. 'Yeah, am I the only one who thinks this is a bad idea?'

Everyone nodded back. I threw my hands up in surrender. 'Okay, okay, I'm in, but I still think it's a terrible idea.'

Tate fixed me with a stern look as if I was challenging his authority. 'Nothing's going to go wrong, as long as we all work together. Stop being such a girl and get ready. Right, places gentlemen, I see movement.'

Tommo walked to the toilets and disappeared while the rest of us loitered at tables nearby, not really concentrating on the games.

I lost another tenner in the first couple of minutes, and then lost interest as I saw Shades walk towards the toilets in company with a slim Iranian-looking male with oily black hair and a jawline beard. As soon as the door swung shut the 'hippy bouncer', as Tate had called him, moved to stand in front of the door. It wasn't the subtlest of operations but no one else in there seemed to be batting an eyelid.

The rest of us converged on the toilet from different directions, with Ralphy somehow getting there first. The chap with the long hair made the mistake of placing his hand on Ralphy's chest to stop him from going any further, and the big man took the proffered hand delicately between finger and thumb and twisted the wrist around sharply, dumping the man on the floor while Eddie stepped in and placed him in a chokehold before he could cry out.

Leaving Eddie and Ralphy outside, Tate, Rudd and I headed into the toilets. The door led onto a short corridor with another swing door at the far end and we bundled through in no particular order to see Shades and his friend swapping a package of cocaine that would have made a rock star start sweating in anticipation.

The marble front of the washstand it was resting on was leaning against the wall nearby and I could see another package almost as large nestled within. Shades turned to look at us, his expression a mixture of shock and outrage, and suddenly threw the first package at us as he bolted for the cubicles, obviously intent on locking himself in and calling for help.

As the package flew towards me I went for a catch but only caught it with my fingertips, tearing the plastic and sending white powder bursting through the air like a cluster bomb. We were instantly covered, and I began coughing as some of the dust hit me in the throat. Shades almost made it to the cubicles when one of the doors flew open and Tommo lurched out, arms wide as he tackled the dealer to the ground.

The Iranian male was still frozen in place, a look of resignation on his face. No one had shown a badge yet and he raised his hands and backed away from the drugs, probably thinking that we were rival dealers.

'Don't move,' Tate warned him, pulling out his mobile phone. 'I'm arresting you both for possession of cocaine with intent to supply; we'll sort out the niceties later.'

Just as he finished speaking, the door behind us burst open and three more blokes ran in, along with a woman that I vaguely recognized. I swung to face them, and then overbalanced as the coke I'd inhaled began to hit my bloodstream.

'Are they who I think they are?' I asked, turning to Rudd.

He grinned at me ludicrously and nodded. I laughed with him as a strange fire ran through my veins and I began to bounce on the balls of my feet. I kept getting funny shivers coursing through me and had a kind of nervous sickness in my stomach. I'd never taken drugs before, and despite the laughter I didn't feel in control and I didn't like it as the cocaine worked its way into my system.

The older of the newcomers, one Detective Sergeant Lucas Wyatt, from the Serious Organised Crime Unit, stepped forward and regarded us with disgust.

'What the hell do you think you lot are doing? You've just ruined a two-month job!'

I shrugged, feeling totally unconcerned. 'Uh, don't blame me; I thought this was a stupid idea. Ask Tate.' I pointed helpfully at Tate, who glared back at me, having been outside the range of the coke explosion.

The other SOCU officers (not to be confused with SOCO – they don't like that) stepped around us carefully, ensuring that they didn't contaminate the area anymore than it had been already. In moments, they had expertly cuffed the two males we'd detained, and then removed them equally carefully.

Wyatt took Tate out into the corridor, and I could hear their voices raised in sharp exchange. Rudd and I looked at each other and began giggling again until he pointed us out in the mirror and we both began roaring with laughter, seeing two ghost-like white figures staring back at us, almost completely covered in cocaine.

Even when we were ordered out by Wyatt and into the back of a van, where we were forced to strip as our clothes were now evidence, I couldn't bring myself to care while wrapped in the haze of the drugs I'd inhaled.

15

I thought that our job of the evening before would be the talk of the office, but it turned out that while we had been busy taking out one lot of dealers, someone else had been busy in Hove and a well-known dealer had been stabbed a couple of times in the chest. He was stable, but rumours were already flying that it had been a murder attempt and that whoever had done it would be out to finish the job.

Tate's theory was that it was the beginning of a war between rival dealers, which is something we all dread. Brighton is fairly safe as far as drug wars go; the last one we had was two groups from London who had tried to define their turf on the beach by beating the hell out of each other with chains and knives every Friday night last summer. Luckily we'd managed to get one of their fights on a hidden CCTV camera (they always managed to avoid the overt ones), and we had put enough of them away for public order offences that the few who were left outside the net had plenty of space to choose from after that.

Rudd chimed in, agreeing with Tate over the drug-war theory. 'I reckon it's the Scousers. They've been coming down here for long enough to know the city now, but they're selling really low-quality stuff so they need to get a monopoly on the market if they want to keep customers.' The Scousers he was talking about were a group led by a man nicknamed Trash, whose real name is Kieran Phelps. He and his gang had been dealing in Brighton for the past couple of years and there was a saying in the office that as soon as you arrested one lot of his runners, another Vauxhall Vectra-full was already leaving Liverpool. They were like cockroaches; you just couldn't get rid of them no matter what you tried.

Sally shook her head. 'I don't think so, Ian, they would never have worked alone and all the witness statements say that it was only one guy. All the stuff we've got on them says that they work in groups if they're going to get violent. What do you think, Gareth?'

I thought for a minute, not sure if it was worth mentioning Davey and his penchant for knives before deciding that it was too unlikely that he would be out stabbing other dealers openly.

'Maybe they hired someone in? We've seen that they don't like getting their hands dirty if they can help it. Or maybe it's one of the London crews, or the Wolverhampton lot?'

As I think I may have mentioned, Brighton is a soft target for dealers, lots of buyers and comparatively few guns to deal with.

Tate folded his arms across his chest. 'I'm with Rudd; I think its Trash's lot. They've been getting a bit cocky lately. Have we got anything on their latest properties?'

Sally turned back to her desk to look through the weekly reports but stopped when Rudd said, 'They're living in a house on Pankhurst Avenue, off Queens Park Road. At least they were two days ago. Do you think we should stir things up a bit and see what floats to the surface?'

Tate nodded. 'I think that's probably a good idea. I'll talk to Kev before the meeting and see what he thinks.'

He left the pod and went to confer with Kev while I looked over the reports from the attack the night before. Apparently three people had seen the fight, but due to distance the descriptions they gave of the assailant were all different, unsurprisingly.

It's very difficult for a lot of people to accurately describe everything that they've seen; most people tend to focus on one detail and the rest blurs.

Just as Tate came back, Kev ushered us upstairs to the daily meeting where everything of note that had happened in the last twenty-four hours was mentioned, and we all crammed in around the conference table in the meeting room with some of us having to use the chairs sprinkled around the edges.

Nothing particularly interesting came out of the meeting except for a series of sex attacks around St Nicholas's Church, just west of the town centre on Dyke Road. A lone male had been busy the night before and had grabbed three separate women on their way back from clubbing in the town centre. We threw that around the table for a while, trying to work out how he could avoid the first two area searches to strike again, and the favourite theory was that he lived in the area and could duck into a house between attacks. Eddie, whose main job was sex offences and violent crime, said that he'd look into it and offered to jack up an operation by the end of the week if he hadn't been caught by then.

I asked for the description again and this time memorized it. A white male, about forty years old with dark hair in a widow's peak. A few days' worth of stubble, medium build and wearing a black jacket and combat trousers. It didn't sound like anyone I knew, but it was always worth remembering a description like that in case you saw them while you were out and about. I hoped that he did get caught before he struck again but, if not, I was more than happy to volunteer for the operation that Eddie was talking about. Even if it did involve hanging around a graveyard for hours.

I was still thinking about it when a pencil hit me in the face, making me shout in surprise, which in turn brought peals of laughter from everybody. Looking up with a face red from embarrassment, I saw Kev waiting with his arms folded.

'Morning, Ding, anything to report on drugs?'

I nodded and went through the list, mostly sightings of known drug users or members of the public calling in to complain about dealing in their area.

'Thanks, Gareth. After the meeting, you and Tate go and swear out a warrant at the court for the Pankhurst address and we'll see what you turn up. Anything else from anybody? No? Okay, thank you.'

We all filed out and back down to the office where I busied myself with digging out all the reports we had on 109 Pankhurst Avenue. There were about a dozen and I picked the most recent and most relevant, printing off hard copies to take to the court.

Tate went down to the typing pool and got a drugs warrant typed up. It's about the only thing that typewriters are still used for; they have one sitting at the back of the station just for warrants. Despite the fact that it's electronic, it's old enough that only two of the ladies in the typing pool know how to use it.

I then dug through my SharePoint and found the form that I needed to get signed by an inspector so that I could go and get the warrant signed.

I wandered through into the CID office and found DI Jones sitting behind her desk. It was the first time I had seen her since the court case and I knocked on the door with no little trepidation. I needn't have worried as she looked up with a smile when she saw me.

'Ah, Gareth, how are you?'

'I'm good, thanks, ma'am. You okay after the whole Davey thing?'

She shook her head, a frown marring her face. 'Not really, but what can you do when security here is like a leaky sieve?'

I shrugged. 'Go out and get drunk?'

She laughed at that. 'Come on, you reprobate, I'm sure you

didn't come to chat. Is that a warrant request in your hand?'

I nodded and passed it over. I then showed her the intel, and she made a note of all of it in her investigator's notebook. Everything has to have an audit trail nowadays and she needed to show that she had considered all the intelligence for its accuracy and relevance before she signed the warrant, or she would be in as much shit as we would if it all went wrong.

Intelligence is graded in a 5 x 5 x 5 system, depending on where it comes from, how much you trust them and what you are allowed to do with the information. So me seeing Quentin Davey sitting in a car would be an A-1-1 report. I'm a trusted source, the information is known to be true without reservation and it can be disseminated to anyone with clearance that it may be relevant to.

Most of the intelligence on 109 Pankhurst was C-2-1, but there were a few As and Bs as well, so there was more than enough for a warrant.

You may ask why, if we had enough, we hadn't just knocked the door down ages ago, so I'll explain. It's a bit like a game, you see. We need to catch them with their pants down. There's no point, usually, knocking a door in if we don't know for sure who is inside or whether or not they have any drugs on the premises. We need to watch it for a while, covertly of course, to see when deliveries are made and when, if ever, it opens for business.

So there's no point hitting it on a Wednesday when they don't re-stock until Thursday night. We're better off hitting it Friday morning, early, while they're all still asleep and dreaming about how rich they'll be when they finally get out of the racket. If we hit them while they're empty, they all get away, move house, and we spend another month trying to track them down while they keep peddling death on our streets.

Except in situations like the one we were trying to crack, where we needed to shake them up and see what fell out. We didn't really care if they moved on or didn't have anything, because all we were interested in was the information they had. Unless, of course, we got lucky and the house was full of drugs.

I took back my signed form and gave her a cheery wave as I left, walking back through the CID office that's a carbon copy of ours, except that everyone wears suits and has mountains of crime files to investigate.

Back in DIU, Tate was sitting there with the warrant, almost bouncing in his chair with his need to go. He is always like that; cool, calm and efficient until it's time to strike, and then he acts like a kid on Christmas Eve.

Being a Saturday, we couldn't simply go next door to the magistrates' court and get a judge to authorise the warrant. Instead, we had to find the out of hours on-call magistrate and drive over to his house, or in this case flat on the edge of Kemptown.

When the door opened after much banging, Tate showed his badge to a tired-looking man in his mid-forties wearing a track-suit and a sleepy expression.

I feel sorry for magistrates; unlike crown or county judges they don't get paid for their work, other than expenses. I knew this one; his name is John Crick and he's a nurse at the Royal Sussex, for some reason volunteering to be a magistrate in what little spare time he has.

Crick led us into his painfully tidy flat and through a long hallway to the lounge. He gestured us towards a sofa and took a chair for himself. As he sat he gave us a brief smile and got straight down to business. 'Gentlemen, I guess you have a warrant to be authorized. Would you like to tell me the intelligence you have and the grading, please?'

Tate went through the material we had, never actually lying but dressing it up in such a way that it sounded far more urgent than it was. I was impressed; I would have struggled and I'm known for my ability to get warrants even the old sergeant, Karl

Darney, wouldn't have been able to get through, despite being the biggest bullshitter to ever be given a badge.

'Any children in the address or any risk of firearms?' Crick asked, showing that despite his tiredness he was still on the ball.

'No, sir,' Tate replied, handing the warrant over to the magistrate.

'Fine, well you go out and get them. Best of luck!' he said as he signed the warrant, tore off the rear copy and handed the rest back to us.

We smiled our way out, almost tripping over each other in our haste to pay a surprise visit on Trash and his friends.

16

An hour later, three plain cars parked on Queens Park Road and eight of us ran in single file towards the target address. We had tried to get LST support for the entry and search but unfortunately they were tied up on another warrant, so I was wearing a PSU helmet (like the cash-carrying ones), a head-over that only showed my eyes, and a long-sleeved tear-resistant PSU jacket which was also fireproof, all to stop any glass that might shatter when I went through the door.

I was also carrying Baby, our door bosher, or enforcer as the proper name should be, hoisted over one shoulder as we ran. The enforcer is 35 lbs of solid steel with a flat strike plate at the business end, capable of turning my puny swing into over a ton of force as it strikes a door, providing that the door is being braced properly. That normally involves another Method of Entry officer placing his feet against the base of the door, ensuring that the force of the strike goes through instead of dissipating as the door flexes.

Rudd, the other MoE officer, was to be the footer. As we reached the door to the threebedroom semi-detached that was our target, he ran up to it and began pushing at it with both hands, checking to see where it was locked. He pointed to, first, the top of the door, then the middle, and lay down on the concrete path to place both feet against the wood.

Time was of the essence. It wasn't the best part of Brighton and already I could see people hanging out of windows along the road and using mobile phones, so I turned the bosher upside down and leaned backwards, swinging up and attacking the top lock first with a resounding boom that echoed down the street and probably could have woken the dead.

I felt the lock go on the first swing and used the momentum of lowering the enforcer to power my next strike at waist height, careful to avoid the safety glass window in the centre of the door. I felt the door shudder but it didn't open so I swung once more, putting all fourteen stone behind it. The door flew open, knocking someone behind it off their feet as they tried to brace it with a bit of two-by-four.

'BREACH!' I shouted, years of training taking over as I stepped out of the way and grounded the bosher, ready to join the flood of officers running over Rudd as he made himself as small as possible. Finally, everyone was in and I followed, Rudd coming in behind me. Tate was already cuffing the guy I had knocked down. Blood seeped from a gash right in the middle of his forehead, but it didn't look serious enough to worry about before we'd secured everyone else in the house.

Most of the others had gone upstairs, so I joined Kev and Rudd in securing the ground floor. The house wasn't huge, just a lounge-diner and a kitchen with a small hallway between the two, but it had an amazing amount of crap stored in it. Boxes and bags were piled up against the walls, and the kitchen looked like a dozen teenagers had been using it for a decade without cleaning up.

The whole place stank of mildew, rotten food, and dog shit, which should have warned me really. Gagging even through my head-over, I opened the back door to get some air then closed it again hurriedly as a massive Rottweiler charged at me from the tiny garden, growling menacingly. I managed to get the door locked just as the dog slammed against it, rattling the whole house, then carefully took the key out and placed it on the windowsill. I did *not* want that thing getting in there.

Eddie called down that they had two people secured upstairs, and Rudd and I cleared the sofa of rubbish, mostly takeaway wrappers, so that we could keep them all in one place. We also searched it carefully, coming up with two kitchen knives, a flick knife and a rubber cosh, all hidden behind the cushions. You couldn't be too careful in the life they'd chosen; it was all too easy to get done-over if you weren't.

Once the sofa was cleared, all three prisoners were sat down. Aside from the man I'd knocked over, there was another man, clearly a user from the marks on his arms, and a scrawny woman with bleach blonde hair and a mouth the size of the Thames Estuary. She was shrieking and calling Eddie all sorts of names, and I stepped in before it could escalate.

'Look, love, just shut up and this'll be over much faster. We don't want to be here,' I looked around pointedly, 'anymore than you do, but we've got a job to do and the sooner you quieten down the sooner we're out of your hair.'

'You can't talk to me like that in my own house, how dare you! Anyway, I'm not the coward with his face covered up!'

I realized that I still had my helmet and head-over on, so I took them off and placed them carefully on top of a search bag where they wouldn't touch the grimy carpet.

Kev split us into search teams and I was again paired with Rudd and given one of the bedrooms upstairs. Kev would act as exhibits officer, writing down and logging everything that we found, as well as guarding the three cuffed prisoners, while the others would act as search teams and clear the other rooms.

It was easily one of the most unpleasant searches I have ever done. I found out through a rather dated passport that the woman was called Nancy Pemble and had been born in Brighton forty-one years before. Clearly that hadn't been enough time to attend a basic hygiene course, however, as not only were there takeaway

114

boxes and dirty plates all over the house but under the bed was a pile of used condoms, and worse, used sanitary towels. I almost gagged when I saw them and warned Rudd about them too.

Joking about and setting your mates up when you are safe is one thing, but when it involves bodily fluids, needles or anything else dangerous it doesn't happen, period, and we always warn the others about anything dangerous we find.

There were dozens of used needles on the floor and in every cupboard and drawer I searched, so we double-gloved and tipped out every drawer before checking the contents.

The hours dragged by and eventually we finished, finding two small bags of heroin that Nancy admitted were hers. Unfortunately though, if they knew anything about the attack they were keeping it to themselves. Not even Kev with all his charm could get a whisper out of them.

We had managed to convince a pair of response officers to act as transport for our lovely lady, and after leaving them in her delightful company we headed back to the nick to book in the drugs and have a much-needed cup of tea.

I also wanted to change my clothes as I felt dirty, as if a sheen of something loathsome had stuck to me while searching the house. I've always hated searching in plain clothes as we don't get an allowance, so they're just normal clothes that we wear in to work. That means you can search a shithole like that and, if you forget yourself, it's all too easy to go home and sit on your sofa, spreading the germs that you've picked up. Officers have contracted everything from bed bugs to scabies that way and just thinking about it makes me itch.

The first thing I did was go down to my locker and put on a spare pair of jeans and a clean Tshirt, kept there for just that kind of moment, then I headed back up to the office, intent on getting my statement done then planning what I would do that evening. Not that I had much in the way of a social life at that time, with

Jimmy in the hospital and most of my friends outside the job married with kids.

As I walked into the pod, though, I saw Sally sitting at her desk twiddling a pencil listlessly with a tight expression on her face as if she was trying not to cry.

'What's up?' I asked, keeping my tone light.

She sighed and looked over at me, her face marred by a frown. 'That bloody wanker cancelled on me again, and then when I complained he dumped me, the bastard!'

Trying to make light of it I gave her a smile. 'Well you can always go out to dinner with me instead?'

She perked up immediately, a smile appearing as if by magic. 'Really?'

I hadn't expected that. 'Uh, yeah, sure. I've got no plans tonight. Jimmy's folks are visiting him, so I'm staying away. His mum thinks I'm the devil, always leading her little boy into mischief, so I try and avoid her.'

Happy now, she unleashed the full force of her smile at me, making me go weak at the knees. 'Do you want to meet at about eight? Where do you want to take me?'

I nearly swallowed my own tongue as I tried to think of an answer that wouldn't get me slapped. 'Errr, how about Browns on Ship Street?' Browns is a particularly nice restaurant, one of the best I've eaten at, and I knew I'd made the right choice as her smile got even wider.

'Fantastic! It's a date!'

I smiled and turned back to my desk, struggling to believe that one of the most beautiful girls I'd ever met wanted to go for dinner with me, even if I was a substitute for the low-life idiot that had stood her up. I realized I'd have to put that night's plans on hold, leaving the pot noodle and DVD that had been calling for another time, but glancing back at the now happily humming Sally, I had the feeling it was probably worth it.

17

Sally only kept me waiting for fifteen minutes, which isn't bad for her, judging by how late she always turns up for work dos. I stood outside, enjoying the late evening sunlight and checked my reflection in the large restaurant windows for the fifteenth time. I'd chosen a grey pinstripe shirt with loose black trousers and no jacket or tie. The shirt had been a gift from Jimmy, who swears that I'd go to weddings in a T-shirt if I had my way. He's probably right. My thinking on the matter is that the way someone dresses doesn't matter as much as the person themselves and being scruffy is at least a talking point; but I took that all back as Sally walked into view.

She was wearing a light cotton summer dress with a floral pattern, and I reckoned that a light breeze would tell me what she was wearing underneath, it was so short. She was also wearing heels, which she never does at work, and had just enough make-up on to enhance her looks without detracting from her natural beauty.

I'd never seen her looking so good – and neither had every bloke she walked past as she came towards me. I was glad the road was quiet or there would have been an accident.

'Sorry I'm late,' she said, leaning over and kissing me on the cheek. 'Damn taxi took ages to arrive.'

I smiled, still slightly dazed by her being here with me. 'That's fine. I booked the table earlier, so they can wait. You look amazing by the way.'

She blushed. 'Really?' she asked, and I honestly think she didn't know.

'Well put it this way, if I had a choice of you, Kate Moss and Jessica Alba I'd still be going in here with you.'

She laughed and batted the back of my head with one hand, but slipped the other through my arm and we walked in together to the envious looks of every other man in the restaurant.

The waiter who seated us seemed equally taken by my date and all but dribbled on her as he spread the napkin on her lap. He caught my warning look though and remembered his manners, offering us the wine list and then moving a discreet distance away.

'And what would madam care to drink?' I asked in a posh voice.

She giggled. 'Um, I think madam would like a nice white wine, but not too much or I'll get tiddly.'

I ordered an expensive bottle of white then tried to make intelligent conversation, which I've never been particularly good at with pretty women. 'So, how was work for you today?' I asked, not finding anything else to say despite the inanity of the question.

'Yeah, it was okay. I get a bit bored sometimes though, I wish I could come out with you lot instead.'

'I wish you could too, we could do with another pair of hands. You should have been at this search we were on this morning. My God, we found some—' I stopped, realizing that I was sounding job-pissed. Too many officers are – and all they ever talk about is work. I would never come across as interesting, funny and intelligent if I kept talking about work, and I badly wanted to seem all three. 'Sorry, here I am, talking about work. So where are you from originally?' I asked, realizing that we never actually talked that much at work, and apart from her terrible

118

taste in men (myself excluded, of course) I knew next to nothing about her.

She looked pleased that I was asking about her. 'Well my dad is from London, but my mum is Russian,' she began, explaining her looks. 'But I was born in Northampton. We moved to London when I was ten, and when I was nineteen I moved to Brighton to go to university.'

'Oh really, what did you study?'

She looked a little shy as she spoke, peering up at me from beneath her eyelashes. 'Architecture – but I never finished the degree, I got bored. Besides, it's not what I really wanted to do.'

'Oh really, what was that?'

Her look went from shy to defiant. 'If you laugh, I'll hit you.'

I held my hands up in mock surrender. 'Okay, no laughing, I promise.'

'I wanted to play the tuba professionally.'

I laughed; she hit me and then joined in with the laughter.

'Can you imagine me, with a tuba? I must have been mad!'

I took a sip of the excellent wine, noticing that her first glass was already almost gone. 'Why the tuba? It's not the most glamorous of professions.'

'And being a drug researcher for Sussex Police is?'

'No, that's fair,' I answered, refilling our glasses from the bottle.

'Anyway, that's enough about me. What about you? You're an intelligent bloke, why did you decide to join the police?'

I swallowed my instant retort about the intelligence comment, knowing that she wasn't being rude about my colleagues. 'Really? It's a long story, are you sure you want to hear it?'

She nodded, and I was about to tell her when the waiter came over to take our order. I knew what I wanted and ordered the peppered steak rare enough that it still might moo, but Sally wasn't sure and took a good few minutes to choose. Once she had finally picked a duck dish that I could barely even pronounce, she reminded me that I had been about to tell my story.

'Okay, well my dad always wanted to join the police and he gave me a very firm idea of right and wrong when I was a kid. Both me and my brother in fact.'

'I didn't know you had a brother!' she interrupted.

'I don't talk about him much; I'll tell you why in a minute. Anyway, so I went away to university to study English, and Mum got ill. It turned out to be cancer, a particularly aggressive form, and she died while I was away. They hadn't told me how bad it was at the time because they didn't want it to ruin my studies.' I tried not to let the bitterness I still feel come out in my voice.

'So, Dad calls me and I come back for the funeral and take a couple of weeks out, staying with Dad and Jake. I hadn't seen my brother for ages and when I came back I noticed that he was different. He looked thinner and ill and he was acting strangely. He kept borrowing money off Dad to go into Brighton, even though he had a job at a local garage as a mechanic. When I asked him about the money, he got aggressive and we had the first proper fight we'd ever had. He nearly knocked me out, but during the fight one of his sleeves got pulled up and I saw track marks all over his arm.'

I stopped for a moment, uncomfortable with the subject. It isn't something that I like to talk about, but Sally was obviously hooked on the story, her head tilted slightly to the left as she listened intently, so I continued.

'As soon as he knew I'd seen them, he got all funny, started apologizing and said that he'd been cut by a chain at work, even though they clearly weren't chain marks. I went back up to university the next day and didn't think anything more about it for a while, other than occasionally asking Dad how Jake was when I phoned.

'Then one day I got a call from Dad saying that Jake had gone missing, and that he'd been burgled as well. He phoned the police, worried that Jake had been kidnapped trying to defend the house or something, and they investigated, but the only fingerprints they could find, even inside Dad's safe, were Jake's. So I left university and came back to stay with Dad. Of course, he wouldn't believe that one of his sons would steal from him, so he kept badgering the police and one day they turned up with some pictures of Jake, taken during a heroin deal that they'd caught on CCTV. Even from a distance you could tell it was Jake and what he was doing. Dad was beside himself but he still spent the next few years looking for Jake, posting his picture on the internet and offering a reward. I still don't think he's really given up hope that Jake will appear on the doorstep one day to beg forgiveness.'

I paused and took another sip of wine to wet my mouth. 'And I joined the police so that I could stop more families being torn apart by heroin. Bit of a sob story, huh?' I laughed, but Sally just looked at me seriously over the top of her wine glass.

'I don't think it's a sob story, I think it's a terrible thing. Do you know how he got started on it?' she asked, her eyes shining with unshed tears.

'No, I've got no idea, but if I ever find the bastard that got him hooked I'm going to rip his lungs out with my bare hands.'

I stopped talking as the main course arrived, realizing that my revenge daydreams weren't exactly polite dinner conversation. My steak was perfect; the sauce creamy and spicy at the same time, and Sally's duck was just as well cooked. We chatted about inconsequential stuff after that, and I have to say that we got on better than I ever thought we would. Sally turned out to have a wicked sense of humour and a sharp intellect that she only allowed a little of to show at work. Yet again I was amazed that a woman this rare allowed herself to be treated like shit by wide boys and wannabe gangsters.

We polished off another bottle of wine over dessert and subsequently we were both quite tipsy as we left the restaurant, strolling arm in arm towards the taxi rank at East Street by the old Hannington's store. Sally smelled almost as good as she looked and I enjoyed the cool evening breeze wafting her scent towards me as we walked. When we got to the rank there were several taxis but no queue, so I prepared myself for a quick goodbye, wishing that things were otherwise.

'Right, you're up towards Lewes Road, aren't you?' I asked, trying not to sound disappointed.

She moved in close to me, holding her face inches away from mine as a tension began to develop that I knew couldn't just be coming from me.

'Do you really want me to go home alone?' she asked, her voice low and throaty.

I looked into her eyes, losing myself in them for a moment as I discovered little gold flecks I had never seen before. Not that I'd ever been that close to her.

'Um, well, that would be rude of me, wouldn't it? And I do pride myself on being a gentleman.'

She leaned forward and touched her lips to mine, keeping eye contact all the while. My body rose to the occasion and she giggled as she snuggled in against me, gyrating her hips ever so slightly. 'It's a shame I don't screw on a first date then, isn't it?'

She pulled away slightly as she spoke, and I tried my best to hide the disappointment that must have been written all over my face.

'Um, yeah, I mean, look, it's not a problem. Part of being a gentleman is being able to wait. It's not like sex is the be-all and end-all, is it?' I could tell by the smile flickering about her lips that she was playing me for laughs, pretending to be awkward, but I couldn't bring myself to play the game.

I think she saw that and relented a little. 'Well, if you really are a gentleman, you won't mind opening the cab door for me, then escorting me home.'

I've never moved so fast in my life. I almost yanked the door off its hinges then slowed down to offer her my arm as she stepped into the back. I joined her and we snuggled together as we headed back to her house on Brading Road, still unable to believe my luck.

The journey seemed to take about thirty years and I honestly don't remember what we talked about on the way there, but I do remember paying the cab driver generously and letting her lead me up the steps to the house she shared with a friend whose name I couldn't remember and didn't particularly care about right then.

As soon as the door closed, Sally slammed me up against it and did her best to devour me (despite my protests, of course). We were undressing each other as we went up the stairs and I nearly tripped and spoiled the moment as she undid my trousers before I had reached the top.

I managed to waddle into the bedroom after her and we both fell on her bed in a giggling heap. By now she was down to her underwear, black lacy items that showed more than they hid. With practised ease, I slipped one hand up her back and undid her bra. She shucked it off, and then disentangled herself to stand outlined against the lamplight like an angel sent to taunt me.

'Do you like what you see?' she asked, her voice suddenly shy.

My answer was to reach for her again and all sense of time fled as I buried myself in her warm curves.

18

I woke up with that sudden surprise you get when you realize that you aren't in your own bed. I rolled over, only to find Sally asleep on my arm with the covers thrown back so that I could admire her sleeping form. For a moment I thought I was dreaming, but the lingering taste of her was too real and I gently began kissing her neck and shoulders until she woke up and turned to kiss me properly.

'Well, PC Bell,' she said, unconcerned at the situation, 'you certainly have a lot of stamina, I don't think I'll be able to walk for a week!'

I smiled and carried on kissing her, moving down until I was over her again and we made love slowly, all the while looking into each other's eyes. I hadn't felt like that with somebody since I was sixteen and new to the game, and I saw an answering look in her eyes to the unspoken question in mine as we moved gently against each other, our breathing fast as sweat gathered on our bodies. The world shuddered as we collapsed against each other, almost laughing with the simultaneous release.

'You do know we're going to be late for work?' she asked some time later as she slid deftly out from under me.

'Yeah, I don't really care right now,' I replied, admiring her body before it disappeared beneath the towel she took off the radiator.

'Well I'm going to shower. Go and find the tea and put some toast on.'

I dug out my boxer shorts and did as I was told, padding down the stairs and into the kitchen at the back, whistling happily. I stopped dead in my tracks as I reached the kitchen, seeing a dark-haired girl in a skimpy shift who I could only assume was the nameless housemate, eating a bowl of cereal and reading a newspaper at the kitchen table. She looked up as I came in and waved me towards the kettle with a vague smile. 'Tea and coffee over there. Hi, I'm Amy.'

'Uh, hi, Gareth. I, uh, work with Sally.'

Amy swung round to look at me properly, suddenly interested. 'Gareth? Really? God, she never stops talking about you; it's nice to finally meet you!'

I wasn't sure what to say to that, so I made a non-committal noise and busied myself with making the tea. I felt more than a little self-conscious in just my underwear but I refused to retreat, so I made two cups of tea and four slices of toast before I left Amy and her inquisitive gaze to the newspaper.

Sally was back in the room by the time I returned and gently but forcefully refused my amorous advances as she dressed and threw me a towel. 'You stink, go and wash.'

Once again I did as I was told and in remarkably short time we were out of the house and in her car, heading towards work.

I rested my hand on her leg all the way in, enjoying the simple human comfort of just touching her, and she kept throwing smiles at me as she drove. I still felt like a sixteen-year-old falling in love for the first time, and I was about to say something along those lines when something else occurred to me.

'Sally, you know we have to keep this quiet at work, right?'

'Why, are you embarrassed?'

I looked at her to see if she was joking, but she stared resolutely ahead and I couldn't tell. 'Of course not, far from it, but you

125

know the rules on relationships in the office. We have to keep it professional and that'll be easier if no one knows.'

She grinned suddenly and the shadow that had been hovering over my heart disappeared. 'I know, you idiot, I was kidding. Can you imagine the piss-taking we'd have to endure if Kev found out?'

I rolled my eyes at the thought. I wouldn't put it past him to somehow get a banner placed on the intranet homepage if he found out; he would think it was hilarious.

For the sake of appearances, Sally dropped me off a couple of streets away from work and I walked the distance trying to wipe the grin off my face. I finally got into the office about five minutes late but no one seemed to care as I sat down in the drugs pod, making sure to greet Sally just the same as everyone else. It would have been easier if flashbacks of her naked body writhing against mine hadn't kept intruding.

It was a busy day and the time flew by as the team went out en masse to follow a new group of dealers that had recently come into town from London. By the time I got back to the office, it was nearing six and Sally had already gone home.

I wrote my reports as fast as I could and went down to the car park to drive home before remembering that Sally had driven me in and my car was still outside my house. Cursing, I walked out through the car park and headed to the bus stop at the Old Steine, managing to jump on a number five just before it pulled off. I sat slumped in my seat, trying to work out what I was going to do that evening. I needed to visit Jimmy but afterwards I was torn between visiting Sally and leaving it a few days so that I didn't seem too keen.

It should have been an easy decision, but this felt like the first time in a long while that something good had happened to me and I didn't want to ruin it. Fate, however, seemed to know exactly what it wanted me to do and as the bus pulled into Norfolk

Square I saw Gordon Edwards, a man reputed to be a fairly large-sized cog in Davey's heroin machine, disappearing up a side road towards Montpelier Terrace while putting a set of car keys into his pocket as he went.

I jumped off the bus, annoying the queue of people trying to board, and followed him at a distance as he headed north. He was looking nervous, so I knew he was up to no good, and this was too fortuitous an opportunity to pass up. I pulled out my mobile and tried to call Kev to let him know what I had, but it just rang without being answered so I pocketed it again and concentrated on my quarry.

He turned left onto Montpelier, disappearing from sight, and I hurried to the end of the road and crossed to the far side as if I had intended to go that way all along. I found him again seconds later heading towards Furze Hill, still looking about to make sure he wasn't being followed. I resisted the urge to pull out my phone and fake a conversation, instead trudging along with my hands in my pockets trying to *think* like I belonged.

He obviously didn't find me suspicious and turned into Furze Hill itself, heading towards St Ann's Well Gardens, one of the most pleasant parks in Brighton (Hove, actually). I turned into the road about thirty seconds behind him only to see him get into the back of a silver Vectra with an 08 plate, a sure sign that it was a hire car. The car drove off before I could take down the full index but stopped fifty yards down the road to drop Edwards off again. I knew that the only reason he would be getting into and out of a car so quickly was to buy or sell drugs and quickly made the decision that with or without backup I was going to stop him and find out what he was up to.

As the car drove off once more, Edwards strolled back towards me then took a right into the park. I began to jog, wanting to catch him in the shady area under the trees before you got into the park proper. I tried to be as quiet as possible but as I approached him he turned and looked at me, so I resolutely looked forward then checked my watch as if late.

As it had outside the jeweller's, the ruse worked and he even stepped out of my way as I jogged past. Just as I passed him, I paused as if lost and began looking around in confusion, actually checking that no one else could see us in case he had someone waiting to meet him. Edwards tried to veer round me but I stepped in front of him, grabbing hold of his left arm with mine while waving my warrant card at him with the other.

'Gordon, police. Don't try anything stupid.'

He froze for a moment and a look of sheer terror crossed his face. I just had time to wonder why he was quite so scared when his right arm came up towards me in a blur with something shiny and dangerous-looking clenched in his fist.

Without thinking I tucked myself back behind his arm, still keeping hold but unable to lock the joints from my current position. Feeling this he pivoted around, trying to stab me with the flick knife he held in his right hand. I didn't dare disengage and let him get room to use the blade properly but I still couldn't get a proper grip on him, so we spun in crazy circles as adrenaline and fear doused me with cold sweat.

'Oi, drop the knife!' I yelled at him, hoping that I didn't sound as scared as I felt.

'Piss off and leave me alone!' he yelled back, sounding terrified.

I tried to think of something useful to do that wouldn't mean a knife in the chest and made an attempt to kick his legs out from under him, hoping that he would fall on his knife arm and trap it under his body. I hooked my right leg over his and placed my foot behind his left, shoving hard at the same time with both hands.

He stumbled forward but as I threw myself on him he managed to twist round so that he landed on his back with the knife held out towards me. I was out of control now, falling towards the blade. My vision narrowed until all I could see was the sunlight reflecting off the steel clenched in his fist. I lurched sideways, trying to move offline. I thought I'd made it until I felt a sharp sting in my left thigh as if I'd scraped it on barbed wire.

I landed hard and the breath rushed out of me, leaving me gasping and trying to hold my stomach and my leg at the same time, while Edwards scrambled to his feet and ran off towards the tennis courts. Ignoring the pain, I forced myself to my feet and ran after him, refusing to look at the leg that burned like fire with every step. He was running as fast as he could but the constant glances over his shoulder at me were slowing him as he had to swerve to avoid obstacles. After a few seconds it was clear that I was gaining and he began to sob and shout at me, screaming, 'Just fuck off and leave me alone!' – over and over.

I was more than a little puzzled but the pain and exertion were taking their toll on my system. I simply didn't have the energy to try and work out why he was so scared. He streaked past the tennis courts and towards Somerhill Avenue and just before he reached the road I caught up with him, hurling myself on his back with a lack of finesse that would have had my kung fu instructor screaming at me.

He toppled, this time with the knife trapped underneath him, and I screamed aloud as my injured leg hit the ground. He tried to writhe out from under me and get his arm free but I crawled up his back and slid my right arm under his neck, curling it around until the palm sat in the crook of my left elbow. I sawed my arm back and across, pulling his windpipe out of position and choking him and gasped, 'Drop the knife and stop fighting me!'

He struggled for a few seconds more but as the chokehold became more painful he went limp and shot his right arm out sans knife. Unsure what to do next, I looked around and saw that a crowd had gathered, comprised mostly of parents with small children, and tennis players, with the odd dog walker here and there.

'Someone dial 999, I'm a police officer!' I barked out, fighting to keep the pain from my voice. I saw a young father pull out a mobile phone and tap the keypad three times. Why no one had called before then is beyond me, but then I've found that generally either everyone thinks that someone else has done it or thirty people call up about the same thing.

Edwards was muttering quietly to himself and kept tensing his muscles as if he was going to fight, but every time he did I put the hold back on and he would subside after making horrible choking noises that were clearly for show as I was barely putting any pressure on. I wasn't trying to hurt him but he'd already stabbed me once and I wasn't about to let it happen again.

One man actually went so far as to come over and lean down to look at Edwards, saying, 'Are you all right? I can get this officer's number if you think that he's using excessive force?'

Edwards looked up at the chap as far as my hold would allow him to and thanked him by saying, 'Fuck off you twat!' and spitting at him.

The man huffed, but continued to hover around, clearly wanting to berate uniform when they arrived for my brutality. I shook my head wearily, wishing that I could feel surprised that someone who was clearly intelligent couldn't see what was really happening, blinded by his prejudice against the Establishment.

What did surprise me was that it took almost half an hour for a unit to make it from Hove police station, two roads away, to where I was still lying on Edwards. I didn't dare move, as the throbbing in my leg was growing steadily worse and I wasn't able to recover the knife from under my prisoner. When the marked car finally pulled into the entrance two officers got out and hurried over to me as if running the last twenty yards would make up for the delay.

'I'm sorry we're late, there was a massive fight between a load of street drinkers and they've reassigned the street drinking team to something else. You okay?' the female officer asked, bending down to take hold of Edwards's outstretched right arm and lever it up behind his back.

'Not really, he stabbed me in the leg. Be careful, the knife's still under his body somewhere.'

She nodded and swung around into a ground pin, kneeling on his shoulder so that he couldn't squirm free. Her colleague did the same on the other side, and I gratefully eased myself backwards, wincing when my injured leg took my weight.

For the first time I looked down and saw a hole in my jeans, right in the middle of the fleshy part of my thigh. Blood had completely soaked my left trouser leg, pumped out of the wound by my exertions as I'd run after Edwards. I couldn't see the wound underneath but it hurt like hell and I knew that I would need stitches. Trying to ignore the pain, I got my colleagues to raise Edwards slightly so that I could find the knife, sweeping my arm carefully under his chest until I knocked against it with my wrist and pulled it clear.

'So,' I asked Edwards conversationally as I began to check his pockets, 'why exactly were you so scared that you felt the need to stab a copper huh? Do you live in some kind of fairyland where it's okay to go around cutting people up?'

Edwards refused to speak to me, turning his head to look the other way. I continued to search in silence, to prevent my anger from making me say something stupid in front of a crowd of people who were clearly hanging on every word. It wasn't every day you saw a police officer get stabbed and catch the guy who did it right in front of you, and I could see a few mobiles raised to immortalize the moment on video.

Searching his pockets turned up nothing of particular interest, but as I searched the waistline at the front of his jeans I felt a large lump hidden under his jumper. My first thought was that it might be a firearm and I felt myself go cold at the thought, but as I dragged it clear I could hardly believe what I was looking at. In my hand was a clear plastic wrap about the size of two house bricks put together, filled to bursting with a brown powder that I recognized immediately.

'Is that what I think it is?' the male officer asked, his eyes almost as big as his face.

I nodded, a fierce grin breaking through my attempt at studied calm. 'Yup. What we have here is about fifty grand's worth of finest heroin. Mr Edwards, I have the greatest pleasure in arresting you for GBH, possession of an offensive weapon and possession with intent to supply a class A drug. It is necessary to arrest you to prevent your disappearance,' I like to vary the reason for arrest – we have a list of about eight to choose from, 'and I'm now going to caution you before I leave you with these fine officers and get my leg seen to.'

Despite the hole in my leg, I felt like laughing out loud. If the gear that I'd found belonged to Davey he was royally screwed. No way could his empire survive the loss of that much product, the system of payment and sale was too fine a line. Not only that, but if Edwards was as close to Davey as the shipment implied, that would also be a major blow. That much heroin found in front of that many witnesses would mean at least ten years inside and suddenly I understood why Edwards had been so scared. Even in prison he wouldn't be safe from Davey, and I sobered as I realized that, wherever he went, Edwards was more than likely going to end up hanging from a rope, thanks to me stopping him today.

'Any chance of some more units and an ambulance?' I asked the officers who were now busily cuffing the prisoner.

'We've called for another car, but almost half our section is on holiday or sick and they haven't got an overtime budget to cover it. We're down to four officers for Hove for the whole late shift.' He sounded a little disgruntled, as well he should be. The budget cuts seemed to be affecting everyone, despite the assurances that it wouldn't affect front-line policing, and I felt sorry for the poor bastards who had to try and keep control of everything from Boundary Passage to the far side of Portslade with only four officers and a few PCSOs.

I nodded at him. 'Ambulance?' I asked again.

'Already on its way: Sharon called for one as soon as she saw you bleeding.'

I nodded my thanks at the female officer, who smiled back as she and her colleague got Edwards carefully to his feet.

'Have you got any exhibit bags in the car?' I asked, not wanting to be left standing in the street holding a knife and a lifetime supply of heroin once they got the prisoner away to custody.

I was handed a knife tube, several exhibit bags and a pen and I sat in the front of the car, careful after my recent court experience to get both officers to countersign the label once it was sealed. The paramedics arrived just as I was finishing and took one look at my leg before bustling me into the back of the ambulance and whizzing me up to the hospital to get stitched up.

Not looking forward to the earbashing I was about to receive, I took the opportunity to pull out my phone and call Kev, making sure to tell him about the drugs before I explained how I'd let myself get stabbed while I was supposed to be off duty.

19

The hospital was quick and efficient, giving me a tetanus shot just in case and then stitching me up in surprisingly short time. Kev arrived before they had finished and stood there cracking jokes and generally being a pain until a somewhat snooty doctor asked him to shut up or leave. As the doctor turned back to me to finish dressing my wound, I shared a smirk with Kev over his bent head.

'So I'm not getting stuck on for getting injured then?' I asked.

Kev shook his head. 'No, Ding, you're probably going to get a commendation for being an idiot and surviving, although you should have called it in rather than jumping him yourself. Whatever possessed you to start a follow on your own?'

I shrugged. 'It seemed like a good idea at the time and, besides, I tried to phone you but you weren't picking up.'

'Ah. The lovely Mrs Sands was dragging me around Comet looking at washing machines. Had I known it was urgent, I would have answered.'

'If you'd answered, you would have known it was urgent.'

We both smiled, and the doctor looked up. 'Right, all done. Try and keep your weight off it for a few days. It's not particularly deep, but if it reopens then you'll have a nasty scar once it finally heals.' He smiled and stepped back, clearly eager for me to get off the bed and give it to the next patient.

I thanked him and we left, Kev walking slowly beside me as I limped through the waiting room and towards the A&E car park.

'I'll give you a lift home,' he said, watching sympathetically as I winced with every step. 'But you'll have to do a quick statement back at the nick first.'

I groaned. 'No rest for the wicked huh?'

'Nope. Serves you right for trying to be a hero.'

The trip back to the nick took about five minutes, with Kev parking in the back yard to minimize the number of stairs I had to climb. Unfortunately the lift was out of order, so I still had to go up two flights to get to the office, but eventually I was tapping away merrily while Kev went to make tea. Occasionally officers would drift in to congratulate me or offer sympathy, depending on how much they had heard – and I have to admit that I basked in the glow of a job well done, if you ignored the injury.

Kev bustled around the office doing bits and bobs that were unnecessary but gave him an excuse to wait for me – he's one of those people who would give you the shirt off his own back but doesn't like you to catch him doing it – so I hurried as much as I could and finished shortly before eight.

Just as we were leaving, Eddie, Tate and Ralphy came up the stairs and into the office, stopping in surprise as they saw us. Ralphy glanced down at my leg and shifted his bulk carefully so that he could bend down and have a closer look. 'What the bloody hell have you done to yourself this time?'

'Long story. What are you doing here this late? I thought you'd be watching the Bravo channel with a beer and a box of Kleenex by now.'

He shook his head. 'Not tonight, we've got a job on with that sex offender by St Nick's.'

'Yeah, Ralphy's going to put on a dress and strap his moobs into a bra and try and get attacked!' Eddie interjected.

'I paid good money for these!' Ralphy exclaimed, cupping his chest with both hands and jiggling it in a manner that made me feel slightly queasy.

'Come on now,' Kev said, trying not to smile, 'leave poor Ding alone, he's been playing hero and getting stabbed and he needs to get home to bed.'

'You've been stabbed?' Tate asked, his face a mask of concern.

'Yeah, I got stabbed chasing down Gordon Edwards, one of Davey's boys. I got about fifty grand's worth of heroin off him though, and all on my own.'

Tate's serious expression didn't waver. 'Yeah, but you got stabbed. You know the rule. If it's too dangerous, hang back and wait until you've got backup, or let them go and catch them another day. You and your bloody hero complex.'

He pushed past me shaking his head in disgust. I raised my eyebrows and looked at Kev who shook his own head and pointed down the stairs. I waved goodbye to the others and limped down the steps, waiting until they were out of earshot before turning to Kev.

'What the hell was that about?'

'He still blames himself for what happened to Jimmy. He thinks that it was his fault as he was in charge the day it happened. He talked to me about it the other day, but don't tell him I told you, okay?'

I nodded, feeling chastened. I hadn't realized that it had hit Tate so hard, and the more I thought about what I had done that night, the more I realized how stupid and dangerous it had been. One slip and I could have been in a bed next to Jimmy, or worse still in the morgue. Maybe this was exactly what I needed, I thought, to wake up to the fact that I wasn't invincible, to take a little more care of myself. I thought about it as we made our way out to the car park, and Kev gave me a little bit of time to myself before the bollocking that I knew was coming.

He waited until we were nearly back at my house before he spoke. 'I know that I'm not going to say anything to you that you're not already saying to yourself, but why didn't you ring in on the nines when you couldn't get hold of me?'

I looked out of the window at the passing traffic as I replied. 'To be honest with you I didn't even think about it. Everything about him shouted that he was carrying; his body language was screaming at me, so I jumped him. I didn't think about him having a blade.'

I could almost feel Kev's disappointment even before he spoke. 'You get paid to think, Gareth. You're an intelligence officer. You tell me where exactly intelligence figured in what you did today?'

I didn't have an answer for him, so I just shrugged. He looked over at me, and I met his gaze to see a deep concern there that touched and worried me at the same time.

'Is there anything that you need to talk about?'

I thought about it, pushing away the memories of the fight with the Budds and the heroin hidden in next door's garden. 'I don't think so, Kev, I think I just got carried away.'

'You nearly got carried away on a bloody stretcher. I can't have someone working for me who I can't trust to do the right thing in a tight spot, and what you did was foolish, stupid and dangerous. Now I assume from your miserable face that you get it, so I won't say anymore about this, but I just want you to know that there won't be a next time. Not on my unit, okay?'

'Okay. I'm sorry. I know I was stupid and it won't happen again, I promise.'

I knew how hard it was for Kev to dress anyone down, particularly someone he liked, and that, more than anything else, made me truly sorry for getting carried away. He nodded, considering me properly bollocked as he dropped me off outside my front door with a cheery wave and a beep that made half my neighbours twitch their curtains.

I entered the house with the intention of calling Sally and telling her what had happened, but instead found myself slumped on the sofa with half a bottle of Scotch, mulling over the events of the last few days as the room began to blur and the bottle emptied.

20

I limped into work the next day with a head that hurt even more than the hole in my leg. I'd woken on the sofa that morning with a full bladder and a taste like dead ferrets in my mouth, then staggered around the house plying myself with water and painkillers until I could see straight. Heads turned to watch me the moment I entered the office, and I lowered my gaze so I didn't have to tell and retell the story a dozen times before I got to my desk.

As I got to our pod, Sally gave me a look that promised me yet more trouble but I was in no state to try and deal with it then. Tate and Rudd were already at their desks, despite the fact that Tate had been in until God only knows what time, working on the sex attacker.

'Any joy last night?' I asked him, acting as if he hadn't thrown his teddy out when he'd seen me.

'No, it was completely dead.' He didn't look at me but at least we were speaking.

'What time did you get off?'

He rubbed his face and for the first time I saw how tired he looked. 'About three. I almost slept under my desk but I had to go home and feed the dog.'

I glanced instinctively at the clock as he spoke. In the retelling, a lot of officers will tack an extra hour onto whatever time they finish to make you think they have a harder job than you. Don't get me wrong, I do it too, but Tate is one of the few who always tells it straight. He lives in Ovingdean, just outside Brighton, so doing the math, I worked out that he had probably managed about three hours' sleep.

'Christ mate, couldn't you have come in late?'

He shook his head wearily and reached for his coffee. 'I've got a RIPA I need to complete by midday; I haven't got the time to spare.'

I nodded, understanding. The Regulation of Investigatory Powers Act is the bane of our life in the intelligence world. Since the Human Rights Act came in, instead of just following someone, we have to complete, from scratch, a seven-page document explaining why it is necessary to use covert surveillance on someone, including all the other factors that have been tried and the reason we feel that being sneaky is the best option. We also have to do it all word perfect, without a single mistake, or it comes back from the Covert Authorities Bureau (CAB) with notes all over it, and we have to iron out the mistakes. I've always wondered but never asked why they couldn't just fix it themselves. It would be far faster than emailing it back and forth, but every department in the force suffers from a dose of 'it's not my job', and I suppose this is theirs.

A wave of giddiness swept over me as I sat down and I managed to hide it by wincing and holding my leg. Having an injury was fair enough, but if Sally found out that I had spent last night sitting on the sofa getting blotto, I was worried that our fling might get flung. As it was, she looked over at me with concern on her face that I almost felt I deserved.

'How's the leg? Are you okay?'

'It's all right, it looks worse than it is. The doctors were pretty efficient actually.'

She smiled and went back to her work, still not having entirely forgiven me.

I woke up my protesting computer and forced it into action, going through the previous day's reports. I had about half a dozen emails from various people of differing ranks, ranging from a stern 'well done, be more careful' from Derek Pearson, to a chirpy 'who's the twat that got stabbed then?' from Andy Coucher.

Curious to know what had happened to my attacker, I looked at his custody record and scrolled down to the interview log. As I was expecting, he had answered 'no comment' to all questions and was back in a cell awaiting CPS advice. Except in extreme cases we aren't allowed to make charging decisions on prisoners anymore and instead have a CPS lawyer permanently stationed at custody. It slows the system down but it does mean that we are often more successful at court.

Kev called everyone for the morning meeting, but as I limped out of our pod he put a restraining hand on my chest. 'Not you, Ding, you've got a far more pressing engagement.'

I looked at him in confusion. 'What?'

Kev grinned and I began to worry what he had in store for me. 'There's a young lady upstairs from *The Argus*, and she wants to take your trousers off.'

I heard muffled laughter from the other officers and frowned at them to no avail. 'But I can't get my picture in the paper, Kev, it'll screw my job!'

His grin got wider. 'And that's why, my boy, you get to have a picture taken of the terrible wound you suffered in the line of duty. I can't think of many criminals who will look at a picture of your chicken thighs and say, "Hang on, I know that man!" Do you?'

I shook my head wearily. There was no point in arguing with Kev when he was like that. He had obviously arranged this as a punishment for my idiocy last night, I thought, knowing full well that I had the surveillance officer's usual aversion to the press.

'Good job I put clean undies on. Git,' I muttered, as I limped down the office and towards the press room.

The trip took me almost five minutes due to it being two floors and four flights of stairs above our office. Trust me to get stabbed in the leg when the lift wasn't working. I finally got there to see an impatient-looking reporter sitting in the small room with a photographer and our press liaison officer, Debbie Price.

I smiled at Debbie then nodded at the reporter and shook hands with the photographer. I've known him for years but he's another one whose bloody name I can never remember, so settle for calling him 'mate' whenever we meet up. Annoyingly, he always remembers mine.

I sat without being asked, easing my injured leg out in front of me as Debbie introduced the reporter.

'Gareth, this is Claire Morgan. She's the new crime reporter for *The Argus*. Claire, this is Gareth Bell.'

Claire threw a smile at me, one of those professional ones that snap on and off. 'Gareth, hi. Do you mind if we get going on the interview?'

I looked up sharply at Debbie. 'Interview? I thought this was a photo shoot?'

The press officer looked a little confused. 'Um, Kev said that you would be giving a full interview on the condition that no photographs are taken of your face. If that's not the case ...' She left it hanging with just the hint of a frown.

I sighed. 'No, no that's fine. I'm just a little sore from yesterday and it's making me cranky. Let's get on with it then.'

For the next thirty minutes I had to relate what had happened over and over until they were satisfied that it sounded suitably heroic and violent. When that was done I was cajoled into removing my trousers and allowing them to take photographs of the stitched wound in my leg. Just as I thought we were done and I was buckling up the trousers that I had struggled to get back on, the final coup de grâce came in the form of the two officers that had assisted me the day before along with the brick of heroin.

The photographer managed to get all three of us in to the frame in such a way that my face was hidden behind the drugs, so he said, but I insisted on seeing the shot on the small views-creen on the back of his camera before I would allow it to get printed. There followed lots of handshakes and commiserations about my leg, and I stumped back down to the office, determined to get my revenge on Kev – even if I did deserve what had just happened.

My mood lifted slightly as I got back to the office and found that Sally was the person who had been designated to staff the office during the morning meeting. It meant that we could clear the air between us without anyone else catching on. She looked up as I approached and smiled at me.

'Did you enjoy the interview?' she asked, too sweetly for my liking.

'You knew as well, didn't you?' I made my way over to my chair as I spoke, and I like to think that I hardly played my injury up for sympathy as I did so.

'You deserve far worse, Gareth. I thought you were a smart bloke but what you did last night was stupid and dangerous, and you didn't even bother to call me and let me know, so I had to find out from Tate this morning and try not to look too upset. You do know that if we are going to see each other we need to trust each other, right? Did you not think that I might want to know that you were injured? Or am I just a bit of fun that isn't that important?'

She was keeping her voice low, but the tone was anything but friendly. 'You always go on about the men that I usually go out with, but you're really taking the biscuit, Gareth. Now I have the choice of worrying about you every time you're not within sight or finishing it here – and having to sit next to you every day. How do you think that makes me feel?'

I considered my answer carefully, more than a little shocked

143

at how angry she was. I had known she would be annoyed but if I'd had any idea that she would take it as such a serious trust issue, I would have done things very differently the previous night.

'Look, I'm really sorry. You're not just a bit of fun, I really do like you. I'm so used to being on my own that I'm not used to thinking about someone else when I take risks, and I was in so much pain last night that I overdid it a bit on the medication and just zonked out on the sofa. If I'd thought about it, which I obviously didn't, I would have at least called you to let you know that I was okay.'

I reached out to take her hand, but she leaned back in her chair and folded her arms across her chest. 'And what about your antics in the park? Am I going to spend my evenings worrying that you're lying dead somewhere every time you're more than a few minutes late? Because I don't think I can live like that. Why do you think I haven't dated coppers before?'

I gestured helplessly, not quite sure how to explain my side of it. 'It's who I am, Sally. I can't just leave things be. I joined the job to stop people like him and how could I look at myself in the mirror if I just let people like Edwards walk away and carry on doing what they're doing? You're right, it was stupid and dangerous, but you have to think that if he wasn't afraid to stab a copper, who else might he have stabbed? Someone less likely to be able to defend themselves maybe. If by getting a knife in the leg I've stopped someone else from getting hurt then I've done my job. I know that work shouldn't interfere with real life this much but I can't just let things like that slide.'

She looked at me with a sudden glimmer of understanding. 'This is why Lucy left you, isn't it?'

I nodded, my gut churning as the old memory resurfaced.

'What happened?' She still sat with her arms folded and I couldn't help but feel that what I said next would make her mind up about me.

144

'We were filling up the car at the petrol station on Ditchling Road, the BP garage, when some arsehole pulled a woman out of her car and drove off with it and her baby still in the back seat. Do you remember the story in the papers?'

She nodded and gestured for me to continue.

'Well, I saw it happen and dumped Lucy out to calm the woman down, then drove off after him. I kept tabs on him right across town and managed to call in enough units to surround him and he finally got rammed by traffic, just enough to get him to stop without hurting the kid in the back. By this time, uniform were with Lucy and the mother and they heard over the radio that there had been a crash. Both of them assumed the worst and thought that the child and I were dead or seriously injured. Apparently it was just too much for Lucy to cope with. She'd already threatened to leave over the amount of overtime I was doing; she loved the money but hated the fact that I was never there. She never really understood how much the job means to me, and she thought I was either deliberately avoiding her or having an affair. The petrol station was the straw that broke the camel's back and she moved out the next day.'

Sally was still looking at me, the expression on her face unreadable. I resisted the urge to reach out to her again.

'Can you put up with someone as job-pissed as I am?' I tried a grin, weak though it was.

'I don't know, Gareth, I really don't. I need to think about it.'

I opened my mouth to try and convince her but suddenly the office was full of noise as everyone came back from the meeting. I swung back to my desk, suddenly wishing that there had been more whisky in the bottle and that I'd taken the day off sick.

21

The rest of the week passed with little of interest happening, apart from I was finally forced to stay in the office long enough to get most of my paperwork done while the others went out and shook up some more of Davey's network.

The enforced convalescence was driving me up the wall, and so when, at about ten to four on Friday – five full days since I'd been out on the streets – Kev came into the pod to ask Rudd if he could come back in later to help out with the sex offender job that they were running again, I would have chewed his arm off for a chance to get out and do something useful.

'Sorry, Kev, hot date,' Rudd replied, picking his gear up and heading towards the door.

Kev looked over at me. 'Well there's no point asking the wounded hero. I don't think you could catch a cold at the moment, let alone a pervert.'

'I could do the log?' I offered, trying not to sound too desperate..

He looked at me thoughtfully. 'Can I trust you not to get out of the car?'

I nodded. 'Scouts honour.'

'Okay. Be back here at eight, ready to go. Leave your fighting kit in your desk.'

I smiled, pleased to be getting out of the office even if it did mean a lack of sleep, and tried to ignore the look that Sally was giving me.

I managed to get home, showered, fed and changed in just enough time to be back at the office an hour early, but occupied my time by running through the intelligence surrounding Davey, looking for another weak spot that we could exploit.

The others came in just before eight, Eddie first, then Tate, Ralphy, Kev and Tommo. Although we all worked separate crime types normally, there simply weren't enough of us not to all pitch in when it came to a big job. Just as we were about to start briefing there was a nervous knock at the office door and I swung around to see Bobby, the probationer that I'd had words with at my house. He was wearing plain clothes and a nervous expression and hovered in the doorway as if unsure of the welcome he would receive. 'Uh, hi, I'm looking for Detective Sergeant Sands?'

Kev waved lazily from his chair. 'Come in, come in. Gents, this is Bobby. He's from the tutor unit and he'll be accompanying us this evening. He needs to get some proactive competencies signed off, so I've arranged to get him out with us.' He introduced us one by one, and I took enough pity on the young officer to actually give him a smile and a wave. There's nothing worse than being new and thinking that an experienced officer hates you, and he was nervous enough already.

As soon as Bobby was seated, Kev got down to details. 'Right. We've had no more attacks this week, but as it's a Friday we expect a lot of through-traffic at the churchyard. Here's a photofit of the male we're looking for.' He passed around a made-up photograph that could have been any one of a dozen sex offenders I knew of.

'The reason we're going out early is to try and catch him setting up. We'll be happy with an early intervention if we're pretty sure we have the male. We don't want to get to the stage where he's attacking someone before we jump him. Teams will be myself and Ralphy, Tate and Eddie, Tommo and Bobby, with Ding in the car nearby doing the log.' He laid out a map of the area on the desk and we all crowded around to look.

'Ding, I want you south-west of the plot on Upper North Street. Tate, you and Eddie on Church Street covering the main churchyard. Tommo and Bobby, you get Clifton Terrace, and Ralphy and I will be inside the graveyard on the west side of the road. One set of night sights per team. Don't lose them, they're bloody expensive. Radio Channel BDivEventsGen6 and the overtime code is the standard DIU central one. Questions?'

I raised a hand. 'Yeah, why aren't I doing the log back here where I can have computer access?'

'I want to swap Bobby around so that he can see how the log works and let him soak up some of your hard-won knowledge, and I don't want him to have to keep leaving the plot to do it. See, there is method in my madness. Any real questions?'

I flicked an elastic band at him in protest – which he nimbly avoided.

'Right. Bobby, go with Ding there and he'll show you the procedure for booking out a logbook and getting it all ready. Welcome to the fast-paced world of surveillance. Out on the ground by nine o'clock, please, gentlemen, with fighting kit but no vests.'

I limped back over to my desk with Bobby in tow. 'So this is your first time on a surveillance job, huh?'

He nodded excitedly. 'Yeah, it's something I've always been interested in. Do you do a lot of jobs like this?'

I nodded, suddenly feeling old. 'Yup, and let me pass on a few basics. Firstly, bring a book, but when you're reading it keep it below window level. Books, magazines and papers make you look like you're ready for a long wait and two blokes in a car already makes you look out of place. Unless you want to snog the driver every time someone walks past.' He began to nod before he realized that I was being sarcastic.

'Next,' I continued, 'whenever you're waiting somewhere, and believe me waiting is mostly what we'll be doing out there, give yourself a reason in your head for being there. Like waiting for a friend who's late, taking a break from work, even being a drug dealer. Thinking it makes you act like it, and body language is the biggest giveaway in this job. Have you ever spotted a criminal in a crowd for no apparent reason, but you just know they're up to no good?'

He nodded.

'Well, that'll be their body language. They know they're up to no good and their body shouts it unless they're really experienced. I normally spot our regulars by body language miles before their face is recognizable.' I stopped burdening him with old-sweat wisdom and took him through the procedures for starting a logbook, which is as complicated as everything else in a system that has to be totally accountable. 'Right, any questions?'

'Um, just one. Why do they call you Ding?'

I laughed. 'That, my friend, is something for the privileged few to know. If you're still around in a year, ask me again and I'll tell you.'

'Ding!' sang Tate and Ralphy at the same time.

Bobby looked over at them in confusion. 'Err, okay, I will.'

Seeing from Ralphy's face that he was about to spill the beans and embarrass me, I quickly changed the subject. 'Oh, and while I remember, Bobby, don't worry about the other day. I used to be called the Section Five king when I was a probationer. Even though I had a mouth like a toilet, I'd threaten to arrest anyone who swore in front of me, even once in someone's own house. I was just in a bad mood when I saw you, so sorry for being a cock.'

I smiled at him to show I meant it, and he smiled back gratefully. Feeling proud of myself for not just dismissing him as a waste of space – which is very easy to do with probationers when you've got a few years in, however unfairly – I gathered up my kit and headed down to the car park.

Twenty minutes later I was sat up near the Hampton pub on Upper North Street, tucking into a bag of Doritos that I didn't really want or need, with the logbook open on my lap and the radio on. After enough surveillance jobs you develop a weird ability to be able to shut your mind off and let the time fly by, while still being alert enough to instantly spot anything suspicious or respond to your radio immediately. Except Ralphy, of course, who is famous for once having slept through a ram raid on the premises he'd been watching. At the time he claimed a radio failure, but eventually the truth got out and he's never quite lived it down.

The evening passed quite pleasantly with the help of Radio 4 and the occasional company of Bobby who, to his credit, sat quietly until prompted into a conversation. A few minutes after he'd left for the fourth time my radio suddenly crackled into life, with Eddie's voice almost making me jump.

'From Eddie, we have contact, contact on a suspect male matching description given. He is westbound up Church Street towards Dyke Road, eyes all about. Male is wearing a black woollen donkey jacket, black combat trousers, and black boots.'

I copied down the relevant parts in the log, making a note of the time. Somehow it was already half one in the morning.

'From Eddie, male is into the churchyard, one final look all about and he veers to the left of the gate and is away from my view.'

Even though I wasn't allowed out to play, I felt the adrenaline flowing through my veins. If this bloke was heading into the graveyard itself, away from the brick paths that cut through the church grounds towards the bottom of Dyke Road, then he was probably up to no good. Or desperate for a piss, but my money was on bad stuff.

150

Kev's voice came through on the radio. *'Kev has control and the male is paused behind a gravestone near the path. He's either having a dump or waiting for someone to pass by.'*

I actually reached for the door handle before remembering myself and taking my hand away.

'From Kev, we have a female walking south to north along the path; it appears the male has seen her and is changing position slightly. I don't want to wait any longer, strike, strike, strike.'

I heard a chorus of clicks as people responded, and this time I did get out of the car, walking towards Dyke Road as fast as I could, still clutching the logbook. I may not have been able to join in, but I figured if the target ran I could point him out to the others if he came my way.

Even from as far away as I was, I heard the female scream. It must have been earsplittingly loud in the churchyard. I began to walk faster, wincing as the stitches pulled but eager to know what was happening.

'Any update for the log?' I called over the radio.

'Runner, over the wall onto Dyke Road, towards the graveyard Kev was in,' came Eddie's voice, breathless as he gave chase.

I reached the corner of the road in time to see a male dressed all in black scrambling over the iron gates at the front of the western churchyard, with Eddie and Tate not far behind. Bobby then ran past them, climbing the gates like a monkey, and disappeared from view in moments.

I limped up the road, seeing Ralphy and Kev moving only slightly faster as Kev talked to someone on his mobile phone. I guessed he was probably calling comms to get uniform out and assisting but I was more interested in what was happening in the graveyard. I needn't have worried, as a few moments later Bobby and Eddie walked up to the inside of the gate with the man in cuffs. As I approached I recognized him as one James Elroy Petersen, a wellknown sex attacker who I had thought was still in prison.

I stopped by the gates at about the same time as Kev and Ralphy. 'Good job, lads. I couldn't have climbed the gate that quick.'

Bobby grinned, as did Eddie, looking very pleased with themselves.

'One thing though, chaps,' I said, glancing down at the thick padlock then back up at the ten foot gates. 'How are you going to get him back over this side?'

22

I was woken at about half past ten by my phone buzzing angrily. I eased myself carefully onto my side and groaned when I saw *Kev* flashing up on the screen. 'What?' I answered, trying not to sound too surly. I only got to wake up naturally two days out of seven – or fewer with all the overtime we'd been working recently – and he'd just spoiled one of them.

'I'm fine, thank you, Gareth, thanks for asking.'

I was still too sleep-fuddled to try and be funny back, so I just grunted in the hope that he would get to the point.

'So, how's the leg?' he asked.

'It hurts a bit but I've got a little more movement in it today.' I flexed it experimentally as I spoke.

'Good. I want you to take today and tomorrow off, just to make sure you heal up properly. Aren't I nice?'

'You'd be nicer if it wasn't my scheduled days off, remember?'

'Are they?' he asked innocently. 'Well isn't that convenient?'

I was tired enough that I wondered if I'd missed the point of the phone call. 'Did you just phone me up to torment me?' I asked, searching with my free hand for the pint of water I always kept by the bed.

'Pretty much. Seriously though, I just wanted to make sure that you're all right.'

'Yeah, I'm fine thanks. It's just been a long week is all, what with working over rest days again.'

'Okay, well you make sure you get rested up. We've got a lot on next week and I need the whole team operational. Don't go doing anything stupid, okay?'

He hung up, and I lay there for a moment wishing that I was still asleep. Thoroughly awake now, I crawled out of bed and forced myself up and down the stairs ten times before breakfast, not wanting my leg to seize up. Then I went through my recently lapsed routine of press-ups and sit-ups, stopping when the strain got too much.

After a brief breakfast, I popped over to see my dad and take Lily out for a walk over the fields at the back of Woodingdean, then called Sally to see if she fancied lunch. She let the phone ring without answering, so instead I spent the day wandering around town, buying crap that I didn't really need.

As I walked around the mall at Churchill Square, dodging squealing children and families with no sense of spatial awareness, I couldn't help but think of the heroin I had hidden in next door's garden. What I'd done was not only stupid, it was criminal, and I kept worrying about the line I'd crossed. I've always thought that the only thing that separates us from the criminals is our morals and, if that were the case, was I any better than the people I was trying to stop?

Much as I wanted to, I couldn't think of any way to come clean without losing my job. I couldn't even risk going to Kev. Despite his relaxed attitude he would have no choice but to throw me in a cell and get PSD over to deal with me.

I didn't think I could bear to be kicked out, losing my job and most of my friends in one swoop. It would be like being divorced all over again but without the support I'd had the first time from my colleagues.

I was so wrapped up in my dark thoughts that I almost didn't notice the two men following me. The first I knew about it was when I came out of the toilets on the middle level of the shopping centre. I exited the corridor back out into the main area, instinctively looking around. Two men, both apparently separate from each other, avoided making eye contact at the same time, and the hackles rose on the back of my neck as I recognized one of them. It was the guy from the hospital with the leather patches on his jacket, the same one who had burgled my house. The other I didn't know but as I walked calmly away, straining my skills to the limit to act as if I hadn't seen them, I saw his reflection in the window of HMV as he began to pace me from the far side of the mall.

I considered calling someone at work but then wondered what I would say. 'Excuse me chaps, but the dealer I nicked a load of heroin off has got a couple of his guys following me?' No, I'd just have to lose them or deal with them myself.

The second guy was wearing a grubby blue shirt and blue jeans, making him easy to spot as few people dress all in one colour, and I kept tabs on him as I used the escalator to go to the lower level. Patches was coming down the escalator on the far side, still trying to act as if he wasn't watching me. Neither of them was particularly good but then they hadn't had the training and experience I'd had, so on someone less aware they probably would have been fine.

I was torn between leading them around town for a bit or heading straight down into the car park and driving off. The twinge in my leg told me that I'd be better off driving, and I guessed that they probably knew what car I drove anyway, so it wasn't like I had to keep it a secret. I walked down the steps to the car park, resisting the urge to turn and see where my tail was. The only time the target has an advantage on a surveillance job is when the followers don't know that they've been blown and I wanted to keep that advantage as long as possible.

If they figured it out, they might do something rash. Without knowing what they wanted I couldn't be sure they wouldn't go for me, and I was in no condition to be rolling around on the floor with people. My adrenaline began to kick in at the thought, making me buzz with unwanted energy. I shoved my hands in my pockets to stop them from shaking and stared resolutely ahead, tensed against a half-expected attack as the crowds thinned out.

I finally reached the level I'd parked on and walked to my car as if nothing was amiss. I hoped that this would be the end of it and that I could just drive off without them making a move, but as I slid into the driver's seat, Patches jogged over and banged on the window with an intense look on his face. I didn't wind the window down, instead looking at him through the dirty glass.

'What?' I asked, not bothering to pretend to be surprised.

'You've got something that belongs to a friend of mine. He wants it back. He told me to tell you that this is the only friendly warning and, after this, bad things start to happen, copper or not. You got that?'

I just stared at him, a cold feeling spreading through my stomach as the implication of what he was saying sank in. Davey wanted his gear back and he was making threats to someone he knew was a copper. Davey was well known by police and criminals alike as a total psychopath, and he had a reputation for never making threats that he didn't carry out. Apparently it was a point of pride.

'Well, I'm waiting.'

Something in his tone made me angry. I wasn't used to people like him making demands. I lowered the window just enough so that I could be heard clearly without him being able to get a hand inside the car. 'You can tell your *friend* that I don't deal with monkeys. If he wants something from me, he's going to have to ask me himself. *You* got that?'

Patches grinned at me as if I'd made a joke. 'Yeah, I'll tell him that. Just don't be surprised if something unpleasant happens between now and our next chat, speaking to him like that.'

I shook my head and closed the window, watching Patches recede in the mirror as I drove away. Somehow I'd managed to get myself into a situation where a psychopathic drug dealer with a penchant for knives was upset with me and making threats, and I couldn't do anything about it. I felt powerless, scared, and, most of all, alone.

23

When I got into the office on Monday morning my leg was barely hurting. I'd spent the rest of the weekend relaxing and it had done me the world of good. I got all the way to my desk before I realized that something was wrong, then saw Tate, Rudd and Kev in the inspector's office. As soon as I made eye contact with Kev he waved me in, and I closed the door behind me.

'We've got a problem, Gareth,' he said before I could even perch on my usual filing cabinet.

'What's up?'

Tate handed me a sheaf of intelligence reports and printed logs.

'We had two more dealers stabbed over the weekend, with a third cut badly. The first two are both critical, one of them probably won't last the day.'

'Is anyone talking to us?' I asked, looking at the reports.

Kev shook his head. 'Not so far. I need you all out on the ground on this one. CID are treating them as attempted murders.'

I scratched my head thoughtfully. 'Who do the victims work for? Surely we can work out who's doing it from the targets?'

'We could,' Kev said, handing me three mugshots with names underneath, 'if they all worked for the same person. The first two work for Trash, and the other one works for Davey. It could be another group trying to muscle in but so far it's all just guesswork.'

'Could it be Davey cleaning house, maybe?' Rudd chipped in.

Kev shrugged. 'Maybe, but why would he be attacking Trash's crew *and* his own?'

I held up a hand. 'What if he's stealing product from Trash now that we've got most of his in the store, and his guy was retaliation by Trash?'

Kev looked at me, clearly impressed. 'You know, Ding, you're not as stupid as you look.'

'Well it makes sense. We know that his operation has ground to a bit of a halt and he's got to get some more gear from somewhere. If I was him I'd go to the easiest free source, which is Trash.'

Kev stood and began rapping out orders. 'Okay. Ding, Rudd, find out where Trash is living and sit up on the house. Tate, you call as many informants as you can and find out everything you can get about who's doing the stabbings. I think Gareth is right. If we can catch these guys in the act, we can hopefully trace them back to Davey and bring the whole crew down in one easy hit.' He looked around the room at the three of us. 'Well what are you waiting for, gentlemen? We have criminals to catch.'

We all but ran out of the office and began flicking through reports, trying to find anything relevant before we got out on the ground. As per usual Sally found what we were looking for before any of the rest of us, handing a sheet of paper to Rudd.

'Got it. Sal, you're a genius!' he said, waving the report at me.

'Where is he then?' I snatched the paper out of his hand. I scanned the report, which had been put in over the weekend by a uniformed officer who had seen Trash kissing a girl goodbye on the doorstep of a house on Elm Grove on Saturday morning. 'Right, let's go. Thanks, Sally.'

She nodded as I grabbed a set of keys from the board and raced Rudd to the car park.

* * *

I had deliberately chosen the nattiest car we had and it didn't look out of place as we parked up at the end of May Road, just across from the target address on Elm Grove.

'So what do we do now?' Rudd asked, lowering the back of his seat so that he could slouch comfortably.

'Well, I could be wrong, but I think we probably sit here and wait until Trash comes out, then we follow him. It's called surveillance, maybe you've heard of it?'

Rudd laughed. 'I think I might have done, once or twice. You hungry?'

'Yeah, starving. What you thinking of?'

What he was thinking of turned out to be a pair of massive all-day breakfast sandwiches from a nearby café. He got back into the car and dumped one of them on my lap, already halfway through his. I ate my sandwich as I studied the front door to the target premises. It was a three-storey house with a single front door but I could see at least five buzzers, meaning that it was split into flats.

I'd never seen any intelligence on this place before and made a mental note to email the officer who had seen Trash and thank him. Too few officers remember to put in intel logs and moments like that prove how vital they are.

I managed to finish the sandwich without getting too much of it down my shirt, and was about to get out and stretch when the house door opened and Trash stepped out. He actually looked like a Scouser, with close-cropped ginger hair and a pale complexion, and he had a face that only a mother could love. He was wearing a green jacket and blue jeans, and I wrote the description and time down as he walked down the steps, looking around himself to make sure that he wasn't being observed.

I tried to think casual, as did Rudd, and we managed to avoid catching our target's eye. He walked over to a silver Vauxhall Astra and, with a final look around, he slipped into the front and drove off down Queens Park Road.

Rudd got on the phone to Kev while I followed, being careful not to get too close. It's always tricky doing a mobile follow with only one vehicle but I stayed as far back as I could and tried not to anticipate what he would do. An early indication from me or anything else out of place would alert him, and then we were screwed.

He reached the end of the road and turned left onto Eastern Road, driving carefully. Trash was normally an awful driver, so I knew that he had to be going somewhere important. I just clipped the red light as I followed him through, keeping a couple of cars between me and him as cover.

'Kev says that they're on their way and not to lose him,' Rudd said helpfully with the phone still stuck to his ear.

'Yeah thanks. Does he want to catch up and take over driving?' I asked as Trash turned right into Upper Bedford Street and drove out of my view.

I automatically started to look for my pressel to give a radio update before cursing as I remembered that we hadn't kitted up before leaving the office. Schoolboy error, I thought, as I turned into the road after him. He was nowhere to be seen and I had a moment of panic as we sped down the road. If someone was out and about stabbing dealers and they got to Trash after I'd lost him, there'd be hell to pay.

On a hunch I turned down Montague Street and sighed with relief as I saw Trash's car pulling into the car park that belonged to a block of flats nearby. I pulled over on the far side of the road, managing to get a space that allowed us a clear view of where he had parked. I resisted the urge to get out for a better view, knowing that I was likely to be spotted if I did. Trash sat in his car facing the road, clearly waiting for someone.

Rudd was off the phone to Kev by then and was sitting there tapping the dashboard, his anticipation finding a vent in physical action. 'Who do you reckon he's going to meet?' he asked, never taking his eyes from Trash.

161

'No idea. He tends to keep his hands clean, so I doubt it'll be a pickup. Maybe he's going to meet up with some of his lads.'

Rudd shook his head. 'Why would he wait in a car park for that? Surely he'd be in one of their houses or make them come to him?'

I shrugged. 'I dunno. I suppose we'll just have to wait and see.'

As I spoke, I saw Kev and Tate drive into the far end of the road and park outside a mechanic's shop. Tate got out and began a conversation with the mechanic, occasionally pointing at the car while Kev stayed in the passenger seat.

My phone rang, and I saw in the distance that Kev had his phone to his ear.

'Go ahead Kev,' I said as I answered.

'*Anything?*' he asked.

'Nope, just sitting there. Have you got eyeball as well?'

'*Just about, although I'm partially blocked by the hedge. Can you give me a heads-up if anything happens?*'

'Will do,' I said and hung up.

We didn't have to wait long. A few minutes after I'd spoken to Kev, Rudd tapped me frantically on the leg, and I looked in the mirror to see a green Jaguar XJS pull into the road behind us. I couldn't make out the driver as it went past, not wanting to turn and stare. I'd been on jobs too many times where the target had felt someone watching and glanced around, and eye contact is the last thing you want in our line of work.

The Jaguar pulled into the car park and stopped a few bays over from where Trash was parked. I stared in shock as the driver got out and looked around, showing me a face that I'd seen up close and personal in the courtroom only a few days before.

Rudd tapped my leg again and a glance at his face showed that he was as unbelieving as I was. 'Is that …?' he began, unable to finish the question.

'Yeah,' I replied as I reached for my phone, 'it is. But what the hell is Trash doing meeting up with Quentin Davey?'

24

I almost dropped my phone as I dialled Kev's number, and then waited impatiently for him to pick up. *'I know, I can see,'* he said as he answered.

'Looks like we might have been right about Davey's lot doing the knife jobs.'

'Maybe. Let's not judge until we've got a better idea. When they split, you take Davey and I'll take Trash.'

I hung up again and returned my attention to the two dealers now standing chatting between the cars. The films would show a meeting like this with an army of goons on either side, all with hands inside coats, but the truth was just two average-looking men standing in a car park having a chat. I dearly longed to get close enough to hear what they were saying, but they had picked the spot well and anyone getting close would be spotted straight away.

I tried to lip-read, but they were too far away and all I could make out was the body language. Trash seemed defensive, and Davey was being his usual bullying self by the looks of things. He was standing square on with his hands waving about, and every so often the wind brought me his raised voice, sadly not clear enough to make out anything but the tone.

Trash suddenly turned as if to walk back to his car and, quick as lightning, Davey grabbed him and spun him around. Trash's fists came up in a guard as Davey struck him in the chest, and I thought we were going to have to intervene before we had another stabbing.

My hand was on the door handle when my phone rang. It was Kev again.

'*Don't do anything unless one of them pulls a weapon,*' he warned me, and I could see him shaking his head in the distance.

'Okay. Let's just make sure we don't leave it too late though,' I replied, not taking my hand off the handle just in case.

'*Don't worry, I'm not about to let someone get stabbed while I'm watching.*'

I put the phone down and turned my attention back to the two men. They seemed to have calmed down now, and Davey had his hands up placatingly. After a bit more chat, Trash actually stuck his hand out and Davey shook it. They got back into their respective cars, and I started the engine as I got ready to follow Davey.

He pulled out and drove on past Kev, deeper into Kemptown, not batting an eyelid as he passed the other car. I knew that Kev and Davey had had dealings with each other a few years back but there was no sign of recognition in the way he drove.

I pulled out and followed at a distance, leaving the others to follow Trash, who still sat behind the wheel of his stationary car. Davey hung a left towards Eastern Road, and I followed him across and up Sutherland towards the racecourse. Yet again I wished for another couple of cars on the follow, but we didn't have anyone spare, so I kept my opinions to myself and concentrated on not losing Davey. He drove all over town, taking random turns and running lights, but I managed to stay with him without being spotted – as far as I could tell.

Eventually we ended up on Dyke Road Drive, cruising past houses that are so far out of my price range it isn't funny. Davey owned one of them though, and every time I drove past the six-bedroom detached house with its two-car drive and security fence,

I always liked to remind myself that crime doesn't pay. Davey pulled in, the gates swinging open as he approached, and I pulled up across the road and slightly past the address.

As soon as we stopped I got back on the phone to Kev. 'He's gone back home. What have you got?'

'*Trash is still driving. We're down past Wilson Avenue now and still going.*'

'What do you want us to do? If we stay here for more than a few minutes we're going to need a RIPA.'

'*Good point. You find an OP and tell Rudd to take the car and go back to the nick and get an urgent authority sorted out.*'

I hung up and turned to Rudd. 'Good news, mate. I get to go and sit in someone's house and you get to go back to the nick and spend an hour sorting out paperwork.'

Rudd rolled his eyes. 'RIPA?'

'Yeah. Get an urgent one; we should be able to sleeve most of the paperwork until later.'

I left the keys in the ignition and got out, scanning the houses opposite Davey's for one that would be suitable to use as an observation post. I marked out two that had cars in the drive, a good sign that someone was in, and then phoned Sally.

'Gareth?' she answered.

'Yeah, hi. I've got a couple of houses I need checked on CIS to make sure that they're clean.' I gave her the house numbers and she put me on hold while she ran me through the system.

'They're clean. The second one you gave me had a burglary a few months ago and we caught the offenders down the road, so they'll probably be more receptive.'

'Okay, thanks, Sally. You're a star.'

She rang off without replying, and I was left with a slightly guilty feeling in the pit of my stomach. I wanted to fix things between us but I wasn't quite sure how to do it. I could see now why Kev didn't like relationships in the office.

* * *

I strolled to the second house, a sprawling red-brick building with a top-of-the-range Mercedes in the drive, and crunched up the gravel to the house. The front door was solid oak with cast iron hinges and as I rang the doorbell I half expected a butler to answer the door. Instead, a slim, harried-looking man in his forties answered.

'Yes, can I help you?' He looked me up and down suspiciously.

'I'm sorry to bother you, I'm PC Bell from Brighton police station. Can I pop in and have a word? It's nothing to worry about.' I showed him my warrant card, making sure that he saw both the badge and the picture.

His frown deepened, his mind obviously churning over trying to work out why I was on his doorstep. 'Yes, yes come in. I'm sorry, I'm right in the middle of some work and I wasn't expecting visitors. Please excuse the mess.'

'The mess' turned out to be one of the magazines on his stylish coffee table being ever so slightly out of place. The house was spotless, expensively decorated and bigger than mine and my dad's put together.

'What's all this about, officer?' he asked as I sat carefully on the edge of the leather sofa.

I found myself slipping easily into the patter that I'd used a hundred times before. 'The reason I'm here is that we're conducting some surveillance in the area, on one of the houses nearby. I can't tell you what the person has done, but suffice it to say that it isn't the sort of thing that you want happening in the area. Your window faces the area that we're looking at and I'd very much like to just sit here for a couple of hours and keep an eye on them if that's all right with you?'

He looked slightly taken aback by the request. 'Erm, are you sure you're really a police officer?'

I nodded. I'm used to that; dressing scruffily doesn't always have advantages. 'Yes, I am. You can call the 0845 number and confirm it if you like?'

'Er, no, I'm sure that's fine, I've just never heard of anything like this before.'

I laughed. 'We tend not to advertise; it lets on to the criminals.'

He smiled. 'I can see that. Of course it's fine. I'll be in the next room working. Just call me if you need anything. Oh, did you want to use upstairs or down here?'

'Upstairs would be great, if you don't mind?'

He led me up to the spare bedroom at the front of the house. I sank into a computer chair and peered through the net curtains, pleased to see that I had a clear view of Davey's house and a fair bit of the road to either side.

'I'll leave you to it,' my host said with a smile, and I returned my attention to the target premises.

I spent the first five minutes getting to know Davey's house as well as I could. He had updated his security since he'd been arrested for stabbing Jimmy and I was keen to get an idea of the sort of security measures he had installed. From where I sat I could make out three CCTV cameras and a burglar alarm, and was searching for more when a black Grand Cherokee four-wheel drive with darkened windows pulled up about twenty feet down the road.

A man in his forties with a bald head got out of the passenger seat and walked towards Davey's gate while talking on his mobile phone. He looked like a bruiser, all bulging muscles and bad attitude, and I couldn't help but wonder if he was part of the hired help I was beginning to suspect Davey had brought in. He certainly looked the part.

I scribbled down the index of the vehicle and was about to phone it through to PNC when the male bolted back to the vehicle and jumped in. A few moments later, I saw Davey's car pull out of the gates and drive towards town. As soon as he was on the road the Cherokee pulled out and followed.

I dialled Kev's number, sprinting out of the room and down the stairs past the startled owner, who was bringing me up a mug of tea. I almost wrenched the front door off its hinges as I ran outside and onto the road, desperate to see where the cars were going. I finally got through to Kev as I reached the kerb, cursing as I scanned the empty road.

'He's gone, mate. He and a second vehicle drove off together. Any joy your end?'

'Well I'd hardly call it joy. I'll send a car to pick you up, there's been another development.'

'What sort of development?'

'Put it this way; I hope you're not squeamish.'

25

'The development' turned out to be a block of flats in Albion Street, just a few roads over from the police station. The outside of the building was taped off, with uniformed officers standing every ten feet or so to keep back the large crowd of onlookers, residents and photographers. I've never known how they got wind of things so fast and have long suspected that someone in the job is getting cash for tip-offs.

I flashed my badge at the officer tasked with the scene log and paused long enough for him to scribble my name down before ducking under the tape and walking into the main entrance to the block. Detectives and SOCOs were everywhere, measuring and scraping and writing in notebooks. I could hear Kev's voice coming from inside the flat nearest to the main door and, as I approached, I could see the flash of a camera going off inside. I pushed the door open carefully, making sure that I didn't touch it anymore than I had to, and stepped into a scene out of *Hellraiser*.

The flat was actually a bedsit with a mattress in one corner covered in filthy blankets. The kitchen area was covered in stains and filthy crockery, but what drew my eyes was the thing hanging from the ceiling. I say 'thing' because you couldn't call it a person anymore. Metal hooks had been driven into the ceiling about five feet apart, and then para-cord had been strung between them to support the weight of the poor bastard hanging there.

Whoever had hung him there had then proceeded to cut pieces off him and had left them lying discarded underneath. The smell was horrendous and blood was liberally splashed all over the floor and ceiling. Even though I was no stranger to death, this was brutal and I had to look away as my stomach churned.

Kev stood nearby talking to Detective Chief Inspector Morris from CID, and waved me over when he saw me. 'Gareth, you know DCI Morris?'

We nodded at each other. 'Sir.'

'Well,' Kev continued, pulling out a hanky to hold over his nose, 'we got a call from the neighbours about four hours ago. It came in as a noise complaint. They thought the victim was having a loud party with lots of screaming and music. A response vehicle finally turned up about half an hour ago and found this.' He gestured to the body hanging there.

As I looked over at it again I had to fight the urge not to retch. Whoever had done it had really gone to town. There wasn't a single part of the torso or face left without brutal-looking slash marks that showed bone glinting white through the lacerated flesh.

'Any idea who he is?' I asked, trying to breathe through my mouth so that I didn't have to smell the stench of death.

'Your unit seems to think that this is Bob Neams, a small cog in Trash's organization. He's been living here for about three months,' Morris answered.

'He used to work for Davey,' Kev interjected, 'but a few months ago he got caught with his hand in the cookie jar. He was quite high up by all accounts but he got kicked out and had to go running to Trash.'

I gave up trying to breathe through my mouth; I swear I could actually taste the smell. My eyes kept straying to the gently swaying body despite my attempts to ignore it, so I forced myself to look rigidly ahead as I spoke. 'Yeah, I know the guy. So this adds weight to the theory that Davey is cleaning house then?'

Kev nodded. 'It does indeed. Who did you see with Davey?'

I filled them both in on the Cherokee and the one occupant I'd spotted.

'Maybe Davey has hired outside help then. Let's get back and run it through the box, see what comes up. Unless there's anything else, sir?'

Morris shook his head, letting Kev and me exit gratefully into the fresh air.

'That was unpleasant,' I said, unable to get the picture of the body out of my mind.

'That it was. You okay?'

I nodded and wished for a cigarette to wash away the aftertaste of the room. 'Yeah. I've seen too many bodies to get worked up over it, but I try and avoid it if I can.' I was lying, of course. No matter how many you see, it can still affect you. I've probably only seen twenty or so bodies in my career but I hate to appear weak, so I brazened it out.

Kev nodded in understanding and motioned me over to his car. We drove back to the nick in silence and headed back up to the office.

The first thing I did was get Sally to run the index of the Cherokee through PNC.

'Stolen from Walthamstow three days ago,' she confirmed when she got off the phone.

'Well that clinches it. What would a stolen vehicle from London be doing hanging around Davey if it wasn't up to no good? Can you put that vehicle out with a "do not divulge police interest" marker?'

She nodded and began trawling for the right form. Then she stopped suddenly and went into the log from the murder in Albion Street.

'What you got?' I asked, puzzled.

'I'm sure I saw that index on the log somewhere. There.' She pointed to an entry made only ten minutes before, about the time Kev and I had left the scene. A member of the public who lived in the next block had seen a black Cherokee drive away from 'the party' in the other block. The index they'd given was two digits out, but it was close enough for me.

'You're brilliant!' I squeezed her shoulder and kissed her on the top of the head.

She looked up at me, half annoyed and half amused.

'Go on then, go tell Kev and get all the credit.'

I all but ran over to Kev's desk and filled him in on the details.

'Right. Get Rudd and go and find that vehicle. I don't care how long it takes you, but I want to prove a link between whoever is in it and Davey, then we'll nick him for conspiracy to commit murder as well as taking them down. Kit up, make sure you've got vests on and don't do anything stupid. Clear?'

I nodded, and Rudd and I left the office once again.

Rudd was driving this time, so I busied myself listening to the divisional channel and looking out of the window for any sign of the vehicle. Rudd and I both agreed that it was probably a wild goose chase, but orders are orders, so we drove around the city, swinging by Davey's house once every half an hour or so in case they had returned there.

'This is pointless!' Rudd complained as we passed the house for the fourth time.

'Have you got a better idea?' I asked, just as frustrated as him.

'No, but … Hang on, what was that?' I turned up the radio and listened to the message that I had tuned out.

'… *have the vehicle, southbound on Grand Parade. It's four up. Permission to stop it, over?*'

'*Negative 107*,' replied the controller, '*we are not to divulge police interest. Keep obs on the vehicle and do not attempt to stop. Received?*'

'Roger; 107 confirm. It's swinging back round now, heading north up Grand Parade towards London Road.'

Rudd immediately floored the accelerator, and I flicked the lights and sirens on. We sped through the traffic on Dyke Road and headed towards the town centre, barely braking as Rudd hurled us around corners at 70 miles an hour.

'Charlie Papa 281, comms,' I called up over the radio, trying to sound calm despite the adrenaline the drive was flooding me with.

'Go ahead 281.'

'We're making from Dyke Road in a plain vehicle, can we get updates on that vehicle's location until we get there, please?'

'Roger that – 107 have you still got the vehicle?'

'Yes, yes. It's now stuck in traffic waiting to head up London Road towards Preston Circus. We're about three cars behind and I don't think he knows we're following.'

Rudd had been following the conversation and now drove down Old Shoreham Road towards Preston Circus. I knew that if the car came out that way it could only go north and we would be able to pick it up easily. We got down to the traffic lights opposite the fire station in less than a minute, turning off the lights and sirens well before we got there. The last thing we wanted to do was spook a car full of people that cut dealers up for fun.

Rudd pulled round the corner and we stopped just past Barclays bank, facing north. The vehicle would have to come past us and it would look perfectly natural if we pulled out after it.

'Charlie Papa 281, comms – we're in position north of Preston Circus, can you ask 107 to back off once we're sure it's coming this way?'

'Roger. 107?'

'Yeah, 107 copy the last. The vehicle is still travelling north on London Road, just passing Richer Sounds now.'

I looked in the mirror and could just see the Cherokee pulling up at the traffic lights. I nudged Rudd who nodded and gripped the steering wheel nervously. The marked car pulled up next to the Cherokee at the lights and even from where we were, I could see the young officer ostentatiously not looking at the occupants of the other vehicle. I shook my head and reached for the radio to tell him to act natural. It's instinctive to look at another vehicle when you're at traffic lights, particularly if you're in a police car, and I really didn't want these guys spooked; they were too dangerous.

Before I could press the button on the handset, it all went wrong. The Cherokee suddenly pulled out through the red traffic lights and took an illegal left up towards New England Hill. The driver of 107 immediately put on his blues and followed, leaving me and Rudd cursing as we tried to turn against the oncoming traffic.

'Drive up on the pavement!' I directed Rudd, and we shot around the corner past startled pedestrians who leapt out of the way.

Once on New England Hill I could see 107's lights up ahead of us under the bridge and towards Old Shoreham Road. We shot up the hill with our lights off, not wanting to show the car out if we caught up. The radio suddenly blared into life.

'*Charlie Charlie 107, I'm in pursuit of the vehicle heading west on Old Shoreham Road. Request permission to continue follow.*'

'*Negative 107, pull off and leave the vehicle, we have plain units in the area. Acknowledge last, please.*'

There was silence on the other end of the radio. Whoever was driving 107 obviously wanted some glory and was willing to get it at the cost of our job.

'Catch up with that idiot, will you?' I asked Rudd, and then clutched desperately at the dashboard for support as he made a sharp turn at almost ninety.

I could see the two vehicles ahead, both tearing up towards Dyke Road. They were going at least twice the speed limit and I was worried what would happen when they hit the traffic lights ahead. By the time we reached the brow of the hill we were only two car lengths behind and I heaved a sigh of relief as the lights turned green. We shot through the lights in convoy and then the Cherokee braked suddenly, almost causing the marked car to plough into it. Rudd braked rapidly and we screeched to a halt with a squeal of tyres.

I hung on for dear life as we just missed the back of 107 and saw out of the corner of my eye the driver's window of the Cherokee sliding down. Even though I could see what was coming I had no time to shout a warning as a pistol was extended through the window and two shots went off, shattering 107's windscreen and making Rudd and me scramble for cover behind the dashboard.

Huddled in the footwell, I threw my hands over my head and prayed that no more shots would follow. I was rewarded with the sound of the four-wheel drive screaming off again, so I opened the door and ran for 107, hoping against hope that the driver was unharmed.

26

I got to the other car in record time and yanked the door open on the driver's side. The officer inside was young and I couldn't put a name to him. He was also bleeding from glass cuts to his face and he stank where he had voided his bowels but otherwise he was unharmed.

'Are you okay?' I asked, gripping the hand he still had glued to the steering wheel.

He turned to look at me, his eyes so wide they seemed about to fall out. 'They shot at me!' he whispered hoarsely. Tears began to fill his eyes and trickle down his cheeks.

'Look, you're okay. Come on; let's get you out of the car.'

He nodded and let me pull him from the vehicle. His eyes were still the size of saucers and probably would have been larger still if he'd seen the bullet hole in the headrest, only millimetres away from where his head had been.

'What's your name, mate?' I asked, trying to bring him back from whatever dark place he was in.

'Me? Gavin. You're Gareth Bell, aren't you? We worked together on that drug job last year.'

I nodded, not remembering him or the job. 'Yeah, I remember. Look, we've got people coming; you just sit here with me.'

I led him to the kerb, ignoring the angry beeps of protest from other drivers who wanted to get past. I looked over to Rudd who was on the radio in our car and pointed to Gavin, then wiggled my hand to indicate he wasn't doing so well. Rudd held up two fingers, which I took to mean that help was only a couple of minutes away.

My relief that Gavin hadn't been too badly injured was beginning to give way to anger at his stupidity. He had been forbidden to carry on the follow but had done so anyway, resulting in him being shot at and losing our chance at catching the Cherokee. After this they would no doubt burn it out somewhere and pick up a new vehicle.

'Do you smoke?'

Gavin began fumbling in his pockets and produced a battered packet of Marlboro's and a lighter.

'Good man.' I took two out of the packet and lit them, passing one back to him. I could hear sirens now; it sounded as though every emergency vehicle in Brighton was converging on our location. I stayed sitting with Gavin, one arm around his shoulder as he began to shake, and let Rudd get on with everything else.

The cuts on the officer's face were superficial, little more than scratches really, and I checked carefully to make sure that he didn't have an extra hole anywhere that shock wasn't letting him feel. By the time I'd finished, an ambulance had arrived along with half a dozen police cars and a fire engine. The paramedics took Gavin straight to the ambulance, and I waved him off, standing up and brushing myself down as Derek Pearson arrived on scene looking more than a little harried. He made a beeline straight for me.

'Well?' he asked, crossing his arms over his chest and glaring at me as if it was all my fault.

'He's fine, sir, just a few cuts and shock.'

'What happened?'

I gestured towards the damaged car. 'He was ordered to pull off the follow and he didn't. They got as far as here and obviously decided that they didn't want to play anymore. They pulled up and fired two shots out of the driver's window with a pistol. By the time we poked our heads back up they were gone.'

He shook his head. 'No one shoots at one of *my* officers in *my* city and gets away with it. Get yourselves back to the nick and write it up. Don't miss anything out. I want these men, Gareth.'

I nodded and went to collect Rudd. We had to leave our car there as part of the crime scene, so we blagged a lift with a marked vehicle. The radio was alive with the sound of units, mostly armed response, calling in as they searched frantically for the Cherokee before it was dumped.

'You okay?' I asked Rudd as we climbed the stairs to the office. We'd both said nothing on the journey back. Even though we hadn't been the target of the shots it was still sobering to be so close to an incident like that.

'Yeah, fine. I reckon Kev's going to tear us off a strip though.'

'Why? We didn't do anything wrong.'

'I know, but what should have been a simple follow turned into a bloody shooting.'

My answer died on my lips as we walked into the office to see Kev standing at his desk, one hand on his hips and the other pointing to the inspector's office. We dutifully filed in and waited until he was seated before speaking.

'Tell me,' he said, doing his best not to look angry and failing miserably.

Rudd explained this time and, by the time he had finished, Kev was looking more concerned than angry.

'Okay. It sounds like you did everything you could. At least no one was seriously hurt. We've got units out scouring the city for the vehicle, so if it's still around we'll find it. Make sure you write it all up properly, this is going right up to the top.'

We both nodded in unison and went to our desks. The office

was almost empty, it now being after four, and we were blessedly free from enquiring colleagues as we bent our heads over our desks and got on with it. It took almost two hours, making sure that absolutely everything we could remember was down on paper.

As we left the office, Rudd invited me out for a beer.

'Thanks mate, but I've got other plans.'

He waved and left me to it. I pulled out my phone and hesitated before dialling Sally's number. I wasn't sure what sort of reaction I would get if I called, but I missed her and I needed her company that night. It rang a good dozen times before she picked up.

'Yes?'

'Uh, hi, it's me. Are you free tonight?'

There was a long silence, then, 'I suppose so. Where are you now?'

'I've literally just finished work. Those guys in the Cherokee shot at an officer in front of us today.'

'Shit, is he okay? Are you okay?'

'Yeah, everyone's fine. I could really use your company though.'

'Of course. Come on over.'

I drove straight to hers, only stopping to pick up a couple of bottles of wine on the way. Despite her concern on the phone I was still nervous as I rang the doorbell, almost jiggling from foot to foot as I waited for her to answer. When the door finally opened, however, my nerves vanished and I stepped into Sally's arms and wrapped mine around her. The contact was more than welcome after a day of death and violence and I felt myself relaxing as I held her.

'Uh, Gareth, are you planning to let go and come in at any point?'

I released her with a laugh and closed the door behind me. 'Sorry, it's been one hell of a day. You look lovely.'

179

'You always say that.'

'You always look lovely.'

'Creep.'

I smiled and went through to the kitchen to find a corkscrew. I might not have been entirely out of the doghouse yet, but I was pretty sure that things were looking up.

27

The next morning found me back at my desk looking at reports. It seemed that the drugs that I'd found the previous week coupled with the stabbings had screwed with Davey's network, and the team headed out to check the streets and confirm what we were reading.

As the intelligence suggested, Davey's crew were nowhere to be seen. We spent the day poking around and calling in favours to find out where they were hiding. No one on the streets wanted to talk to us, however, so just after six I took a car over to the hospital to see Jimmy and give him the good news.

He was sitting up in bed when I got there, propped up on several pillows and watching a film on a portable DVD player. As I approached the bed he looked up and flicked it off.

'Thank God, that's the third time I've watched that film in the last week.'

'Oh I see, so I'm only a diversion from your endless boredom now?'

'Stop being so bloody melodramatic. That's always been your issue, Gareth, you never appreciate other people's problems. Take mine, for example, I'm stuck here with a hole in my lung that isn't healing properly, bored to tears because my so-called best friend can't be bothered to bring me any new films, and he makes the papers, gets stabbed, and I have to find out about it from aforesaid newspapers. That's nice, that is.'

I sat down on the bed hard enough to make him wince. 'Jesus, Jimmy, how long have we been married? You go on worse than Lucy did.'

He looked away for a moment, as he always does when I mention Lucy. He always had a thing for her, and in fact he had been the one who'd introduced us after he met her in a club one night, to his eternal annoyance. She'd seemed interested in him until I came along but had shaken him off and clung to me immediately. I still wasn't sure why; not that it matters anymore.

'So,' I said, trying to think of something to move past the awkwardness, 'you saw the newspaper article then. What did you think?'

'You should have shaved your legs first.'

'There's nothing wrong with hairy legs, they're manly.'

'Not when you can't see the skin underneath.'

'They're not that bad.'

We both grinned, feeling a shared camaraderie in knowing but never mentioning the whole Lucy thing, as if it drew us closer instead of being a problem. Every time it comes up, we dive headlong into a ridiculous argument about anything, just to let the moment pass.

'So what else have you been up to?' he asked, and I filled him in on the events of the previous few days. 'Bloody hell,' he said when I finished explaining, 'I'm out of the game for a few weeks and the whole division gets turned upside down. Did SOCU have their job logged anywhere?'

I shook my head. 'Of course they didn't, they're cowboys. They had it logged with their own people but they don't trust us mere mortals back on division, so we wouldn't have known even if we had called it in.'

It wasn't fair calling SOCU cowboys as they actually do a bloody good job, but I was annoyed and venting and Jimmy knew it.

'So how did it feel?'

'The coke? Horrible. It was like being on a fairground ride that doesn't stop. You know what I'm like about being in control and I couldn't shut it off.' I shuddered at the memory.

'Do you think that's the last we've seen of Davey then?' he asked, changing the subject again.

I shrugged. 'I hope so, although I suspect that he'll surface again like the bad penny he is. He's too much of a psycho to go down gracefully. If those shooters yesterday were his, they'll probably be long gone as well.'

'What about the streets; has it made a difference?'

'Nah, it's still crazy out there and only getting worse. It always will be, you know that. Every other dealer in the city has just started expanding. Nature abhors a vacuum.'

Which is the problem with Brighton. You can dent the supply, or the demand, but never both at the same time, which is what we need to do to cut the number of users and dealers and hence the crime rate. Someone once told me that if someone has a £100 a day habit, they steal £1,0000 worth of stuff a month in order to feed it. So you do the math and work out where most of the money from burglaries, robberies and other thefts goes. Most of the users only steal to get their next fix, so remove the supply for long enough and the users will go elsewhere to find their drugs. But if you only strike at the dealers, the demand is still there and someone will always be willing to turn that to their profit despite the risks.

'So you *did* come to cheer me up then?'

'Sorry, Jimmy, I just get so bloody fed up sometimes. It feels like we're doing all this for nothing. We nick one lot and another just steps in. It's like trying to put out a fire with a water pistol.'

'You don't have to tell me, mate, I work there too, remember?'

'Yeah, I know. Anyway, that's enough being miserable. What have the docs said about your lung?'

His expression immediately made me wish I hadn't asked.

'They think I'm developing pneumonia, so they've got me on all sorts of antibiotics. I can't eat without being sick, and to be honest with you I'm just bloody fed up and I want to go home.'

I reached over and squeezed his arm affectionately. 'I know, mate, but just stick it out. I'm sure they'll kick it into touch soon and then you'll be out and about and getting into trouble with the rest of us, I promise you. Look, I've got to go, mate, I've got things to do, but I'll come see you for longer in the morning and bring you some different films, okay?'

He nodded, and I shook his hand as I got up and left.

I walked back past Bramber ward to see if Billy Budd was still there, only to discover that the bed he had been in was now occupied by an elderly gentleman. At least that was one problem solved.

I left the hospital via the main entrance, then turned and walked back into the shop to pick up a paper. I wanted to see if anything had made the nationals yet about my drug bust or the shooting the day before.

As I turned, a man further down the corridor suddenly ducked to his left and out of my sight. I wouldn't even have noticed him if not for the quick movement, but I carried on into the shop as if nothing had alerted me. I wasn't sure if it was PSD or one of Davey's goons but either way it didn't bode well. Not wanting to give the game away, I bought a paper which I ostentatiously placed under my arm as I walked out.

I headed over to my car, parked in one of the bays at the front by Eastern Road, and sat in the driver's seat for a few minutes pretending to talk on the phone while I watched people going in and out of the building. I'd only managed to get a glimpse of the man following me – late twenties, shaven head, blue T-shirt and jeans – and I wanted to get a proper look at him before I left so that I would recognize his face and not just his clothes.

That's why so many mid-level criminals wear outfits that we

think look ridiculous. So you see a bloke in a red tracksuit top and trousers with a stupid hat that stands up off the top of his head. He does something criminal, deals drugs, steals something, take your pick, and you call the police. When they arrive – probably later than you or they would like – they ask for a description and you tell them about the horrible tracksuit and hat the guy was wearing. I can promise you that ninety per cent of the time the guy that you're talking about could walk past you as you're giving the description to the police and, if he's changed out of the tracksuit and hat, you won't recognize him. The more garish the outfit, the harder it is to remember the face. A good surveillance officer – and I'd like to think I am one – will memorize all sorts of things about a target, like the way they walk, habits and mannerisms, how they slouch, that sort of thing. It makes a real difference when you can spot someone in a crowd from a hundred yards just because of their body language, believe me.

So I sat and waited, careful not to be too obvious as I had a pretend conversation on the phone with my ex-wife. It helps to imagine the person you're making up the conversation with; it makes your body language change, which will get picked up by anyone watching you and make you seem more convincing. No one told me in training how hard it could be just to look and act like any other person on the street, and I wouldn't have believed them if they had. Irritatingly, despite the fact that I was making up the argument I was having with Lucy, I still lost. My therapist would have found that interesting, I was sure, not that I ever went to see him anymore.

Just as I put the phone down, convinced that my mark wasn't coming out, he appeared and began walking across the car park in my direction, scanning left and right as he looked for me. I began to get a little worried as he got closer; he didn't look, or act, like a copper, but I knew his face from somewhere – only I couldn't place it for the life of me. As he walked past the car, somehow not seeing me, it clicked and I remembered seeing him

185

in an intelligence photograph on Davey's association chart. So not PSD at all, in fact, but instead one of Davey's crew.

Shit. I wondered whether he had seen me there and decided to follow me off his own back or whether Davey had him tailing me in the hopes that I would lead them to the heroin. I nearly drove away and left him to it, but I needed to find out what he wanted for my own peace of mind if nothing else.

I waited until he disappeared around the corner of the building towards the service road that runs through the centre of the hospital grounds, then got out of the car and ran after him. I paused at the corner, counted to five and walked round slowly, just in time to see him slip down the side of a building, still looking right and left, but not behind. I moved quickly across the open space and followed him down the alley, stopping dead when I saw him turn to face me only a few feet along.

Up close his face resembled nothing so much as an angry bulldog as he grinned at me in a manner that told me he had known I was following him.

'Davey's got a message for you, mate,' he stated in a hard Brighton accent. 'He wants you to know that what happens now is all your fault. He tried to be nice and you told him to fuck off.'

I laughed at him, positioning myself in solid stance so that I could fight easily if it came to it, feet firmly grounded and facing forward, shoulder-width apart, knees slightly bent and hips tilted forward.

'You can tell Davey that he can go and eat his own shit. I told your man the other day that I only deal with the big boys, not the muppets. If you've got a problem with that I suggest you take it up with him.'

I began to edge away slowly, still facing him, but I could almost feel the adrenaline begin to hit his system as his face began to drain of colour, the blood flowing to the muscles instead.

'You don't understand, mate,' he continued as he began to edge closer to me. 'If you don't do as he says, your mate up there's

gonna find himself with a whole new set of illnesses. You get me?'
His voice was getting lower and more aggressive as his body
prepared to fight, and I could feel my own body yearning to do
the same, sensing the threat my adversary was presenting. Not
for a minute did I take the threat to Jimmy seriously – there were
too many people and CCTV cameras around there for them to
hurt him without being caught.

'Yeah, I get you and you wouldn't dare. If you even so much
as touch him, I'll break your fingers.'

I should have turned and walked away but I suspected that if
I did he would jump me, so I stayed facing him as he inched
closer. Finally, it became too much to bear and I lashed out with
a foot as he came within range, his fists up in a boxer's guard.

He skipped forwards rather than backwards, as I was expecting,
and the foot that should have hit his chin discharged its energy
on his thigh instead as he closed. He stumbled, and I moved in
quickly, throwing three rapid punches into his chest. He collapsed,
struggling for breath, and I grabbed his face between my hands,
squeezing hard enough to bring tears to his eyes.

I leaned over him so that I was close enough to smell the
cigarettes and coffee on his breath and growled, 'If you ever
threaten Jimmy again, I'll kill you. Then Davey and anyone else
who stands in my way. The drugs are where you'll never find
them, so don't even bother looking, okay?'

He struggled for breath for a moment longer then finally got
enough to speak. 'Too late, mate, you've fucked it now!' He cocked
his head to one side as if listening and I suddenly became aware
of shouting, the banging of a car door and then the screeching
of tyres in the car park I had just left.

Dropping my opponent I ran back to the front of the hospital
to see a host of angrylooking medical staff milling around as a
white panel van screamed off east along the main road. I grabbed
hold of a confused-looking nurse and shook her, just a little, to
make her look at me.

'What's going on?' I shouted, having to raise my voice over the general hubbub in the car park.

She looked up at me and pulled away from my grip. 'They just came in and took a man from the ward! They knocked the sister out and just took him from the bed; four of them in balaclavas. One of them had a gun!'

I knew the answer before I asked the question but I had to ask anyway. 'Which ward, which bed?'

'Catherine James ward, bed four. They took the police officer that got stabbed.'

28

The ward was a mass of confusion, shouting voices and angry staff and patients as I tried to work out exactly what had happened. As soon as the nurse told me that Jimmy was missing, I'd run into the building and sealed the area off as a crime scene, already on my mobile for backup.

I was holding down the fort, just, my badge unfolded and hanging from my jacket pocket so that people would listen to me as I barked instructions, demanding that anything the kidnappers may have touched be left well alone. The ward sister had a nasty gash on her forehead that looked as if it had been done with a baton or torch and was being dealt with by two other nurses, one of whom was crying silently as she worked.

Apparently the men had burst in at about the time I had been fighting in the alleyway and had grabbed Jimmy, hauling him out of the bed, heedless of the drip and other pipes and tubes attached to him. There was blood on his sheets from the cannula coming loose, and just looking at it made guilt hit me harder than anything I had felt before. There was no escaping it; it was my fault. If I had just done things properly instead of going out and stealing from Davey, Jimmy would still be lying there trying to chat up the nurses instead of being taken God only knew where in the back of a van. I crossed to the bed and felt under the pillow. My hand closed on something cold and hard and I pulled out the spray I had left with Jimmy.

I heard booted feet pounding down the corridor as backup arrived in the form of two entire vans of LST, four response officers and three detectives, all racing to get to the scene first. I shoved the can in my pocket before anyone noticed and walked quickly away from the bed. As they entered the ward I gave them a brief sit-rep, explaining what had been touched, who had seen them and how long ago it had happened. I had given the description of the van and the direction of travel over the phone and traffic and firearms units were already scouring the city in an attempt to find the vehicle before it disappeared.

Sam Moran, the senior LST sergeant, took charge of the scene with cool professionalism, organizing the milling staff, patients and visitors into two gaggles; those who had seen the kidnappers and those that hadn't. Officers began to seal the ward off with tape, much to the annoyance of the staff who were still trying to work around the sudden wave of uniforms that surrounded them, and I took the chance to step into the corridor and phone Kev. Despite the fact he was probably at home by now, he would kick my arse from here to Sunday if he was left out of the loop when one of his officers had been kidnapped.

He answered after two rings and I could hear that he was on a car hands-free kit.

'*I already know,*' he said before I could say anything. '*They called me as soon as you called it in. I'm on my way.*'

'Okay, I'll be here,' I said as he hung up. I turned back to the ward, trying to work out what to say that wouldn't implicate me in his disappearance. As much as I wanted to get Jimmy back, I had a feeling that it would only be resolved through returning the heroin I had taken and not through police work. If I told them what I had been up to I would be in prison, Davey would never see his heroin and Jimmy would wind up dead. I couldn't let that happen, so I thought furiously about what I would say when they got around to questioning me.

Even more officers turned up, including Superintendent Doyle, a stern-looking woman in her early fifties with steel grey hair and the crispest uniform I'd ever seen. I assumed that she was the duty Gold Commander, which meant that she was nominally in charge of the force for the shift. Doyle frequently dropped into various divisions while she was Gold, and I knew that for her to get there so quickly she must already have been in Brighton.

She looked around, clearly waiting for someone to notice and give her an update, and I stepped towards her without really thinking about it. Some habits die hard.

'Ma'am,' I said, nodding respectfully.

She looked me up and down, noting my badge. 'DC ...?'

'Uh, PC Bell, ma'am, DIU. Jimmy's my friend; I'd just finished visiting him when he got taken.'

She was silent for a moment as she absorbed the information. 'Right. So you left and they took him. Did you get to see anyone or anything useful?'

I shook my head. 'No, ma'am, I was around the back trying to find the café for a bite of food before I left, and I ran back when I heard the shouting and screeching of tyres.'

She looked at me, her fierce blue eyes boring into mine. I could feel the intelligence in her gaze hit me like a physical weight as she assessed what I was telling her.

'I assume that they knew who you were too and were waiting until you had left before kidnapping PC, uh—'

'Holdsworth,' I finished for her. 'Yes, ma'am, that's what I'd assumed too. If there's nothing else, ma'am, I'd like to do what I came here to do: find Jimmy.'

She nodded, and I gratefully escaped, finding Sam Morgan talking to the newly arrived Kev. Kev reached out his hand for me to shake without stopping talking to Sam.

'So the cameras were all out? This is starting to sound like a very professional job.'

My head turned sharply as I heard him say that and he turned to include me in the conversation. 'Sam was just telling me that there was a power cut in the security office, so all the recorders were offline, as were the monitors from about five minutes before the grab until about thirty seconds ago. That means we haven't even got a chance of footage showing the van index.' He sounded angry, his usual laconic air missing.

'Have you got any idea who might have done it or why?' I asked, knowing that there was only one sensible answer.

He shrugged. 'Until we get something else, the only link we've got is to the court case with Davey, but I can't see a reason why they'd take him, unless you know something we don't?'

Shaking my head while maintaining eye contact with Kev was one of the hardest things I've ever done; it made me feel dirty inside. 'No idea, but I intend to find out. I don't mean to sound alarmist but do you think it could be the guys in the Cherokee?' I instantly regretted my dissembling as I saw the look of alarm cross the sergeants' faces.

'I hope not. We'll log it as a possibility just in case but we're going to have to keep an open mind. We're doing everything we can think of fast-time. Brighton's too small a place for someone to do this and keep it quiet for long, so we'll hear something. Look, I need an intel officer on this. Are you happy to go back to the nick and do it?'

I nodded, glad to be away from eyes that were trained to see too much for my comfort. Every major job has an intelligence officer assigned to it, a person to research anything that the officers on the ground might need checking for relevance and add it to the log so that there's an easily readable trail to follow for everyone involved in the job. I'd done it plenty of times but never for something like that. I could easily be adding information to the log that would be incriminating myself. Still, it was better than being there, waiting for someone to spot or realize something that I hadn't thought of and put two and two together. So, with a wave, I headed out into the car park and drove back to the nick, all the while worrying about Jimmy and wondering how Davey would make contact with me.

Back at the station I swiped myself into the deserted office and headed to my desk, taking my radio off charge and switching it on so that I could hear the units on the ground. When I didn't hear anything I called comms as I logged into my computer and OIS, the system that kept the logs that I needed to access.

'Charlie Papa 281, comms.'

'Go ahead 281.'

'I've been tasked as intelligence officer for the kidnapping, can you derestrict it to my terminal, please, and let me know which channel we're working on?'

I knew that the serial would be restricted before I even got into the system: it would have to be for a job like that one, and due to the lack of radio traffic, they also had to have dedicated a separate radio channel to the job.

'Roger 281, serial 1355 derestricted to your terminal and it's channel B-DIV-A.'

'Roger, many thanks. I'll be here if you need me.'

A double blip told me that they had received my last and I turned the dial on the back of my Nokia handset to the right channel, hearing controlled chaos as white panel vans were stopped by units right across the city.

I read the log, beginning from the moment that I had called in and working through to the current time. Barely half an hour had passed since I had alerted them but it felt as if years had gone by already. I fretted as I read through the log, worrying about Jimmy. The pneumonia had hit him hard according to what the nurses had said, and he needed the antibiotics that they were pumping into him intravenously or it would begin to spread again. I knew why he'd hidden from me just how bad it was. I'd once had pneumonia and, even healthy and whole as I'd been, it had nearly killed me. Doubtless he hadn't wanted me to worry like I was then.

I had that sick feeling in the pit of my stomach that you get when you know you've done something wrong and don't know how to fix it, and my hands wouldn't stop shaking as I sat there waiting to be useful.

'*Charlie Echo 104, comms?*' came an excited female voice over the radio, making me jump.

'*Go ahead 104?*'

'*We've got a white panel van on fire at the top of Wilson Avenue, partial index W79 something, the rest is obscured by flames, over?*'

'*Received, we'll get Trumpton en route.*'

Trumpton is police slang for the fire brigade, and I wasn't sure if I was hoping for or dreading their arrival. It was recent enough that they might be in time to put out the fire before all the forensics were scoured away, and if the kidnappers weren't top notch it would give us something to work with.

My thoughts were racing, alternating between wanting them to find Jimmy before his kidnappers went to ground and not finding him until I could get the heroin back to them. I hated myself for not telling all, but I knew that Davey was capable of killing if he didn't get what he wanted, and I also knew that the only thing he wanted was the heroin. If I handed it over to my bosses, the chances were that Jimmy would end up dead in a ditch as revenge and I would end up dead in a prison cell a few months later. Shaking my head to try and clear it I turned back to the log, searching for anything I may have missed the first time.

Six hours later I was startled by Kev coming into the office, where I sat slumped in front of my computer screen. The log was now over a hundred pages long, which was pretty impressive even for a job of that magnitude. I was so tired from my relentless hours of screen work that my eyes felt like they had been packed with sand, and when Kev offered to make me a cup of tea, I could have kissed him. Being the only one in the office, I hadn't even dared leave for a piss, just in case I missed something, and I hoped a cup of tea would wake me up enough to keep going.

Kev brought the promised tea over a few minutes later then pulled up Sally's chair to sit next to me. 'How's it going?' he asked, his face full of sympathy that I didn't want or deserve.

'Shite. You?'

He settled back into the chair, looking tired and worn. 'About the same. A nationwide bulletin has gone out and they've called an Aftan, so it's just a waiting game now.'

An Aftan is a rule buried deep in some regulation book somewhere that forcibly prevents any officer on division from leaving work until the job is called off. Needless to say they are extremely unpopular, although with the present case I suspected that people wouldn't mind. I drank my tea in silence, staring at the screen in front of me as I tried not to think about Jimmy. Kev startled me yet again by suddenly speaking; I'd almost forgotten he was there.

'How are the checks on that partial index from the van going?'

'So far, 1,212 possible matches on PNC, none stolen in the force for over a year and the PNC bureau is working to narrow the list down. Hopefully they'll have something by morning prayers.'

'Morning prayers' is the nickname for the meeting that the command team has every morning to discuss what has happened on the division over the previous twenty-four hours, just after our daily intelligence meeting. But by then I knew that the trail would be colder than my marriage and we would be into 'slow-time', which meant that we would be wallowing further and further behind as we used reactive instead of proactive methods to try and find Jimmy.

'Okay, well I'm going to check in with Gold but I suspect that we'll be stood down shortly. CID are providing someone to do anymore intel stuff.' He glanced at the clock on the wall; the red LEDs showing that it was some time after 2.00 a.m. 'Can you make it in for seven thirty?'

I nodded, suspecting that I would struggle to sleep anyway. 'Yeah, no problem. In fact I don't mind staying for the duration if you need me to?'

'No, I want you to get *some* sleep at least. I'm going upstairs to speak to Gold; I'll let you know as soon as we get the stand-down.'

He squeezed my shoulder as he left and walked out of the office while I idly scanned through the other logs to see what was happening on division. My attention was starting to waver by that point and I couldn't concentrate properly, so I stared into space until I was jolted back to wakefulness by Kev coming back in.

'Go home, I'll see you in a few hours,' he called, and I waved as he left again.

I called comms to let them know I was logging off and closed everything down before leaving, trudging down to the car park through deserted corridors that felt more like home than my house did.

29

Two hours' sleep, two Pro-Plus and one large coffee later, I was sat in the briefing room on the fourth floor of the police station with about fifty other officers, all of whom had the look on their faces that we tend to reserve for when someone has done something to one of our own. The whole force had been mobilized for this, unsurprisingly, and this briefing was one of many that was going on across Sussex as they prepared to turn over every stone in the county looking for Jimmy.

I still hadn't been contacted by Davey and I was growing more concerned by the minute. What if this was purely revenge and not an attempt to get the drugs back? If that were the case, I figured, it wouldn't make any difference if I told the whole story; but I knew I couldn't rely on that in case Davey was just letting me sweat a little before making his demands. I was so tired that my brain refused to think in a straight line and I kept going round in circles trying to work out what to do. I began to get frustrated with just sitting and waiting and shifted impatiently.

Rudd was sitting next to me, staring into his own coffee and ignoring the world in general but as I began squirming he looked up at me. 'You all right, Gareth?'

I shook my head, feeling my brain rattle as I did so. 'Not really. I want to be out there and looking for him, not waiting for the command team to pull their finger out and get this briefing started.'

He smiled sympathetically at me. 'I know, mate, I feel the same, but if we all go haring off in different directions we'll never find Jimmy.'

'I know; I just don't like the waiting.'

Whatever Rudd was going to say next was lost as Superintendent John Decker came into the room and walked to the podium at the far end, leaving a trail of silence in his wake as officers shut up and prepared to listen.

'Good morning everyone, I'll keep this as brief as possible. I'm Superintendent Decker from Brighton division. Most of you know me already but for those of you who don't, let me just tell you that we are committing every resource to finding PC Holdsworth as quickly as possible, and I *will* get this done.'

He paused to look out over the sea of faces staring up at him. 'This has now been named Operation Hunt. Just after 20.00 hours last night, PC Holdsworth was abducted from the Royal Sussex by four men, all with balaclavas, and one was carrying a handgun which was not discharged. They assaulted a senior nurse and took PC Holdsworth from his bed, despite the fact he's suffering from pneumonia after a stab wound that collapsed one of his lungs.'

He pulled up a map on the large computer screen attached to the wall behind him and used a laser pointer to indicate several red circles superimposed on the map. 'These are the areas we have searched already, doing complete house-to-house enquiries on the route that they took, then areas where someone might have seen the vehicle they used after they burned the van out at the top of Wilson Avenue. Although we have nothing forensics-wise, we are working on the assumption that Quentin Davey, the drug dealer who stabbed PC Holdsworth, is responsible for the abduction until something else presents itself. We don't know a lot more at this stage but we will be working around the clock until our colleague is found. You will be given assignments by your supervisors. Can sergeants and inspectors stay behind please; the rest of you get ready to deploy. Thank you.'

I filed out with the others. Another typical Sussex briefing: they drag everyone in to tell them how we'll get the job done, then kick us all out so that only the supervisors know the ins and outs, wasting precious time that we could be using to find Jimmy.

I thundered down the stairs, not wanting to talk to anybody despite my name being called a few times as I ran past people. I made it back to the office in record time, ignoring Sally as I switched on my terminal and waited impatiently for it to wake up.

'Gareth?' Sally asked tentatively, looking as though she'd just been slapped.

'I'm sorry, what?'

'Um, nothing, I just wanted to know if you're okay? Kev called me last night and told me what happened, so I know why you didn't call me.'

I sighed. I had totally forgotten that we'd arranged a dinner date and, despite what had happened, the least I could have done was call her and let her know.

'I'm sorry, Sally, I've only had a couple of hours' sleep and I'm exhausted. I couldn't stop thinking about Jimmy last night; I just want to find him safe and well.'

'I know, we all do. Everyone in the nick is doing everything they can to help.'

I nodded and turned back to my computer, which as usual was taking forever to wake up. The office was muted this morning, the usual buzz absent as people went about their work in near silence. The lack of noise immediately got on my nerves. It was as if they already thought that Jimmy was dead.

As soon as my system chugged into slow and painful life, I booted up OIS and checked Jimmy's log, skimming through the hundred and fifty plus pages, years of experience allowing me to skip the information that wasn't relevant, such as which call signs had been assigned and requests for PNC checks.

Nothing vital had been added, so I began to search the rest of the serials. Initially I just searched central Brighton, then moved on to include Hove as well and was about to go back to the kidnapping log when something caught my eye.

An elderly woman had phoned in to complain that the people downstairs were having a party and that one of the men going into the flat was wearing a dress. She claimed that it wasn't right and that not only were they banging and crashing all the time, but now the 'gays' were invading Hove and we should do something.

The woman had been given advice by the operator to call Environmental Health about the noise and the log had been closed off without police attendance. It wouldn't have meant anything to me, either, had I not tailed a dealer back to that block of flats a couple of weeks before during a follow, and although I hadn't recognized him, he had been selling to Davey's customers.

It was probably nothing, but a hospital gown could look a little like a dress and I couldn't discount the possibility that it could be where they had taken Jimmy. The time on the log said that it had come in at 22.10, which was about two hours after Jimmy had been taken.

'Sal, come and look at this,' I said, excitedly. 'I think I might have found something.'

Sally leaned over, reading the log, and when she had finished our eyes met.

'Do you think the dress could be a hospital gown?' she asked, looking animated.

I nodded. 'That's what I reckon. Where's Kev?'

'I think he's still in the briefing,' she replied, checking over the divider.

As if summoned by her look, Kev appeared at the door, seeming remarkably awake considering the time he left the night before.

'Kev, I think I've got something,' I called, as he approached then came into the pod at my call. I pointed to the computer screen, and he read the serial.

'It's a bit of a long shot,' he said, rubbing his chin the way he always does when thinking.

'I'm pretty sure that I saw one of Davey's boys going into that flat the other day.'

He looked at me sharply. 'Did you put an intel log in?'

'I thought I did, maybe not. I'll check and see.'

He nodded. 'Right. You do that; I'll go see the super.'

I immediately checked through my CIMS outbox and cursed when I couldn't find the intel log. 'I must have forgotten,' I said to Sally, who was still watching over my shoulder.

'Well write it now and get them to put it on the system,' she suggested, which I did immediately before pinging it off to Kate at the centre desk, who would then sanitize it by taking out any information that would show the source of the log and place it on the system.

Rudd and Eddie came back from getting coffee, placing a large one on the desk in front of me. I showed them the serial and told them my little snippet about having seen a dealer there recently. As soon as I mentioned it Rudd got excited.

'I lost Davey there a couple of weeks ago. I saw him go into the estate but I lost him when I parked up. I'll bet that's where they're keeping Jimmy.' He pushed me out of the way and used my CIMS login to dig up the report which he then printed along with mine.

Kev came back through the door with Superintendent Decker and we had a brief powwow, which rapidly turned into a plan for a strike on the flat. Decker then took Kev away with instructions to Rudd to go over to the magistrate's court and swear out a warrant, something which he is particularly good at, and for the rest of us to stand by for further instructions.

A tense twenty minutes later we pulled up all the intelligence we had on the flat, which sadly wasn't much, but we managed to find a floor plan from a previous warrant buried in the filing cabinet where they are all kept, which made the job a lot easier.

Eddie and I discussed possible avenues of approach, settling for using the alleyway that led into the estate from the street next to it and approaching the target flat from behind. We agreed this would be the safest way to get into position without alerting the occupants to our presence.

We had just finished making maps and plans from Google Earth, drawing over the top in thick black pen, when Kev came back into the office.

'Eddie, Gareth, you two with me. Rudd is going straight to the plot to watch the front; he's got the warrant with him. We're briefing a firearms team in five minutes, so get everything you've got and see you on the fourth floor.'

Now that the plans were made, everything seemed to be happening all at once and I could only pray that I wasn't mistaken and that we would find Jimmy alive and well.

30

An hour later, I was sitting in the driver's seat of a beaten-up old panel van parked up on Bolsover Road, just east of the target flat. Only the occasional jostle gave away the fact that eight heavily armed officers were hidden in the back. I felt sorry for them, all loaded up with tactical vests and rifles, then crammed into the rear of the van as the temperature hit the low twenties, but they were used to it and not one of them made a noise in complaint.

I had my covert set on and was to give the go as, for tactical reasons, firearms officers use a different channel on their radios. Rudd hadn't seen any movement from the flat and ideally Kev wanted to see something before we went in, even if it was just the curtains twitching so that we could get an idea of what we might be facing. Finally, as the clock on the dash ticked over to 11.03, my radio crackled into life and Kev's voice whispered in my ear.

'Ding, we're good to go. Confirm strike, strike, strike.'

I turned to the small hole cut in the wooden panel that blocked the rear of the van from view and said, 'Sarge, we're good to go.'

I heard a double tap on the panel and the door slid open to spill armed officers into the bright sunlight, their black helmets and tactical vests dusty from the time spent in the van. They filed out in silence, running for the alleyway that led to the flat. In moments the street was empty, and I clicked my radio.

'They're away, Kev,' I said, and heard a click in response.

Then my job was to wait in the van and cover the alleyway in case anyone managed to run out that way; not that I was allowed to do anything as they may have been armed, but at least I could call up and follow at a safe distance. The seconds ticked by and I chewed my lip nervously as I waited, hoping that I wouldn't hear shots. That's always the worst thing about a firearms job; you pray the officers never have to use their weapons as they'll instantly get suspended and investigated even if they were clearly in danger. It's one of the reasons that I never went the firearms route; that and the psychological trauma of having to shoot someone.

My fears were groundless, and after an agonizing wait the firearms sergeant called up on our channel.

'Hotel Foxtrot 96, premises is clear.'

I was out of the van and running before he had finished speaking, wanting to know if there was any sign of Jimmy. I was a little breathless when I got to the flat, which was up two flights of concrete stairs, and my injured leg was painful but holding up surprisingly well. I was allowed in by the officer guarding the now broken shards of the front door, mute testament to the speed at which they had entered.

Inside the flat stank of damp, blood and piss, and the bare chipboard floor was littered with needles, most of which were uncapped. The sergeant, a stocky man in his late forties with a shock of curly brown hair that was currently plastered to his head with sweat, came out of the front room to meet me.

'Sorry, mate, your friend isn't here. There is a hospital gown in the second bedroom though and it's got blood on it, so it's safe to assume that we just missed him.'

I cursed and entered the room he had indicated. It was bare apart from yet more needles, a filthy mattress on the floor and a hospital gown with blood all over one side. It looked fairly fresh too. I swore again and walked out of the flat, almost knocking Kev over on the stairs.

'Well?' he asked, putting a hand on my shoulder to stop me from walking away.

'Sorry, Kev, it looks like he was there; there's a gown with blood on it but no sign of him or anyone else. I'll get SOCO rolling.'

He nodded and let me continue, and I fiddled about until I could reach my radio and call for scenes of crime officers to attend while Kev went into the flat.

Outside, Eddie and Rudd were sharing a rare cigarette which I immediately stole from them, almost draining it in one puff. I explained what had been found, and I could tell by the looks on their faces that they weren't particularly happy about it either.

'So what do we do now, just sit back and wait?' Rudd asked, his face sombre.

'I don't know, mate. There's not a lot we can do until SOCO have been, except maybe get a name for the tenant from the housing association.'

We had tried earlier that morning by phone, trying to explain the need for expediency as well as confidentiality but, as usual, the housing trust in question had to go through the proper channels, which meant waiting hours until the right person came into the office. God forbid they should actually carry a mobile phone.

Eddie took back the cigarette, teasing a last puff out of it. 'I'll go back and do that. I've got a few other calls to make anyway.'

Kev came out and joined us. 'Rudd, I've got a few more things to check out, you okay to drive?'

Rudd nodded, and Kev turned to me. 'Gareth, can you take their van back?'

'Will do.'

Now that they were in plain sight, the firearms boys wouldn't go near the unmarked van until next time they needed it. They had a marked carrier waiting nearby for pickup. If they all climbed back into the unmarked one, some enterprising git would write down the index and it would be on the web by lunchtime.

I threw a wave at the others and walked back to the van, deciding that I would stop in at home on the way back just in case there was anything waiting for me. It didn't make sense that Davey would go to all this trouble and then not contact me. He didn't have anything to gain by having Jimmy if he didn't make demands, and the silence was making me nervous.

The drive back to my house took minutes, and for once I was blessed with a parking space only a few doors down. I opened the door, pushing a flood of mail out of the way, and then stopped as one in particular flipped over. It was a plain brown envelope with just my first name printed in biro on the front.

I closed the door and took the letter into the front room, my hands shaking as I sat on the sofa and tore the envelope open. Inside was a piece of plain A4 paper, written with the same neat hand. It just said:

'Rikitiks, 7.00 p.m. Don't be late.'

Rikitiks is a bar in the centre of town on Bond Street, and as far as I was aware it had no criminal connections whatsoever. Probably why they wanted to meet there, I thought, as it was unlikely to be under any form of surveillance.

I put the note in the fireplace and burned it, envelope and all, then leafed through the other mail, most of which were bills. Leaving them on the sofa, I took the van back to work, my thoughts once again churning as I drove along the seafront.

Back at work the office was still ominously quiet, people beavering away at their desks with barely a whisper. I didn't even have time to sit down myself, however, before Kev waved me over to his desk.

'Gareth, I've got a job for you. LST are sending people out to ask the local pond life about Jimmy and they could do with one extra, are you okay to go?'

I nodded, glad to have a chance to stay out of the office. I was too busy worrying about the meeting that night to sit down for long without someone noticing that something was wrong. 'Yeah sure, I'll pop down there now.'

I headed down to the LST office, stepping into the organised chaos that always fills the room.

Mike Barker looked up from his computer screen and waved. He was wearing his usual blue jeans and denim jacket and had a cigarette tucked behind one ear. 'Ah, Gareth, glad you could join us. You ready?'

'Uh, yeah, I suppose. Where we going?'

He smiled, showing white teeth that offset his shop-bought tan. 'You and I are going to visit all the shops along the Broadway in Whitehawk in case anybody has seen anything.'

I looked at him in amazement. 'You what? What's the bloody point in that? We know that he was in Hove.'

He shrugged. 'I know, but there are other officers doing Portland Road and, as we have no idea where they moved him to, the command team want people out all over the city, just in case.'

'Okay, I suppose it makes sense, sort of. You ready?'

He nodded and locked his terminal before leading me out of the door and down to the car park, where we got into the battered Vauxhall Astra that had to serve all eighteen LST officers as their only plain car.

As soon as we headed onto William Street, he lit his cigarette despite the strict no smoking policy in police vehicles, marked or otherwise. I didn't mind, as not only am I an occasional smoker myself but it looks very strange on surveillance jobs when blokes keep getting out of the car to smoke; it screams 'copper'.

'How are you holding up?' Barker asked, blowing smoke out of the driver's window.

'Yeah, okay. I just wish that I'd been there when it happened, then maybe I could have done something.' I thought that the more I played the guilt card, the less strange any change in my behaviour would be, or at least the less it would be commented on. Not that I needed to pretend to feel guilty, I just had to establish a different reason in the eyes of my colleagues.

'It's not your fault, matey, you couldn't have done anything; they were armed. Anyway, they probably waited until you were gone, so don't feel like you're to blame.'

I gave him my best reassured smile and, although he didn't look convinced, he did change the subject.

'So you think this is linked to Davey?'

It was such an obvious question that it had to be an excuse to talk about something else. 'I don't see how it can be anything else. Unless Jimmy was into some weird shit that I didn't know about, but I find that hard to believe.'

He flicked his cigarette butt out of the window before bursting out angrily. 'Damn it! I wish we could take them down properly instead of pissing about nicking the small fry and not being able to touch the ringleaders. It's one rule for us and as many rules for them as they can get away with. Do you ever wish you'd just worked in an office instead?'

I considered the question carefully. I'd been a copper for so long that I never really thought about doing anything else; in fact, I wasn't sure if there was anything else that I *could* do. I was too used to having the authority and the means to make a difference. It wouldn't have been an easy thing to give up no matter what job was offered in its place. 'Honestly? No, I don't. Can you imagine me selling photocopiers or something?'

He laughed and pulled over at the side of the road as we reached our destination. 'Okay. You take the shops on the left; I'll take the shops on the right.'

We split up and went into the shops, my first one being a local TV and electrical goods store. No one in there had seen anyone matching the photo of Jimmy I showed them, so I moved on, getting the same response at each shop.

Although the shopkeepers themselves were pleasant enough, the customers were another thing altogether. Whitehawkers, while some are perfectly normal, law-abiding citizens, for the most part hate the police with a real 'us against them' mentality. A few years ago a police car was lured into the estate with a fake 999 call and then ambushed by about thirty people throwing rocks and petrol bombs when it entered the close that the call had come from.

The officers somehow managed to escape without serious injury but we had all been called in to get kitted up in riot gear and quell the angry mob. I can't even remember what started it all off but I do remember that it had been mine and Lucy's second anniversary. I'd taken her out to dinner at Casa Don Carlos, a particularly fine tapas restaurant in the South Lanes, and leaving her at the table had probably been one of the thousand reasons she'd finally left.

So, predictably, the customers ranged from surly to downright rude, with one drunken idiot swearing that he had seen Jimmy abducted by aliens the night before. I left the shop empty-handed and the whole thing put me in a foul mood, the anger mixing with the guilt until I wasn't sure which was worse – or if I could even tell them apart anymore.

'This is bloody useless!' I spat at Mike Barker as he rejoined me at the car.

'Steady on, mate, what would you rather be doing?' he asked, his hands raised as if to ward off a blow.

'I don't know, but something that doesn't involve having the piss ripped out of us.'

He looked at me sympathetically. 'Have you thought about taking a couple of days off?'

I looked at him in astonishment. 'Why on earth would I want to do that?'

He looked at the ground, avoiding eye contact. 'Well, everyone has noticed how badly it's hit you, mate, and it's no shame to need a bit of time. Jimmy is your best mate, after all.'

I rattled the door handle on the car, urging him to unlock it. 'I'm fine. I'd be even worse at home. Honestly, mate, I need to be working on this right now.'

Barker nodded and unlocked the door, sliding into the driver's seat. He sparked up a cigarette and offered me one, which I accepted and lit in silence. He turned to me before starting the engine. 'Look, I know it's not easy, but just remember we're all here if you need us, okay?'

'The only thing I need is for everyone to be a hundred per cent committed to finding Jimmy. He's out there somewhere and they've got us doing Mickey Mouse door-to-door enquiries when we should be booting in doors and shaking people until their teeth rattle to find out where he is.'

Barker turned back to the wheel. 'Easy, Gareth, I'm on your side, remember? We'll find him; we've got the whole bloody force out looking.'

I sighed. 'Sorry, mate, I know I'm preaching to the converted. Let's just get back and see what else there is to do.'

He smiled and started the car, pulling a U-turn almost before he was in gear. His driving always makes me grip the dashboard and that day was apparently no exception.

The car that was just passing us beeped its horn angrily, and I glanced at the driver as we shot past, ready to wave in apology. My hand froze halfway, however, as I saw DC Steve Barnett sitting in the passenger seat, looking all around him as if searching for someone, and I felt a sudden chill as I realized that, despite what they'd said, PSD were still hot on my trail.

31

The rest of the morning passed too quickly for my liking, with me spending most of it looking over my shoulder. I couldn't believe that seeing Barnett in Whitehawk was a coincidence, but why would they still be following me? And if they were following me, surely they knew about the drugs by now, so why wasn't I in custody?

I'd spoken to Kev back at the office and told him that I thought PSD were still on me, but all he did was shrug and assure me that he hadn't heard anything. Not that he would be allowed to tell me if he had but it still reassured me a little.

I got back to my desk and sat down, trying to work out if there was anything more I could do to find Jimmy before I met with Davey later that day, when all hell broke loose.

I was jarred out of my musings when Eddie came running into the office shouting that the Cherokee had been found at a house in Wilson Avenue, and I stood up and began getting my kit on before he had finished speaking.

Kev stood as well and began snapping out orders. 'I want full containment on the premises. Anyone out of it gets followed. Eddie, give me details!'

Eddie paused to catch his breath before speaking. 'A PCSO was doing house-to-house enquiries after the burned-out van was found yesterday. There was no answer at one of the bunga-lows there, so she went around the back to see if the occupants were in the garden. She gets round there and sees a four-wheel drive with a tarp over it. Looks underneath and gets the index. It's the one we're looking for.'

Kev immediately made a phone call while ushering us out of the office with one hand. Every single officer in the room, even the ones who were deskbound due to age or injury, kitted up and made their way to the car park. As we ran through the nick, the whole place was in uproar. Officers were pulling out kit bags and, in some cases, dusting them off as they got out riot gear that hadn't been worn for years. Everyone wanted in on catching the kidnappers.

I got into the first available car with space in it, finding myself wedged between Tate and Ralphy in the back of a Mondeo. We joined the line of cars streaming out of the car park and drove full tilt towards Wilson Avenue, Eddie driving like a loon as he ran lights and crossed into the oncoming lane where necessary.

In record time we were crawling up the hill towards the target address. I could hear on the radio that armed units were being deployed and briefed en route and suddenly I felt as if I might be able to get Jimmy back safe and well without having to meet Davey. I allowed myself a small smile at the thought.

We stopped about a hundred yards short of the address, dumping Tate out into the bushes across the road so that he could crawl up and get a good position to observe the premises. The bungalows faced open fields so there was no other way of doing it.

Tommo was sitting in the front passenger seat and he turned to me and Ralphy. 'Which one of you fine fellows wants to crawl into the bushes further up?'

For once, Ralphy actually offered to do something that didn't involve sitting down. 'Yeah, I'll do it.'

'Great. Ding, we'll drop you further up and you can use the phone box.'

Ralphy started to protest, not having seen the phone box, but he was ignored and climbed out as the car stopped again. I got out at the same time and waved as they drove away, trying to look for all the world as if I was saying goodbye to some friends.

I made it to the phone box without seeing anything untoward and picked up the receiver, holding it to my ear and pretending to have a conversation. I studied the target address, an innocent-looking detached bungalow with a green Saab sitting in the drive.

'From Gareth, they have alternative transport. There's a green Saab in the drive, index unknown at this time.' I got a series of clicks in acknowledgement as I went back to watching the place.

My mobile suddenly rang, making me jump before I scrabbled to answer it. 'Hello?'

'Ding, it's Kev. We've got two armed teams on standby. They're going to go in once the targets leave the house. Tate has got at least three targets inside. The rest of us will follow them and see where they go in case they're not holding Jimmy here. Once they've moved I'll pick you up. If they don't move, we'll be going in anyway at 5 p.m. Be ready for a long wait.'

He hung up before I could reply, and I picked up the payphone receiver again to carry on with my pretend call. I could feel a ball of nerves in my stomach writhing around like a live thing and I had to breathe deeply to stop myself from being sick. Thoughts kept churning around in my mind. What if Jimmy wasn't there and Davey got wind of our job? Surely he would just kill him and be done with it? What if Jimmy was there and Davey pointed the finger in revenge for stealing the heroin? I couldn't bring myself to care, to be honest. The only thing that mattered right then was getting Jimmy back alive.

Three clicks on the radio brought me back and I looked towards the bungalow to see three men getting into the Saab. They were all tough-looking and one was the man who I'd seen get out of the car outside Davey's house. The car pulled out and drove past me, giving me a good look at them until one of them stared right back at me and I averted my eyes. I didn't want them to get suspicious, and most people will drop eye contact as soon as it's made.

As the car disappeared around the bend towards Warren Road, Kev rolled up in a battered old Rover. I ran over and climbed in and we shot off after the vehicle.

'As soon as we have the vehicle you take control,' he told me as he put his foot down.

I nodded and moved my pressel out of my pocket so that I could press it easily as the Saab came into view. 'We have contact, contact on green Saab heading north on Wilson Avenue. Vehicle is three up and held at traffic lights with Warren Road and indicating right towards Woodingdean. Vehicle is now away right. Three vehicles for cover.'

We just scraped through as the lights changed, and I kept up the commentary. 'Vehicle is now approaching right-hand bend at four zero miles per hour. Standby.'

The Saab suddenly made a U-turn, almost spinning in position as the driver hurled it around.

'*Tate permission,*' Tate's voice came over the radio.

'Vehicle is now heading back towards address; go ahead, Tate.'

'*Yeah from Tate, the strike teams are in the building and have one detained. Negative on Jimmy, but they think the prisoner made a phone call before they grabbed him.*'

Kev and I looked at each other. There was no way we could spin the car without them seeing us and there was no doubt in my mind that their colleague at home had called them as soon as he heard the strike team.

Kev grabbed my radio pressel and shouted to be heard over my microphone. 'From Kev, teams three and four strike the Saab as it passes you, we have to stop them and find out where Jimmy is. They'll never lead us to him now.'

As he spoke he spun our car out into the oncoming lane and

did a sharp three-point turn. I looked at him in surprise but it all became clear as two cars in the line behind us drove out in front of and behind the Saab at the same time, neatly boxing it off. The car in front of it actually rammed the front wing, driving the Saab into the verge on the far side of the road. Both cars then erupted with plain-clothed officers toting G36 assault rifles, all pointed at the vehicle now stuck on the grass.

As we approached, I saw one of the officers raise the butt of his rifle and smash the driver's window. Even from fifty feet away I could see the men in the car flinch as an officer did the same to the passenger's window and yet another to the windscreen. Suddenly the car doors were pulled open and the occupants were dragged out and pushed to the ground while rifle barrels were pointed at their heads. They were searched and cuffed, and each searching officer held up a pistol retrieved from a prisoner. Those guys don't screw around.

Kev pulled up and we both got out, waving our badges so that we didn't get the same treatment as the prisoners. Another car pulled up the other side and Tate and Ralphy got out and joined us. Kev took the firearms sergeant aside and conferred with him about something in a voice I couldn't make out, then went to the Saab driver and crouched down to make eye contact.

'Right. I haven't got time to screw about. We know you're working for Davey, so tell us where Jimmy is and maybe we'll be able to come to some arrangement. If you don't tell us where he is, I'll personally make sure that you never see daylight again.'

The driver laughed, then spoke in a south London accent. 'Tell you what, mate, you've got no frigging clue. Do whatever.'

Kev bit back an angry retort. 'Okay sunshine, if you want to play it like that, fine. We'll throw you in a cell for a couple of days and then see if you feel like talking.'

It was a lie, of course; we couldn't hold him for more than twenty-four hours. I could hear the frustration in Kev's voice. Quite simply, we had nothing to threaten these guys with.

I heard sirens and looked up to see a police van approaching, fighting against rubberneckers who were all out of their cars watching what was going on.

I had a sudden idea and pulled Kev aside. 'Stick them in the van with me in the middle bit, outside the cage. Throw some coats over me and leave them alone for a few minutes. Hopefully one of them will say something we can use.'

It was unorthodox and probably illegal but Kev shrugged and nodded. We needed to find out where they were holding Jimmy, and he was obviously as willing as I was to get the job done, no matter the cost or the methods used.

When the van arrived, I stepped around it and opened the side door out of the prisoners' view. The back third of the van is a cage with enough room for four prisoners, with the middle third being a storage area with a backwards facing seat for escorting officers to keep an eye on the prisoners through the cage door.

I slipped into the middle and pulled a tarp, a space blanket and the driver's coat over me. It wasn't ideal but it was dark and the chances were that they wouldn't see me as long as the lights stayed off. I began to sweat but I forced myself to stay still and listen. I heard booted feet approaching the van and then the back door clunked open.

I could see through a gap in the front of the coat covering my head that the prisoners were being loaded in. As the last one was placed on a seat, I heard Kev calling someone from outside. The officer at the back door looked around at the prisoners. 'I'll be back in a minute, no trouble from you lot, right?'

They all ignored him and the door slammed shut.

'What the fuck we gonna do?' one of them whispered.

'Listen. They think we work for Davey and that we've got this Jimmy bloke. We keep it like that. If they find out we're down here looking to do Davey, they'll start asking a load more questions we really don't want to answer.'

216

'Like what?' the first voice asked.

'Well if they find out he owes us for the drugs, they'll probably try and stick us with dealing as well. Keep your mouths shut until we get solicitors, not even names. Okay?'

My heart sank. Not only did they not know where Jimmy was, they were after Davey instead of working for him, so they couldn't even let anything slip by accident. Suddenly all the knife attacks on the dealers clicked into place. They must have been cutting people to find out where Davey was so that they could find him and kill him. I wondered if they knew how close they had come to him the previous day.

I stood up suddenly, making them all jump, and opened the door of the van without a word.

'Oi,' I heard one of them call, but I ignored him as I stepped back out into the sunlight.

'Well?' Kev asked, standing just outside.

I shook my head. 'They don't work for Davey; they were looking to do him over for a drug debt. Looks like our plan worked a little too well.'

'Maybe it did, but the trouble is we've spent all day chasing these guys while Jimmy is God only knows where. Still, at least they're off the streets.'

Our part in it done, we headed back to the car and Kev drove us back to the station. I felt like pounding my fist against the dashboard in frustration as I thought about the time we'd wasted. I had no choice then but to go and face Davey and somehow convince him to give me Jimmy back in one piece.

32

Once we had finished the log for the follow, Kev made us all leave on time, wanting us to be fresh to start searching the next day. I was secretly relieved as I thought I might have had to meet Davey on work time. I headed home and sank onto the sofa, intending to watch the telly and get an hour's sleep so that I would have a clear head for my meeting that night.

I woke with a jolt, seeing the light begin to fade outside and swore as I glanced at my watch. It was already quarter past six and if I didn't get my arse in gear I was going to be late for the meet. I didn't have time to shower, so I just pulled on a clean T-shirt and headed out, catching a bus into town. I didn't want to take the car as not only was parking a problem, but also if I was still being followed it would be harder to give my pursuers the slip.

Worry still gnawed at me regarding how much PSD knew. Surely if they knew about my theft of the drugs I would already be inside? It didn't make sense, but I didn't have time to think about it properly as I made my way through town, swapping buses regularly to make sure I wasn't being followed and blessing my warrant card for the free travel it allowed.

Forty minutes later I was sat in a booth at the back of Rikitiks, nursing a double Talisker, one of my favourite single malts. The bar itself is fairly dingy, with one way in or out at the front if you didn't count the fire exits. I was admiring the somewhat surreal painting of Ollie Reed and approaching the bottom of my drink when two men walked past me, making me look up.

Sure enough one of them was Davey, dressed in jeans and a short-sleeved shirt. The other was a man I didn't recognize, a huge lump of muscle with a crew cut and a nasty leer.

'Thanks, John, take a seat over there,' Davey said to his companion as he sat opposite me. The muscle gave me one final leer before doing as he was told and sitting on the far side of the bar, far enough away not to overhear, but close enough to get involved quickly if I started causing trouble. The barman raised the music and electronica pumped out loud enough to make my teeth rattle.

Davey looked at me and smiled, the expression making him look more rodent-like. 'So, Gareth – you don't mind if I call you Gareth, do you?'

'Call me what the fuck you like, just give me Jimmy back in one piece.'

He held up his hands as if warding off a blow. 'Hey now, not so hasty. There's a few things I want to make sure of first. Lift your top.'

I looked at him, surprised. 'What on earth for?'

'Er, bugs, officer?' he asked in a condescending tone.

I sighed and obliged, lifting my T-shirt to show that I wasn't wired. I still could have been, technology had obviously moved on a lot since last time he saw a cop show, but if he didn't know that, I wasn't going to disabuse him.

'Right,' he continued, casting constant looks around the bar as he spoke, 'I suppose you want to know what this little meeting is all about?'

I drained the rest of my drink in a single swallow, keeping my hand on the glass in case I needed to use it as a weapon.

'Let me guess. I give you your stuff back and you give me Jimmy back, and then we all go away happy, right?'

He laughed, an unpleasant grating sound that rubbed my already jangling nerves raw. 'You really don't know a lot about the art of conversation, do you, Gareth? You're as bad as your brother, you really are!'

I sat up straight as he mentioned Jake, my hand tightening on the whisky glass. Davey saw the motion and grinned again, showing crooked teeth.

'You didn't know that I knew Jake, did you? I sold him his first ten bag of brown. I thought it was really sad when he sold me your mum's jewellery for skag.'

He watched me carefully as I absorbed what he was telling me. He was deliberately trying to provoke me but I refused to let myself be drawn in. I clenched my teeth to stop myself from saying anything I'd regret later. 'Just tell me what you want and then we're done.'

He leaned back, obviously enjoying my reaction. 'Well, you see, before you wrecked one of my flats today, I was just going to ask for the drugs back, and then you and your mate Jimmy could have had a touching reunion. But seeing as you've caused me all sorts of trouble I'm going to have to ask for a favour as well as my gear. I want you to get into your police computers and get rid of all the stuff you've got on me and my lads, as well as every other dealer in Brighton, just to make sure it doesn't lead back to me. That shouldn't be too hard for a bright lad like you, should it?'

I laughed in astonishment. 'You've got to be kidding! Do you have any idea how hard that would be? I'd have to find a way into the servers, find the information, then erase it from the database and destroy any backed-up copies. Even if I had a PhD in computing that would take me weeks to do.'

He shook his head, waggling an admonishing finger at me. 'I don't think so. One of my lads tells me that all the police

220

computers are linked, so if you can get into one you can get into them all. Stop trying to be smart with me.'

I wondered how someone so good at running a business, even if it was selling heroin, could be so stupid about computers. 'Have you ever heard of access levels? Even if I worked for tech support, I still wouldn't have the access necessary to do what you want. I. Can't. Do. It. Can I be anymore specific? Just accept your drugs for Jimmy and then we're done.'

Davey sighed and leaned back, pulling a mobile phone out of his trouser pocket. 'Well, if you won't do it, I'll have to try a different tack. Are you sure you won't help me?'

I shook my head. 'Not won't, can't. Not that I would if I could.'

He tapped a number into his phone from memory then began speaking to someone on the other end. 'Yeah, it's me. I'm having a bit of a problem. Yeah. Okay, now you remember Jake, the copper's brother? Yeah, that's right, the one who ran off to Bristol. You remember where his dad lives—'

The words were barely out of his mouth when I swung the whisky glass, shattering it against his temple hard enough that he flew sideways out of the seat and landed on the floor. His muscle bounded across the bar towards me, leaping his boss and literally hurling himself on me WWF-style.

I couldn't move out of the way in the booth as the table had me hemmed in, so I turned on my side and brought both feet up, just managing to tuck them in tight as the bruiser sprawled over me with his meaty hands searching for a grip on my face. I pushed backwards, letting both feet fly. My adversary shot backwards towards the table he had come from, smacking into it and disappearing over the top.

I slid myself out and glanced down at Davey, whose face was a mask of blood as he lay there clutching his head with one hand while the other grasped for something in his pocket. Not wanting to hang around and find out what he was looking for I ran

221

towards the front of the bar, only to collapse in a heap as something hard and heavy hit me in the legs.

I dropped like a stone, banging my head on a nearby table and half turned to see my legs tangled in a chair that the now triumphant-looking John had thrown. I tried to stand up again as he lumbered towards me, but my bruised legs and pounding head were enough to slow me and I was pinned to the floor before I could get my legs under me. John lay there on top of me, bellowing over the music, which a scared-looking barman kept turning up between keeping a watch on the front door. Obviously he was under Davey's sway as much as everyone else in this bloody town seemed to be.

I tried to flip my aggressor onto his back, but he was too heavy and I couldn't get the leverage without using my ankles to wrap around his. One try convinced me that the pain would probably knock me out. After a few moments Davey appeared, staggering as if drunk with an extendable baton clutched in his right hand, his left still holding his temple where the glass had smashed. Blood poured down his face and dripped onto his shirt and his eyes were blazing as though he was about to kill me. Which, I thought, he probably was.

He leaned in close, holding himself up against a table for support. Not even bothering to use the baton, he instead began hurling kicks into my unprotected face. By the third kick my face felt as if it had split from forehead to chin and my right cheek felt slippery and warm. I screamed with the pain, but there was no release and the boot kept coming back, again and again, until unconsciousness reached out to claim me.

33

I woke up with a start, the sudden movement making my whole head flare up with pain. I couldn't work out where I was and I tried to roll into a sitting position, only to find myself unable to move my arms or legs. I tried to open my eyes, then realized that they were already open and that I had some kind of sack over my head, scraping my already raw face and making me want to scream with the pain as I accidentally rolled onto my front.

All that came out was a strangled grunt and I realized that whoever had done this to me had placed a gag in my mouth so tightly that it was stuck to my parched tongue, preventing me from making any kind of loud noise. My tongue seemed about twelve sizes too big for my mouth, and my need for a drink was only exceeded by my need to urinate. I could taste and smell old blood but had no choice but to lie there waiting for someone to free me.

As all of my other senses were useless I tried listening, trying to work out where I was. I couldn't hear anything other than my own breathing, except the occasional creak that told me I was in some kind of wooden building. It felt like there was quite a bit of space around me but I couldn't tell for sure, trussed as I was. I tried making as much noise as I could but after a few minutes I almost choked on what little spit I could produce chewing on my gag, leaving me dangerously close to panicking as I tried to get my breathing under control.

A long while later I heard what sounded like a car engine, then a door slamming followed by approaching footsteps. Another creak and a gust of air hit me, only half felt through the material over my head, followed by a burst of laughter.

'Look, he's gone and pissed himself,' a coarse male voice said, and I felt embarrassment burn through me.

Another voice answered the first, younger but no less coarse. 'I'm not touching him without gloves on, he's soaked.'

'Look, we've got to get him to the farmhouse and we haven't got much time. We've got to be back in town by midnight.'

I felt rough hands grab me, avoiding my urine-stained front as I was hauled upright, the pain in my arms, legs and head making me cry with strangled grunts. I must have passed out from the pain because the next thing I remember is having water thrown in my face and a painfully bright light being pointed at me.

'Stick him in the corner,' a familiar voice said as I frantically licked the water off my face, realizing that both gag and mask had been removed.

I was grabbed and hauled from my position against the wall, instead being wedged into a corner where the wall and floor were both cold enough to make me shiver. It smelled musty but it was clearly a different room. The other had felt like a barn, this one felt more like a cellar.

I heard footsteps recede and a door close and slowly became aware of a flickering light as my eyes adjusted and focused. Sitting next to the lantern was Davey, looking angry and battered with a large bandage over his left temple and an evil glint in his eye.

'Thought you were clever, didn't you? Thought you could have one over on me and get away with it. Well now you're in the shit and being a copper won't save you.'

He shifted position, and I saw that we were indeed in a cellar, with a set of rickety wooden steps leading up into the gloom and a plain wooden door some way behind where Davey sat on a packing crate. Odds and ends were stacked against the walls, looking like the detritus gained from years of living in the same place.

'I'll make it easy for you, just for the sake of 'speediency. I need those drugs back before midnight tomorrow, which gives you just a bit over twenty-four hours to tell me where you hid them. A lot can happen to someone in that amount of time.'

I tried to speak, but I couldn't force any words out past my oversized tongue. Davey noticed but left it a moment, clearly enjoying my distress, before he opened a bottle of water and allowed me a few small sips.

'More,' I gasped, desperate and not caring if he was enjoying it.

'Oh no, not until you give me what I want.'

I began to shake my head and then stopped as pain wracked my whole upper body. 'And you're just going to let me go after I tell you, after you've done *this*? Yeah right!'

He laughed and dragged his packing crate over so that he was sitting within arm's reach.

'Oh no, mate, I'm afraid you're for it. I can't let you go after this, but if you want your mate Jimmy to survive you'll tell me where the gear is. You see, your little stunt in the park, playing the hero and getting yourself stabbed, well that fucked me, see? I haven't got anything left to sell and if I don't get something soon my business will go down the pan. And if my business goes down I may as well take a couple of coppers with me. I've always wanted to kill a copper.'

'Go to hell,' I gasped as my tongue began to dry up again.

He smiled at me and leaned forward, producing a knife from inside his jacket. He waved the blade backwards and forwards slowly in front of my eyes, making sure I could see it clearly.

'You know the great thing about knives?' he asked in a conversational tone.

I just stared at him, too hurt and scared to do more than that as the blade drew ever closer to my face on each pass.

'Well the thing is, they don't make any noise and you can draw the pain out for as long as you want.' As he finished speaking, the blade darted in, piercing my left cheek and making me cry out with pain.

'Don't be such a baby, that was just a little prick,' he said scornfully. 'My dad used to give me worse for just talking back to him. Stealing now, he would have taken a strip of flesh for that.'

As if to demonstrate, he stood and lifted his bloodstained shirt, showing a flat stomach that had little squares of scar tissue rather like a human chessboard.

'He never caught me; these were just warnings when he couldn't find anyone else to blame. I was never stupid enough to actually steal from him.'

He sat again, and I tried to shrink away as he brought the knife close to my chest. 'Now don't go running away, I've hardly started,' he laughed. In that laugh I heard barely suppressed madness and an involuntary whimper escaped my lips.

His head snapped up as if tasting my fear, and he grinned at me as the knife slid up and down my chest, almost caressing me in a manner that made me want to vomit. His spare hand leaned over and gripped my chin, forcing my head round to look at him.

'Of course, with a dad like mine it was hard to do anything right, but you wouldn't know about that, would you? You and your perfect family. I had a psychologist see me once, in prison, and he said that my violent urges weren't my fault. He said that what my dad did to me made me angry and the only way I could let the anger out was to hurt people.'

He leaned back and fumbled for a cigarette with his spare hand, lighting it from the lantern but never taking the knife away from me. 'I had to agree, so I took his pencil and stuck it in his eye. I didn't get anymore head doctors coming to see me after that.'

What made this monologue worse was that I knew he was telling the truth. He had been charged with GBH with intent while in prison for assaulting a doctor, only no one ever knew what was said between them to make him snap. Apparently that came under patient-doctor privilege even after the doctor was half blinded.

'Look, I'll get you your drugs back, just don't do this. Do you know what'll happen to you for killing a copper?'

He laughed his grating laugh again. 'Oh they'll never catch me; you can be sure of that. I've got a whole load of people in London that will say that I was at parties all this weekend, and some of them are even judges and lawyers. So it's just you and me, a nice little cosy evening getting to know each other.'

He took the knife and slid it up my left arm from the elbow to halfway up the bicep, leaving a trickle of blood as its razor-sharp edge sliced through my skin. I shouted in pain and tried to pull away, and he removed the knife, looking at me strangely.

'You afraid of a little pain? I thought you were stronger than that. Gareth Bell, hero of the hour, disarming Davey and saving Jimmy's life. If I'd known before that all I had to do to get the drugs back was cut you, I wouldn't have bothered with any of this.' He waved the knife at the walls as he spoke.

'Why did you drag me out here?' I asked.

He shrugged. 'You made me lose my rag. Now which bit do you think you can live without the most?' He held up the knife again.

I tried reasoning with him, not liking the glint that lurked just underneath the surface of his eyes. 'Look, Davey, I've told you I can get you the drugs back so there's no need to start cutting me, is there? What happens if there's an accident and you kill me before I get the drugs for you?'

He paused for a second, thinking. 'You've got a point there. So tell me where the drugs are and then I'll start playing.'

I shook my head carefully, not wanting to pass out from the

pain. 'It doesn't work like that. I need to go myself or you'll never find them.'

Davey laughed his psychotic grating laugh again. 'Oh, of course I'm going to let you go wandering around out there, because you'll definitely come back, won't you?'

I looked at him as steadily as I could. 'You've still got Jimmy; of course I'll come back.'

He paused then, staring into my eyes as if he could read my mind. 'Okay. I'll send one of my lads with you; no, two I think, and you can go and get the drugs. You come back here with them, and I'll let your friend go. If you're good I might even let you go too, as long as we can come to a suitable ... business arrangement.'

'I want to see Jimmy first,' I demanded, 'make sure he's still alive and that you're treating him okay.'

Davey smiled innocently. 'Oh don't worry, he's in the best of health, I promise. Let's get you cleaned up and then you can go see him; but no funny stuff or I'll slit his throat and then yours even if it means I have to tear Brighton apart to find the drugs myself.'

The evil glint in his eye as he spoke told me that it wouldn't take much for him to follow through on his promise. My shoulders sagged and I nodded once, hoping that somehow I'd be able to get both myself and Jimmy out of it alive. Looking at the armed madman in front of me though, I had my doubts.

34

Cleaning me up involved another bucket of water being thrown over me before I was hauled up by Davey and one of his goons and dragged stumbling up the stairs and through a door at the top.

I found myself led into a farmhouse kitchen, a large room with an Aga and neat wooden furniture. The work surfaces were littered with rubbish and the place smelled of old food and cigarettes. The large window showed me that it was still night outside with just a hint of dawn showing on the horizon. Before I could get my bearings by taking a good look through the window, I was pulled through another door that led to a hallway and up another flight of stairs. None of the lights were on and we only had torchlight to lead us as we reached the top. I was shoved through another door into a dark room that stank of shit and infection.

Someone flicked a light on and my eyes watered as the glare hit me. I blinked away the tears and saw a bare floor with a single mattress on it and a huddled form lying still under a blanket. I staggered over with my hands still bound behind me and dropped to my knees next to the figure, recognizing Jimmy as I got close. He looked terrible, pale and sickly, and a smell like cheese and rotting meat was emanating from him in waves.

'Untie me and let me check him, please?'

I felt cold steel against my wrist as my bonds were cut, and I immediately threw back the blanket, ignoring the pain in my hands as circulation returned. I gasped when I saw Jimmy's body; he was naked under the blanket and his back and arms were a mess of halfhealed cuts and bruises. They had clearly been beating him regularly, old wounds overlaid by new ones. My temper flared, overriding the fear that had been my constant companion since I had been taken.

'He needs a doctor. What the fuck have you done to him? Jimmy, Jimmy mate, it's Gareth. Can you hear me?'

He lay silent and unmoving, and I checked his pulse with shaking hands. It took me an age to find it and when I did it was weak and thready, just a flutter of life remaining in his broken body. I pulled the blanket back up and turned to Davey, somehow managing not to throw myself at him. I knew that in the state I was in I would last about two seconds against my captors, and then Jimmy *would* die.

'You fucking arsehole!' I raged, clenching my hands into fists. 'How could you do this to him? What has he done to deserve this?'

Davey stepped back, knife raised warningly. 'Don't blame me; you're the one who made me do this. If you hadn't decided to screw around with my business, he'd still be having cute nurses play with his cock. Did you really think that you could step into my world and beat me?'

He laughed harshly. 'The sooner you leave and get my drugs the sooner you get back and Jimmy here gets a doctor. We wouldn't want him to die now, would we? Tie him back up.'

I bit back an angry retort as my wrists were rebound, not wanting Davey to change his mind about letting me go. Even escorted, I realized, I stood a better chance of getting out of it by leaving than I ever could by staying there. 'Okay, I'm ready. Let's go.'

'That's better. Just remember though, *Ding*, that if you try and mess me around, Jimmy dies. I don't even need to do it myself, I reckon. One more day is all he's got and he'll be dead anyway, and it'll be your fault. Chop chop.'

I nearly made a play then and there, despite my wrists being tied, but instead I walked meekly out of the room, clenching my fists so hard that my fingernails gouged my palms. His use of my nickname, Ding, had made me go cold. Only a few people ever call me that. I've made heroic efforts to make sure that it doesn't get used outside of the office, and I think few people even know it. That meant that Davey's mole was someone in my own office, someone that Jimmy and I had worked, eaten and got drunk with.

I was guided downstairs and made to sit at the kitchen table while his goon, a stocky chap in his forties with a ridiculous quiff, went to get a car and another pair of hands to guard me.

Davey sat opposite me, rolling a cigarette with one hand while the other held the everpresent knife. 'Now, Gareth, I want you to know something just so that you know I'm not mucking about.'

I looked at the weeping cut on my left arm. He saw the look and smiled.

'That's right. You know that I'm a man of my word; you have to be in this business. So when I tell you that if you screw me over, not only will Jimmy die but that your dad will as well, you'll know I'm telling the truth.'

He sat back and lit his roll-up, apparently oblivious to my struggle not to leap over the table and kill him. 'And don't be thinking that if you kill me it won't happen. The order is already in place and if they don't hear from me to cancel it, it's bye bye, Daddy. Clear?'

I nodded jerkily, angry enough that I didn't trust myself to speak.

'Good. Ah, the car's here. Have fun.' He waved me up with the knife and pushed me out of the door in front of him, heading first into the hall then out of the main door and into a farmyard.

The whole place was eerily silent and smelled deserted. The place looked run-down from the outside and clearly hadn't been a working farm for quite some time. A battered red Nissan Primera sat outside the front door with Quiff driving and another man sitting in the back seat behind the driver.

I got into the rear passenger seat and wasn't overly surprised when a bag was pulled over my head. Before they could get the bag over my eyes, I looked up at Davey. 'I need my warrant card; I won't be able to get the drugs without it.'

He looked at me grimly. 'You'll manage; you don't have a lot of choice.'

I shook my head, gambling on his lack of computer and technical knowledge. 'No, really, I can't get at them without it. It's got a chip inside it that allows me to access where they're hidden.'

Grumbling, he leafed through his pockets, pulling out my mobile phone and keys, then my warrant card. 'Oh, and I'll need my keys as well.'

He threw the warrant card and keys at me, tucking the phone back into his pocket, then slammed the door shut and we drove away.

I tried to use my teeth on the cloth, attempting to smooth the folds so that I could see something, but in the dark it was hopeless.

Quiff turned the radio on and it blared loud enough to annoy me, further spoiling any attempts I might have made to listen to the road surfaces as I sought any clue as to where the farmhouse was.

The drive lasted for about an hour, and I had been half dozing for some time when the bag was pulled from my head. I blinked and sat up, seeing that we were on the A27 just approaching Brighton.

'Where we going?' Quiff asked, never taking his eyes from the road.

232

'My house. You know where that is?'

'Yup.'

He swung round the roundabout and up Mill Lane onto the flyover and within twenty minutes we were looking for somewhere to park on Wordsworth Street.

As I climbed out, the sky was lightening perceptibly and I guessed it was around 5.00 a.m. I shivered, the cool breeze stinging the cuts on my face, and headed up the steps to my front door wondering if I really was going to give the drugs back or if I could manage to pull some last-minute heroics out of my arse and save the day. I didn't feel much like a hero though, but I suppose stinking of your own piss will do that to you. Neither of my escorts had said anything about it but they had both opened their windows on the way and Quiff had kept the blowers going full whack.

The second escort appeared to be a Michael Thewlis clone, even down to the belly and the out-thrust lower jaw, and he prodded me impatiently as I fumbled with the keys. Eventually I got the door open and they shoved me inside, closing the door behind them.

'So where is it?' Quiff asked impatiently.

'Hang on a second, I need some painkillers if I'm going to do this; I need to remember a lot of numbers for the combination. You'll need to untie me as well.'

I was stalling them, but my head really was splitting and just necking a couple of pills might make all the difference between me being able to think my way out of it or just having to go along with their plan instead.

Thewlis grunted and I took that as assent, walking into the kitchen and carefully staying away from the knife block in case they felt threatened. Quiff untied my hands, and I opened the odds-and-ends drawer, pulling out some industrial strength Co-dydramol that I had left over from an operation a couple of years before. I ignored the advice on the label and took four, then turned to my captors.

'Any chance I can take a piss?'

Quiff stepped forward, pulling a baton from his belt and racking it out. 'Stop fucking about and do what you're here for,' he demanded, brandishing the baton at me.

I held up my hands. 'Easy mate, I'm not trying to cause trouble. I need to get to the cupboard behind you.' I pointed to the cupboard under the stairs, a plan forming in my mind. I was beginning to realize that no matter what I did, Davey would kill me and Jimmy. He didn't stand to lose anything by doing it and he had everything to lose if he let us go, so I was frantically working on a plan that would get us out of this in one piece.

My new friends obediently moved out of the way, and I opened the cupboard door, having to get down on my hands and knees to get into the space once the door was removed and placed to one side. I was starting to run out of ideas to stall.

Somewhere in there, I knew I had the golf clubs that I never used anymore. I was toying with the idea of grabbing them and trying to use one to bludgeon Pinky and Perky to death when my eyes settled on my PSU kit bag. Not only did it contain my PSU baton, twentyseven inches of black hardened rubber, but just underneath it, hidden away in a space beneath the carpet was the spare can of Captor that was totally against regulations and indeed illegal for me to own, let alone have at home.

I moved the PSU bag aside and pulled the carpet up, groping blindly in the dark for what felt like an age, unable to find anything in the concealed compartment. Finally, my hand closed around something small, cylindrical and cold with a lump of plastic at one end and I almost cried with relief as I flicked the safety lid and wriggled backwards out of the low cupboard.

'Have you got it?' Quiff asked, leaning over and putting himself in perfect line for what I was about to do.

'Yeah,' I replied, twisting to spray him point-blank.

The first thing they teach you about using the spray is that you should never spray someone from less than three feet away as the force of the spray can drill out the eyeball and damage the retina. It appeared they were right: Quiff screamed, staggering back against the wall with his baton forgotten as both hands flew to his suddenly bloody eye.

The second thing they teach you is that the spray only affects the person you're spraying and doesn't fill the air with fumes. I knew from experience that they were wrong on this one and I was already holding my breath, feeling my eyes tear as I straightened and unleashed a blast at Thewlis who was backing into the kitchen and reaching under his coat.

The spray hit him on the bridge of the nose and splashed into both eyes, making him blink instinctively for a second before shouting in pain. His hand, however, completed the movement beneath his coat and came out clutching a pistol which he waved in my direction, trying to flick the safety catch off with his thumb.

I launched myself at him, spray forgotten as adrenaline dumped into my system at the sight of the weapon. We collapsed to the ground together in a heap, the jolt almost enough to jar me loose as pain shot through my damaged body. I grabbed his right wrist in a death grip, knowing that if he brought the pistol to bear I was dead, while I drove my free hand into his stomach and groin repeatedly as we fought for control of the weapon.

He was strong, far stronger than me, but desperation gave me the edge and I banged his hand repeatedly against the wall until his fingers spasmed and dropped the pistol. He tried to curl up in a ball to prevent my fists from striking the sensitive areas I was attacking, but my fury was pouring adrenaline into me and I pinned one of his arms with my knee and began to beat his chest and stomach with my fists, ignoring the yells of pain as his struggles grew weaker.

He began to fight back again and I redoubled my efforts, but as his guard finally dropped the improbable happened and there was a loud crash and the front door flew open, clearly audible even over the shrieking coming from Quiff. Booted feet pounded down the hallway, and I turned in surprise to see Steve Barnett and two other officers, these in full riot gear, entering the kitchen. I could hear others in the hallway and suddenly the air was alive with shouts and the crackle of radios as someone called for an ambulance.

Barnett stopped at the kitchen door, already halfway through the words, 'Gareth Bell, I'm arresting you for—' when he stopped and took in the scene in front of him. His eyes widened in amazement, but then he was shoved rudely out of the way as one of the uniformed officers saw the pistol and ran to retrieve it.

I slumped backwards as the adrenaline left my system, smiling weakly at the PSD officer. 'Any chance of an ambulance? I've been kidnapped, beaten and cut, and I think I know where Jimmy is.'

35

Barnett wasn't a happy man. He paced up and down in front of the sofa as a paramedic checked out my injuries, politely ignoring the whiff of urine that still clung to me.

The detective had been all for arresting me still, wanting to ask further questions about my involvement with Davey. Luckily for me, the sergeant with the uniformed officers had pulled rank and insisted that a senior officer be brought to the scene before a decision was made. The sergeant, Peter Goble, had joined the job at the same time as me and in fact had always copied my homework at Ashford, but we took pains to do no more than nod at each other, not wanting Barnett to spot the connection.

'So you're telling me that you got kidnapped and managed to convince them that you would be able to get the heroin back?'

I nodded, hoping that the half-lie didn't sound as weak to everyone else as it did to me. 'What can I say, they're criminals. They told me that if I returned the heroin then they would let me and Jimmy go. I knew they wouldn't but I thought I stood a better chance if I got a couple of them back here.'

Barnett stopped pacing to look at me. 'Why did they kidnap you in the first place?'

I thought furiously for a moment then threw out the first

thing I could think of. I hadn't thought that far ahead and the whole thing felt dangerously close to unravelling before my eyes. 'Davey seemed to be under the impression that I could get the drugs back that I seized from Edwards after he stabbed me. He chose me because apparently I'm personally responsible for his business going down the pan if those drugs don't come back. He's not acting like a rational person, is he Steve? He's a psychopath who's been cornered with no way out. There's no telling what he's really thinking.'

'And you say Davey was the one who did *all* this?'

I nodded again. 'Yeah. He told me that it's also revenge for making him go through the court case. He said that he's going to kill every officer involved, one by one.'

Barnett's gaze could have drilled through rock. 'So he told you all this, then just let you go? Somehow I doubt you were even kidnapped. This is all a set-up.'

I gestured down at myself angrily. 'And I let myself get cut to shit and beaten to make it look real? Grow up. Anyway, how did you know I was back?'

He instantly broke the eye contact, looking away guiltily. 'Uh, you don't need to know that.'

Suddenly it clicked. 'You've still got cameras in here.'

His refusal to make eye contact confirmed my suspicions.

I shook my head in amazement. 'So that whole "we found another fingerprint, you're free to go" thing was all bullshit and you still think I'm working with Davey?'

Barnett finally looked back at me, angry now. 'And you didn't give us any reason not to suspect you. What do you do when you're not at work or seeing your girlfriend? Nothing. Or so it seems on the surface, but you keep getting into interesting situations, just happen to find someone with enough heroin to make you into a bloody hero and get heroically stabbed in the leg – somewhere non-vital – at the same time. I find that a bit odd, personally. And what about burning that letter yesterday? You can't tell me that's normal behaviour. I know a rotten apple when I see one.'

I stood up quickly, dislodging the paramedic, but stopped when a deep voice came from the hallway.

'Look in the mirror often, do you?'

Barnett whirled around, eyes snapping with anger. 'Who said that?'

Derek Pearson, chief superintendent for the division, stepped into the room looking sleepy and out of sorts. He was wearing a pair of jeans and a black sweatshirt, and he looked strange out of uniform, his hair still tousled from sleep. 'I did. And I assume you don't have a problem with that?'

Barnett stopped in his tracks, smart enough to know when he was beaten. 'Uh, no, sir, no I don't.'

'Good. Because I'm more than a little upset that you've bugged my intelligence unit without informing me, in the middle of a hunt to find someone who's taking orders from a drug dealer.'

Barnett stepped backwards as if Pearson was actually radiating the anger clear in his face.

'Uh, that wasn't my idea, sir; you'd have to speak to my supervisors about that.'

'Oh don't worry, I will. Now have you finished trying to blame Gareth for everything that's happened, or can we get on with trying to save PC Holdsworth's life?'

Barnett's shoulders slumped and he mumbled something unintelligible before sloping out with the air of the thoroughly defeated.

Pearson walked over and laid a meaty hand on my shoulder. 'I hear you've been through the mill, son.' He paused and sniffed. 'How about you have a bath and get a change of clothes and we'll have someone chat to you about what happened? But first, have you got a location on Jimmy?'

I shook my head, glad to finally have someone on my side, but also more aware than ever of just how much hot water I could land myself in if I said the wrong thing. Pearson had just made an enemy of PSD by standing up for me and if anything about the drugs came out he would come crashing down with me.

'No, sir. I'm sorry, but they had me hooded in the car. Which is parked outside, by the way. It's the red Nissan.'

'I know. There are already officers searching it.'

I must have told someone already then. I was so tired and drained that I was amazed that I'd managed to stay coherent for that long. A thought suddenly wormed its way out of my subconscious, making me sit bolt upright despite the pain. 'Sir, Davey threatened my father. He said that if I caused any problems then he would kill him. He knows where he lives!' I all but gripped his arm as I stood.

'Give me the address and I'll have a car go and collect him immediately. We'll have to find somewhere for him to stay until this is over. Leave it with me, he'll be safe.'

I sank back down with relief and borrowed one of the officers' notebooks to write down Dad's address. Pearson took the notebook and disappeared, making me feel a little better. I felt that I could trust him to do the right thing, and it was a huge relief to know that Dad would be safe.

Something else important was trying to yammer at me through the haze in my brain but it kept slipping away as I tried to focus on it, finally dismissing it as I was helped to my feet and packed off towards the bathroom.

The bath was agony and it was more than a little strange to be lying there, a towel over my privates, with a police officer noting down everything that I could remember. I was beginning to wish that I wasn't so tired, as I needed to concentrate to make sure that my lies remained consistent. I was terrified of slipping up, despite the fact that they'd probably put it down to fatigue or stress. Eventually I'd told them everything that I could remember and I was left alone to soak.

I must have dozed for a few minutes as I woke up with a start, remembering what had been so important and cursing myself for a fool. I hadn't told Pearson that Davey's mole worked in DIU. I knew if we didn't find whoever it was before they phoned Davey and told him that I was free, Jimmy would end up dead and Davey would be on the first flight out of the country before we could stop him.

36

By the time I managed to get Pearson on the phone, the damage had been done and all the DIU officers had been called to come in early. Putting together the pieces of the puzzle that I had provided is what our office do best and, aside from one or two who couldn't be reached, everyone had arrived at work in varying states of readiness.

I got one of the officers at my house to drive me to John Street, still talking to Pearson on the phone – the officer's mobile; mine was with Davey – as we drove. He agreed to delay their briefing until after I got there and, despite my assurances, he would not even trust Kev to be told about it in case he was the mole.

'The simple fact is, Gareth,' he said as I hurtled towards the police station, 'that I need every officer we've got in DIU working on this or I would just take all their phones and shut them in a room for the day, but I can't do that. Besides, we need to know who it is.'

I thought through the possibilities as we neared the nick, discarding them one by one. Rudd was too passionate about his work for it to be him; Eddie was too bad at lying to hide anything that big. Tate had been a police officer for too many years and was too well known for us not to hear if it was him, the same for Kev.

One of the things that I feel keeps so many officers straight, apart from their dedication to duty, of course, is that in a place like Brighton everyone shits on everyone else. It's only a matter of time before you get caught if you step outside the rules. Unless, like me, you don't tell anyone.

Ralphy hated Davey; in fact I'd even had to pull them apart before when they went at it during a job, and no one else in the office sprang to mind either. So who was it?

My head hurt too much to let me think about it properly, and anyway, how do you decide which one of your friends is most likely to have betrayed you?

My driver dropped me at the station, and I took the newly fixed lift up to the fourth floor, not having the energy to climb the stairs. When I entered the briefing room, Pearson was already standing at the front, chatting to Chief Inspector Lawrence Tyson who looked equally tired.

A few people looked up as I entered the room and I heard exclamations of surprise as they saw my battered face. I tried to spot whether any of them were a little *too* surprised, but no one leapt out as suspicious. The room was full of plain-clothed officers from DIU and CID and a couple I recognized from MCB (Major Crime Branch), with the odd uniform dotted here and there.

Tate, Rudd and Eddie were all sitting together and they shuffled up to make room on the end of their row, placing me on the outside next to Tate.

'Hard night?' he asked, eyeing me.

'Yeah, you could say that. Hopefully, though, today will be payback.'

He raised an eyebrow at me but I refused to be drawn out, instead catching Pearson's eye and nodding at him. He nodded back and cleared his throat, getting the attention of everyone immediately.

'Good morning, ladies and gentlemen. The reason you've all been called in early is that last night, the same person who kidnapped PC Holdsworth also took PC Bell.' He paused while people looked at me and whispers ran among the throng.

'PC Bell managed to get away, but unfortunately he was unable to identify a location for us. The only thing we know is that it is within an hour's drive of Brighton and is likely somewhere to the north, perhaps as far as the Surrey border.' He paused here and looked around the room.

'We now know that PC Holdsworth is likely to be killed by midnight if we don't find him and get him back, so today is going to be a massive effort for everyone. Your taskings will be given to your sergeants, but don't expect to be seeing your homes or loved ones for a good twenty-four hours. Can DIU officers please stay behind? Everyone else, thank you and good hunting.'

As people filed out, a cough from the front of the room caught my attention. Pearson stood at parade rest, looking extremely uncomfortable and avoiding eye contact with me as he said, 'It has come to my attention while debriefing PC Bell that Davey has someone on his payroll within the DIU office.' He paused to let this sink in and to give the angry muttering a chance to die down.

'Now, I would ask each of you to be extremely vigilant and report anything suspicious to myself, skipping the usual chain of command. I would like to think that it's a member of support staff rather than an officer, but the sad fact is that it is most likely someone within this very room.'

The dozen or so officers looked at each other, and then all of them at me before Pearson spoke again. 'Until we find PC Holdsworth, all of you will be paired up. That means all day, even in the toilet. If you have to take a crap, your partner will search to make sure you don't have a mobile phone on you. Your personal and usual work mobiles will be confiscated and you will be issued with new mobiles for the day.'

The angry muttering rose in volume until the chief super banged his hand on the windowsill to get attention, and when he spoke his voice was hard and unfriendly. 'I don't care if you think I'm treating you like children, and I don't care if you want to take out a grievance after the day is done. Today, my only issue is finding PC Holdsworth and bringing him back alive. Anyone who has a problem with that can consider themselves suspended from duty.'

He glared around the room and no one met his stare.

'Right, good.' He let out a huge breath, sounding calmer. 'I'm sorry it has to be this way, but Jimmy's life is more important than anything else. I also promise you that when we find whoever it is that Davey is paying, well, if it's one of you, you had better come to my office and explain yourself before we find out another way.'

Kev raised his hand and Pearson waved at him to speak. 'I assume the pairing is to be for civilian staff as well?'

'Yes. I'll leave it to you to pick the pairings, Kev, but you also need to have someone with you, too.'

Kev nodded and sat back while Pearson finished off. 'Right, that's about it. Your mobiles will be collected by Kev, and then brought to my office for storage. Any questions?'

I raised my hand, causing him to raise his eyebrows in return. 'Go on.'

I licked my lips nervously. 'Well, sir, it all seems a bit extreme to me; I mean, he'll know by now that I haven't come back, so surely it doesn't make a difference whether he gets told or not?'

I was more than a little annoyed by Pearson letting the cat out of the bag about the mole; the man had no subtlety. I tried to keep the annoyance out of my voice as I asked my question, which I had only put to him to try and divert some of the wrathful looks that officers were throwing my way.

'He may well know that you haven't come back, but he won't know what's happened to you. He certainly won't know for sure that you're back here with us, so every second longer that he doesn't know, we're a second closer to finding Jimmy in one piece.'

I nodded, not really listening to the answer. I was a little worried about Davey's reaction to my disappearance, but guessed that he would keep Jimmy alive as a bargaining tool while he thought I would come back for him on my own. The moment he found out I had gone back to the police, he would kill Jimmy and move on, hiding any evidence of the murder so that it was just my word against his.

I couldn't let that happen, so we had to find out where he was *today* or it was all over.

I looked up as Tate nudged me impatiently, realizing that we had been dismissed. We were stopped at the back of the room and I held my hands out so that the chief inspector collecting the phones could check that I didn't have one.

Kev then paired me off with Rudd, and we walked down the stairs together in silence. My head still hurt abominably and I wasn't much in the mood for conversation, which was just as well, because Rudd didn't seem to be either.

As we trudged into the office, researchers were starting to arrive. Looking at the wall clock, I was surprised to see that it was almost eight o'clock already. I slipped into my chair before most of them saw my battered face and just beat Sally, who was looking annoyed and out of sorts. She sat down without talking to me, and I sighed as I turned around to address the problem, despite the fact that Rudd was there.

'Morning, Sally.'

'Morning, Gareth.' Her voice was frosty and she kept her back to me.

'You'll never guess what happened to me last night,' I tried, hoping for a response.

'I think I have a fair idea,' she replied, angry now and spinning to face me. 'I got your texts, thanks.' The last word faltered as she saw my face, then her expression hardened again. 'Did you slip it up her too hard and she beat you up?'

I shook my head to clear it, unsure if we were having the same

246

conversation. 'Um, excuse me, but I got kidnapped last night by Davey after he and a mate kicked the living shit out of me. He took my phone and he's still got it. Tell me you weren't texting him?'

She looked at Rudd for confirmation, and he nodded, trying hard not to grin as he guessed what was going on between me and Sally.

'Oh God, Gareth, I'm so sorry, but you should see what he sent!'

'Have you deleted them?' I asked, and she shook her head and took her phone out of her bag.

She passed me the phone, gripping my hand as she did so and giving me a look that made up for everything she'd just said. I smiled back and began to read through the texts. Apparently she had sent one first, asking if I wanted to come over and, well, you get the idea, and Davey had sent back:

sorry luv im fukin a fat bitch coz she takes it up the ars. Yor shit in bed.

Sally had then replied, saying:

Very funny, are you coming over or not?

Without any Xs on the end, which I knew meant that she was annoyed.

Davey had then replied:

No, seerously, yor shit in bed fuk of.

'And you really thought this was me?' I asked incredulously.

She shrugged, and I handed the phone back.

The thought of Davey sending Sally texts made me angry. Was there no part of my life he didn't want to tear apart and ruin? Was that why he had kept my phone, I wondered.

I shook my head, wishing that he'd thrown it away instead of using it, and then it hit me. *He had my phone.* I jumped up, scattering paperwork everywhere and began to look around frantically for Kev. Guessing he was still in the briefing I began to run for the stairs.

'Oi, where are you going?' Rudd yelled at me, trying to catch up.

I didn't slow as I called over my shoulder. 'He's got my phone; I know how to find Jimmy!'

37

'Cell-site analysis,' I said, slapping both of my hands on the table next to Kev. After tearing upstairs to find that he'd already left, I'd come back down to find him at his desk tucking into a bowl of cereal while he read through a pile of intelligence reports.

'Come again?' Kev asked, looking startled.

'Davey has been texting Sally from my phone to upset her. If he's still got my phone on, we can track him with cell-site analysis.'

Mobile phones have become one of the best tools for us to find people and I was amazed that none of us had thought about it before. Mobiles regularly send out a signal to the nearest antenna, making sure that they switch to the nearest and most effective mast, and we've got boffins hidden in a basement somewhere who excel at tracking people through these connections.

Kev looked at me for a moment. 'Good idea, but why was he texting Sally to upset her? Oh!' An evil grin lit his face as he worked it out. Kev is a lot of things but slow isn't one of them. 'Well I hope the poor lamb wasn't too upset or you'll have a lot of consoling to do, and you really don't look up to it. If you need my help …'

He was already out of his chair as he spoke and for a moment I thought he was going to rib Sally, but then he paired Rudd up with Tate as his partner for the day and took me up to see Pearson. We barged straight into his office, and he looked up from his computer, clearly a little surprised to see us.

'Gareth has an idea, sir,' Kev said, and I launched into my explanation. I was only halfway through when Pearson picked up his phone and dialled a number from memory.

'Kathy? Hi, it's Derek Pearson here. I need an urgent cell-site done for the job with the missing officer. That's right. No, there isn't any paperwork yet. NO, you get your man over here, and the paperwork will be completed when we have a chance. I don't care; a man's life is at stake. Oh, we have the owner of the phone's permission, does that make a difference? It does? Oh good, I'll pass you over and you can get started.'

He looked up at me and held the phone across the desk. 'Here you go, they'll need your number and network.'

I took the phone and gave the necessary details over, and was assured that there would be a result for me within minutes. I hung up the phone and looked at Kev. 'A few minutes, they reckon. Should we start gearing up?'

Pearson held up a hand. 'Hang on, we'll need firearms in on this; we've already had two incidents with these chaps having weapons and I'm not about to go off half cocked.'

I started to protest but he talked over me.

'There's no point getting PC Holdsworth back and losing other officers in the process. Not when it can be done properly.'

I nodded, knowing he was right but wanting to be doing something, anything, now that we were so close to finding Jimmy and getting this whole ordeal over and done with. 'You're right, sir. I'm sorry.'

He nodded and ushered us out, promising to come straight down when he received a phone call from the telecoms unit.

Kev and I rushed back downstairs, and he called every officer into the inspector's office. We could barely move once everybody was in and several of us had to slide out of the way to close the door while Kev explained the situation. 'So,' he concluded, 'we're going to be ready to put teams into the area once we have a location, just to observe and locate, not do anything stupid. Ding says he saw the outside of the farmhouse, so we should be able to identify it almost immediately as long as there aren't dozens.'

Rudd piped up. 'There shouldn't be, cell-site normally gets it down to about a hundred metres.'

Kev nodded. 'Yup, so hopefully we won't even be needed, but in rural areas it can stretch up to a couple of miles and that's a lot of ground to cover.' He kicked us all out, and I swear the swivelling of heads in the office was actually audible as Pearson walked into the room.

He motioned myself and Kev back into the office. We followed him in, closing the door and ignoring the curious looks we were getting through the windows. 'South Godstone,' Pearson said, taking the only chair.

'Where's that?' Kev asked, looking at the map of Sussex hanging on the wall.

'It's in Surrey, not far from Redhill. The tech chap says that it's the closest antenna that the phone is pinging, but it's also hitting another couple further out at Oxted and Edenbridge, so he thinks there are a good few square miles to cover. I will speak to my opposite numbers in Surrey, and in Kent. This could end up in either county. How quickly can you get your officers out there looking?'

Kev glanced through the window and made the hand signal for 'kit up', pulling his fists together across his chest. There was a flurry of activity as all the officers began putting on their covert gear. 'About five minutes. We'll travel in pairs, sir, we'll cover more ground like that than with full cars. We'll be on B-Div-Events-Gen6,' he said, giving the superintendent the radio channel we would be working on.

Pearson stood, holding out his hand for us both to shake. 'Good luck. Wish I was going with you, but I'm briefing the firearms team in half an hour and I won't make you wait.'

We both smiled, catching each other's eye as we left. While Pearson is a good senior officer, it was rare to see him anywhere other than behind a desk and rumour has it that he quite likes it that way. Personally, I would have chewed my own arm off to get away from a desk job, but luckily most of my time was spent out and about, so I didn't need to worry about that yet.

Just before we left, Pearson called Kev and insisted that he and Rudd stay behind too, to help with the briefing – Rudd is firearms liaison for the office – and instead I partnered up with Tate who was as eager as I was to get out and looking for Jimmy.

We had been given instructions to search the area, given maps that had been divided into grids by Sally so that we wouldn't just be searching blind.

The tech chap from the telecoms unit had promised to keep checking and would update us if the phone moved or was switched off, so we left with high hopes of bringing Jimmy back in one piece, even if Davey got wind of us and decided to move him. Despite our care, there was still a chance that the mole had tipped him off, and we were no closer to discovering the identity than we had been first thing that morning.

38

By the time we got to the village of South Godstone, the clock on the dash said that it was 09.32. The day was cloudy but hot already, and it was nice to be driving through country lanes instead of the main road. I'd opened my window and the fresh smells of summer woodland floated into the car on the light breeze as Tate drove through the pleasant morning. Our conversation had been limited, partly due to the nervousness that we both seemed to share and partly because of the unease of knowing that someone on the team was working for the man we were trying to find.

Tate could pretty much rule me out unless I'd cut myself up for show, and I could rule him out unless I was a worse judge of character than I thought I was. There were few people more solid or dependable in the office and he had saved me from being badly hurt on more than one occasion.

'Our map says we should go east and cover the area out towards Crowhurst,' Tate said, breaking the silence.

'Yeah, it's that road,' I said, pointing to a small lane with a half-concealed road sign in white.

He obligingly turned into the lane, and I slid my window up as branches from the steep verge whipped into the car and clawed at my face.

The sun peeked out from behind the clouds, turning everything golden for a moment but, instead of making me feel happy as it usually did, it made me think of Jimmy, lying alone in that room, stinking of infection and his own mess. I silently vowed that when we found Davey, I would make him regret every moment of pain and hurt he had given Jimmy, paying him back a thousandfold. Of course I would have to find a way to do it through a full armed assault team, but I was sure I would think of something. If not, all sorts of accidents could happen to a man in prison. I'd stopped that thought almost as soon as I had it. Just because I had stepped outside the law once didn't mean that I should ever let myself do it again. That way lay madness.

I could only hope that Davey wouldn't spill the whole story if caught, hoping that he would still be able to get his drugs back if he kept quiet, but at that moment I wouldn't have put it past him to tell everything and take the heat so that I would go down with him. As we drove along the lane, looking for any side turnings that would lead to a farmhouse, I ran through in my mind any evidence that he might be able to use to get me in front of a court.

He could get the Budds to identify me as the person who had attacked them and stolen their heroin, but not only would that mean them admitting possession and doing time themselves, their evidence would be viewed with suspicion as they worked for Davey.

Other than that, he had nothing – but what little he had was probably enough to ruin me. Thinking about it though, I couldn't bring myself to care as long as we got Jimmy back in one piece.

'So how long you been shagging Sally then?' Tate asked, disrupting my chain of thought.

I looked at him sharply, a little annoyed at his choice of words. 'We're not *shagging*, we're seeing each other,' I replied, not bothering to hide my annoyance.

'Oh, I'm sorry,' he said, sounding anything but, 'so she hasn't let you shag her yet then?'

'Of course she has … You git!' So much for me keeping the details of our relationship quiet.

Tate smirked. 'Come on, mate, I know you may be *seeing* each other and obviously, being a gentleman, you won't want to talk about it, but how did a scruffy oik like you manage to charm your way into the bed of someone like Sally?' I heard a hint of wistfulness in his tone that I had never heard in Tate before. Usually he was quiet and workmanlike, rarely involving himself in conversations that didn't concern the job.

I looked out of the window as I spoke, hoping to catch a glimpse of something that looked familiar. 'She got stood up by one of her string of idiots and I offered to take her out to dinner. She said yes and we got on really well, far better than I'd hoped or expected, to be honest.'

'So it's true that women don't always go for looks then?'

'Shut up and drive.'

A little over an hour later we had almost finished our area, having checked out three farmhouses that weren't at all familiar, and my pencil scratchings covered most of our area of the map.

'There,' I said, pointing to an overgrown driveway that showed recent signs of use, the plants overhanging the road bent and torn by vehicles.

Tate pulled over a little way down the road, and we scrambled up a bank and into a field, making sure to stay close to the hedgerows to stay out of sight of any buildings we might find. We jogged along the edge of the field and through a clump of trees, coming eventually to a rutted farm track that turned sharply to the left and disappeared down a dip before rising again and heading off towards a group of buildings in the distance.

I looked at Tate, who shrugged, and we began to jog along the dried mud of the track, slipping occasionally and adding to the build-up of mud that already caked our shoes and the bottom of our jeans. After we had gone less than a quarter of the distance, my wind ran out, proof that I was far from being healed after my ordeal. I walked along for a bit with Tate hovering worriedly over me like a mother hen.

'Leave it, Tate, I'll be fine, I just need to get my breath back.'

He nodded and moved away, then called up over his radio as we should have done when we stopped. 'Kev from Tate, receiving?' he asked, but I only heard it out loud rather than in my earpiece.

'You're not coming through,' I said. 'Let me try.'

'Kev from Ding, receiving?' I shook my head. 'Nothing. We must be in a dead spot.'

Tate fumbled his radio out of its concealed holder and looked at it. 'Dead,' he said with disgust.

'Did you have GPS on?' I asked.

'How do you tell if you do?' he replied.

'Let's have a look.'

He tossed me his radio.

I tried turning it on, a process that is harder than it should be, and discovered that he was right. It was totally dead. 'Can you get mine out?' I asked.

'Sure, stand still a minute.'

He managed to free my radio from where I had hidden it in the small of my back, passing it to me.

I checked it and it showed a signal bar of one, which is about as good as using two cups and a piece of string. 'Bollocks. Should we go back to the car and update with the mobile set?'

Tate looked at how far we had come and shook his head. 'Nah, let's just check this out and get it over and done with, then we can get back and report in.'

I nodded, turning to let him put my radio back in its holder before we continued to walk down the track, my head aching more and more with every step. Finally, we reached the end of the track and it became a mixture of concrete and gravel. We edged forward carefully with me in the lead, being the one who would recognize it if it was the right place. The yard came into view and I felt a thrill of excitement as I realized that it was indeed the house that I had left only a few hours before.

'This is it!' I whispered to Tate, turning to share the news.

'I know,' he whispered back, and the world went dark.

39

I woke to the taste of blood in my mouth and the sound of two men arguing. My head felt as if it was about to split open, and as I tried to raise a hand to feel a particularly tender spot on the back I found that once again my hands were tied.

Suddenly the memory came back, and I cursed as I realized that Tate must be the mole.

I was in a different room this time, this one with a window that spilled the morning sunlight across mouldy walls that were too grimy to make out the colour of the wallpaper. The room smelled damp and musty, but at least this time I hadn't added the smell of my own piss to the mix.

Depression wrapped me in its miserable embrace as I thought about my situation. Davey would now know about the phone and switch it off, leaving the others with no clue as to our location. I was so upset by Tate's betrayal that I couldn't even muster up a single spark of anger, instead berating myself for being too trusting. I had always prided myself on being a good judge of character, but here I was lying on a bare wooden floor with my hands tied up tightly enough to cut off the circulation to prove that my trust had been misplaced. I tried to wriggle around so that I could see the rest of the room, but the movement made my head spin and I was almost sick. I laid my head down carefully, recognizing the effects of concussion, and wondered what Tate had hit me with. Lying there with nothing better to do, I closed my eyes and focused on the argument, slowly beginning to make out the two individual voices as Tate and Davey, both sounding tense and angry.

'… we're screwed. He knows it's me now, there's no way we can let him go back, but I can't let you kill him either. He's my friend for Christ's sake!'

'You should have thought of that before you let me clear up your gambling debts. Look, don't worry, we'll sort something out.'

'Oh yeah, like what?'

'I don't know, maybe we can make it look like he was the one who was working for me?'

'Don't be daft; they all saw the state of him. Anyway, what about you? They all know it was you now, so you're done too.'

'Don't you worry about me; I've got houses in three different countries and enough money to keep me comfy for a while. I can't stand the weather here anyway.'

'Oh I see, so you're just going to piss off and leave me in the firing line, is that it?'

Silence, then Davey's voice, threatening and low. 'If you'd done what I asked you and kept them off my back in the first place, none of this would have happened. I told you I needed to be left alone that day and instead you turn up with the whole lot and jump me. You may as well have stabbed that bloke yourself. All this blood is on your hands and don't you forget it!'

Tate's voice lowered so that I had to strain to hear it. 'Hang on; I swapped that knife for you, didn't I? I risked my job, my freedom, everything. And now you accuse me of not doing what you ask me? Are you crazy? I work my—'

There was a shout then the sounds of a scuffle as pots and pans banged below, making me guess that they were in the kitchen.

259

The fight went on for a few seconds, then I heard Tate cry out and the noise ceased.

'That's right, you forgot I always carry a knife. Don't you ever call me crazy again or I'll cut your fucking ears off.'

'All right, all right, I'm sorry. Let's just get this over and done with and I'll think of something to tell them. Maybe I can say we were both jumped and they killed him but I managed to get away. I've got the wounds to prove it now.'

Davey laughed. 'You're cleverer than you look. Grab the others and we'll go and find out where your man is hiding my gear, then I can start up again, keep my suppliers from cutting my throat and sod off to Portugal.'

I heard footsteps and a door slam and waited in silence, feeling numb after what I had heard. Tate was doing this because he owed Davey *money*? Since when did money count more than friendship, or loyalty or even honour? I was saddened by the betrayal in a way I can't explain, and as I lay there waiting for them to come and finish it, finally, the anger came back. How dare he? How *dare* he do this over money? I freely admit that I had started the events of that last week by doing over the Budds, but at least I was fighting for the right reasons. I was trying to make my city safer and get some justice for what had happened to Jimmy, never mind the fact that it had nearly got him killed. But Tate, he was doing it because of a debt, and that made him so dirty that I wanted to wash myself until the stink of sitting next to him in the car was gone. What hurt the worst, though, was the fact that he had swapped the evidence so that Davey could get away with stabbing Jimmy. He'd crossed the line and there was no way I would let him get away with it. I decided then that no matter what else happened, I would find a way to drag him to PSD in cuffs and give him over willingly.

My plotting was interrupted by the creak of a door opening somewhere below me followed by the sounds of several sets of footsteps on the stairs. Moments later, I heard the door to my room open and four pairs of legs walked into view.

Tate leaned over and hauled me upright, refusing to look me in the eye. He stepped back as if he could feel the heat of my anger, and I found myself looking at Davey and the two Budd brothers, one still in a cast and looking as if he wanted payback. The double-barrelled side-by-side shotgun one of them was carrying reinforced this image, and for the first time since I had awoken, real fear took root deep inside me and I began to tremble.

Davey crouched down, careful to stay out of range. 'Well well, lookie here. And I thought you weren't going to come back.'

I forced myself to meet his gaze, drawing on the anger that still lurked behind the fear as if using it for a shield. 'I haven't got time to play games with you, Davey, so say what you have to say and either kill me or get out.'

He laughed the grating laugh that made my head hurt and pulled his knife from inside his jacket. 'What I've got to say, *Gareth*, is best said with a little dose of pain to help the truth along.'

I looked at the blade, trying to force back the memory of how much it had hurt when he had cut my arm. 'That won't help you; I'll bite my tongue off before I tell you where the drugs are.'

He took a step forward, moving too rapidly for me to do more than blink as he seized my jaw with his left hand, the fingers digging painfully into my face.

'You won't do that, because if you do I'll go and find your girlfriend before I leave and take the money those drugs cost me out of her pretty little arse, get me?'

I couldn't disguise the fear in my eyes as I thought of this psychopath going anywhere near Sally. 'You touch her and you're dead,' I blustered, knowing how weak the threat was, even before he laughed.

'I'll tell you what, being the good employer that I am, I've promised my lads here that they can have a bit of quality time with you, kind of payback, like. I'm going to give them a few minutes, and all the while I want you to be thinking about Tate here giving me your girlfriend's address. Maybe when I come back you'll have something to tell me.'

I looked up at Tate who was staring fixedly at a point on the wall above my head. 'You can't do this, Simon, don't let this psycho near Sally.'

Tate looked down at me for a moment, his eyes radiating pain, then they hardened again and he walked away, leaving me with the two grinning brothers who owed me payback.

40

If it had been a Bond film the brothers would have placed the shotgun down within easy reach and wandered off to get some tools to hurt me with, but sadly it was real life and Dave carefully placed the weapon in the far corner of the room before returning and rolling up his sleeves.

Billy stood over me and began to undo his flies but Dave stopped him with a hand to the chest. 'What the fuck you doing?'

'I'm gonna piss on 'im, ent I?'

'Not before I've punched the shit out of him yer not. I don't want my hands covered in your piss!'

'Oh, yeah. Good thinking.'

He zipped back up again and leaned down to breathe his stinking breath in my face. 'I owe you. I'm gonna make you squeal like a pig!' They both laughed at his ever-so-clever joke, then Billy pulled back a foot to kick me in the face.

I knew that I would probably not survive the beating that these two were about to give me and, to be honest, I wondered if I really deserved to, but my desire for life was too strong and, without realizing what I was doing, I dropped to my side and rolled under the kick, taking Billy's standing leg out from under him. He collapsed in front of me with the breath rushing out of his lungs, and I staggered to my feet in time to dodge backwards as Dave swung a haymaker at my head.

As he came forward, I suddenly reversed my movement and ran towards him, bringing a knee up and connecting with his balls. It was just as satisfying as the first time I'd done it to him, and he collapsed with a shout of pain.

Billy had just managed to get back to his feet as I turned to him, unleashing a roundhouse kick that caught him on the jaw and threw him clear across the room to crack against the wall. His eyes rolled up in his head and he slumped to the floor, clearly unconscious.

The noise downstairs must have been deafening and I heard Davey shout from below. 'Oi, don't kill him, I need him to talk!'

Neither of the brothers was in a fit state to answer but, to give him his credit, Dave was shakily trying to stand, a kitchen knife now clutched in his right hand while the other still cupped his aching balls. He staggered towards me with the knife held low, and as he came close enough I spun into a kick called the tiger whips its tail, which I'd never been able to do properly in training, but that day it seemed exactly the right thing to do.

I spun in a circle, allowing my left leg to arch out backwards up and over my shoulder as I turned, hitting Dave in the face so hard that I actually heard his jaw crack. He fell to the floor, unconscious before he hit the boards.

Gasping for breath from the sudden exertion, I waddled over and managed to pick up the knife with my bound hands, cutting myself several times but eventually getting the rope as well.

Ignoring the pain from the new cuts to my wrists that mingled with the agony in my head, I picked up the shotgun and broke the barrels, making sure that it was loaded. Seeing the cartridges inside I snapped it shut again and opened the door, intent on going down to the kitchen and finishing this once and for all.

I moved down the stairs carefully, trying not to make too much noise, but the old house gave me away and the wood creaked and groaned under my weight.

'You finished already?' Davey asked as I walked into the kitchen, shotgun first.

'Not yet, but I'm about to,' I replied, and was gratified to see them both swing round from where they were sitting at the kitchen table, jaws hanging open.

'Now, there's no need to be hasty,' Davey said, standing and beginning to back away.

'I haven't been hasty; I've been anything but. If I'd been hasty, this whole thing would have been dealt with long ago and you'd be dead or behind bars.'

Tate stood as well, edging towards the far door.

'I wouldn't bother going that way,' I said, motioning with the shotgun. 'That only leads to the cellar. Believe me, I have first-hand experience.'

Tate raised his hands in submission and as he did a flicker of movement warned me, giving me time to duck the knife that Davey threw at my head. I spun to cover him, my finger already on the trigger but Tate lunged at me, grabbing hold of the end of the barrels. He tried to pull instead of push, and I felt my finger depress the trigger at the same time as he heard it, his mouth a wide 'O' of surprise as the first barrel fired, throwing him backwards across the kitchen with most of his stomach hanging out.

Blood and gore splattered everywhere, and I froze in shock, my mind trying to take in what had just happened. While I stood there staring at the insides of someone I used to call a friend, Davey threw himself at me, going wide of the barrel and pinning it to my body with his. His eyes were wide, almost ecstatic as we fought, our grunts and moans sounding like a horrible parody of lovemaking.

I was bigger and stronger than my opponent but I was also badly hurt, and after a few moments he began to get the better of me, throwing tight punches into my ribs and stomach while I frantically tried to keep control of the weapon. He stopped punching, instead grabbing my legs and trying to haul me off my feet, but I countered and ended up on top of him on the floor, grateful for the soft landing.

I jammed the top edge of the barrel under his chin and used my weight to force the metal down onto his windpipe, choking him and crushing his larynx. Wounded as I was, I wasn't fast enough to stop the knee that he drove into my privates, and my world erupted in pain as I howled and rolled off him.

Before I could recover, Davey was up and out of the door, not even pausing to kick me on the way out. I struggled to my feet, sore and angry, and heard a car start outside. I raced for the door and got there in time to see him driving a Jaguar XJS, wheels spinning in his haste to get away. Without thinking I raised the shotgun to my shoulder and fired, shattering the back window and peppering the smooth paintwork around the boot with buckshot.

I heard a cry at the same time but if I had managed to hit him, he was still healthy enough to scream off down the driveway and out of sight.

Suddenly drained and feeling sick, I returned to the kitchen to see if Tate was still alive.

41

The smell of Tate's blood and guts filled the room like a butcher's shop first thing in the morning. I dropped the gun on the table and walked over to where he lay slumped against the Aga, trying not to slip in the bloody slime that coated the floor.

I bent down to take his pulse and jumped when his eyes flicked open, staring at me in obvious agony. 'Okay, Tate, I'm going to get you an ambulance. Just try not to move.'

I looked at the mess the shot had made of his stomach and grimaced, forcing myself not to turn away and vomit. One whole side of his torso from groin to ribs on the left was missing, his guts and intestines hanging out and pumping a steady flow of blood. From somewhere deep inside an artery was spurting in an ever-lessening arc as he bled out. I didn't need medic training to know that his remaining life was measured in minutes.

He tried to speak, grabbing my arm with a blood-soaked hand and, despite his betrayal, I felt tears gather in my eyes and flood down my cheeks as I realized what I had done.

'Shh, don't try and talk. I'm so sorry, Simon, but you grabbed the gun. I wasn't going to shoot you, just him.' I didn't know if it was a lie or not, but he clumsily patted my arm as his eyes began to dim.

'Sorry,' he mumbled, blood spilling out of his mouth and staining his chin.

'There's no need to be sorry,' I said, squeezing his arm. 'It's all over now.'

His eyes sharpened for a second and he grabbed my hand so hard that I winced. 'No,' he said, speaking slowly so that I could understand, 'I ... gave ... him ... Sally.'

My compassion drained away as the words hit me. 'You gave him Sally? You told him where she lives?'

He nodded, sagging back now that his message was given.

I stood, fists clenching in anger. 'You arsehole, I hope you rot in hell!'

He waved a hand up at me as if to apologize but I kicked it away.

'No, you die damned, you die *fucking damned*!' I shouted, turning and running for the yard, before a sudden thought brought me up short. *Jimmy*.

I raced up the stairs, taking them two at a time with all thoughts of pain forgotten. My hands reached for my radio even as I realized they must have taken it. Seeing the room that they'd taken me to last time, I kicked the door open and almost cried with relief as I saw that he was still there. 'Jimmy, Jimmy mate, I've come to get you out of here.'

I shook him gently and he murmured something before a coughing fit racked him, each cough making him scream with pain. I stopped for a second, trying to find a way to get Jimmy out and save Sally from Davey, but my thoughts kept going in circles.

Exhausted and hurt as I was, I almost missed the noise coming from the room I'd woken up in. I got to my feet and crossed the landing to see Billy trying to push himself up, a pistol halfway out of a shoulder holster. I ran over to him before he could draw, kicking him in the face again for good measure. His nose split, gushing blood all over him as the weapon fell from his fingers.

I grabbed the pistol and tucked it into the back of my belt, then dragged him over to his brother and bound them both as securely as I could using the cut rope from my wrists and the sleeves from their jackets.

Finally satisfied, I ran downstairs and searched Tate, covering myself in his blood in the process. He moved his arms feebly but I ignored him, refusing to feel anything but hate for the man who had given up his colleague, my girlfriend, to a psychopath with a penchant for cutting people.

I found my radio, car keys and warrant card, all bloody but undamaged. My fingers were trembling as I turned the radio on and waited for it to start up. Miraculously I had a signal, and I turned the dial to the main Brighton channel and pressed my emergency button, taking strange comfort from the horrific blatting noise.

'*Charlie Papa 281, do you need assistance?*' The operator's voice was tense with worry.

'I've got two officers down, one dying from a gunshot wound to the stomach, the other is PC Holdsworth and he needs medical attention urgently. Quentin Davey is arrestable for attempted murder and is currently driving towards Brighton in a green J reg Jaguar XJS from the direction of the Redhill area. I need someone to go and find Sally Carter in DIU and stay with her until he's caught; he's gone after her.'

It was too much for one breath but somehow I managed it. 'Confirm you got my last?'

'*Yes, confirmed, what's your location 281?*'

'We're at a farmhouse somewhere near Crowhurst, in Surrey, I don't know exactly where.'

Another voice came on the radio and I recognized the clipped tones of Chief Superintendent Pearson. '*Gareth, this is Derek Pearson. Is there anymore detail you can give us on your location?*'

I thought for a moment. 'Hang on, I'm going to turn my GPS on, then you can track this handset, right?'

The operator confirmed that they could, and I fiddled with the radio, checking the battery level and seeing that it had just enough charge. 'There, done. Confirm you're getting my location comms?'

'*Confirmed, we're on the phone to Surrey ambulance now.*'

'Roger. I'll leave my radio here, I'm going after Davey.'

Pearson's voice came back on the radio, hard and insistent. '*That's negative, Gareth, you will stay there and wait for backup to arrive. We've just assigned units to look for Sally.*'

'Look for her? What do you mean look for her?'

'*Apparently she had a phone call and left work, something about a problem at home. Don't worry, Gareth, I'm sure she'll be fine.*'

The words fell on deaf ears as I dropped the handset on the blood-spattered table and sprinted out of the house, barely hearing Pearson's angry shouts as I left.

42

I made it back to the car in record time, not stopping once even when my breath ran out, cold fear driving me instead. I nearly broke the key in the lock in my haste and forced myself to slow down, taking a deep breath before I started the car. I turned it around in the tight lane, ignoring the angry honks of a driver trying to get past. As soon as I was travelling back towards Brighton I flicked the switch to turn the sirens and flashers on.

I was probably driving towards my own suspension and dismissal, but none of that mattered as much as making sure that Sally was safe. I was back on the M23 in minutes, breaking every rule in the handbook and nearly crashing more times than I care to count, but I couldn't find it in me to care as I pushed the car to its absolute limit and screamed towards Brighton at a 120 miles per hour.

Traffic flashed past in a blur and I risked taking one hand off the wheel for long enough to turn the car kit on, which was hidden in the glove compartment. The main channel was frantic with units all trying to call up one after the other, assigning themselves to the search for Sally.

One unit came on air and their message made me scream with frustration as drivers, confused by the sirens but barely visible grille lights, refused to get out of my way.

'*Charlie Charlie 102, we've reached the home address and the housemate has told us that a man came to the house and forced his way in, tying her up. When Sally got here he took her; she's not sure where as she was still tied up.*'

Davey couldn't have got there before me, I thought; in fact I was surprised that I hadn't caught him up already. My eyes were constantly scanning for his Jaguar as I sped along. I turned the radio up, hoping for anything that would help me find Sally.

'*Roger 102, confirm the kidnapper was Davey?*'

'*That's a negative, he was an Eastern European, stocky, five foot ten with a scar on his cheek.*'

'*Received, all units, be on the lookout for an Eastern European male, stocky build, five foot ten inches tall, with a scar on his cheek.*'

I tuned out then, knowing that Davey had beaten me again. He had obviously phoned ahead and managed to get one of his men to grab Sally for him. They could be anywhere now. I thumped the steering wheel in frustration, nearly losing control of the car as I did so, and let forth a scream so loud that it hurt my already aching head. I turned the flashers and sirens off; there was no point driving aimlessly round Brighton when he would have her tucked away somewhere, waiting to do whatever it was that his twisted mind would come up with.

As I approached the Bolney turn-off, I glanced at the slip road and saw something out of place. I almost cried with relief when I realized that it was the rear end of a Jaguar with a shattered windscreen just disappearing out of sight. I slammed the brakes on, ignoring the beeps of protest and screeching of tyres from behind me, and reversed back to the slip road. I turned into it and put my foot down again, tearing after the Jaguar.

I caught up as it drove over the other side and back down onto the A23 and realized that he had only turned off to see if he was being followed. I slowed to match the other traffic and tried to drive casual. It worked, or at least it seemed to, and he returned to the main road without doing anything out of the ordinary. I followed, keeping several cars between us for cover, intent on finding out where he was going, as I knew that he would be heading for Sally.

I agonized over whether or not to call comms and let them know that I'd found the vehicle, but I knew if I did, uniform would stop the car and we'd never find Sally, so I stayed off the radio and followed him instead.

We drove along London Road and through Patcham, getting bogged down in traffic before we reached the bottom of Preston Drove. Davey suddenly pulled into the bus lane and up Harrington Road, skipping the traffic and heading towards Surrenden Road at the back of Preston Park. I nosed out carefully, giving him a few seconds to get ahead before I turned into the road and followed him at a safe distance.

This was where it could have got dangerous. If I let the gap widen too much, I would lose him in Brighton's twisting streets, but if I got too close he would notice and take me on a wild goose chase until he lost me. Better the latter than the former though, I thought; at least if he saw me following I could still call other units in. If he lost me, well, my mind shied away from what he would do to Sally if he got hold of her.

He reached the end of the road and turned right. I lost sight of him again as he drove south on Surrenden Road towards the park. I still hadn't regained sight of him by the time I reached the end of the road, and my heart began to flutter wildly as I looked right and left. There was no sign either direction, so the only logical choice was Preston Park Avenue.

I shot across both lanes of traffic, missing another car by inches as I swerved into the road I was aiming for. I breathed a sigh of relief as I saw the Jag pull into a driveway about halfway down and thanked any deity that chose to listen for helping me to make the right choice. I pulled into a space across the road on the edge of the park and killed the engine, taking a moment to breathe before getting out.

Every fibre of me was screaming to get out of the car and race after Davey, but I had to be sure that it wasn't just another test to check that he wasn't being followed. I sat there for a full thirty seconds, my hands gripping the wheel so tightly that I thought it might snap as I ticked the seconds off in my head. Once I had reached thirty, I got out and locked the car, walking along the edge of the park towards the driveway where Davey had parked.

As I got closer I began to worry that he had somehow slipped away, as I couldn't see the car. Could there be some alleyway I didn't know about that was wide enough to drive a car through? I hoped not. I drew level and saw that the driveway disappeared around the side of the Victorian house which appeared from the number of doorbells to be split into flats.

Taking a risk, I crossed the road and crunched as quietly as I could up the gravel to the rear of the house, peering around the corner first and being rewarded by the sight of the battered Jag sitting all alone, the engine still ticking as it cooled.

He hadn't come back round to the front and there was a twelve-foot wall guarding the rear and sides of the car park, so I turned my attention instead to the back of the building, which had two private entrances nestled next to each other: '31g' and '31f' – Davey must be in one of them, I figured. Presumably Sally and her captor too, but which one?

I could hardly knock and ask if they were in, as I suspected that my only answer would be a shotgun through the letterbox.

I was uncomfortably aware of the solid weight of the pistol tucked into the back of my waistband and wished that I had left it in the car. If I used it, no matter if it was in selfdefence, I would be screwed as I had brought the weapon with me. I put it firmly out of my mind for now, needing instead to concentrate on finding out which flat was my target. I stood on the corner for what felt like an age, then finally an idea came to me.

I went back to the front of the building and climbed the steps to the multi-occupancy buzzer and pressed the tradesmen's button. The door obligingly clicked open and I went inside, finding the thing I was looking for – a shelf full of post. It was a matter of moments to find post for both of the flats at the back. I've never been into a block of flats where the post always got delivered to the right door and this place was clearly no exception. The tenant of flat 'f' was a Ms Dawson, which was no help whatsoever, but flat 'g' was apparently occupied by one Mr Lek Mierza. *Bingo*.

I recognized the name. He was freelance Polish muscle; for some time prior, he'd been rumoured to be working for Davey; so, I figured, he must have grabbed Sally and brought her back here knowing that all of Davey's properties would be watched.

I jogged down the steps and around to the back again, making and discarding plans as I went and finally settling for the simplest option. I didn't stop as I reached the corner but ploughed on and hit the door to the flat at full tilt, almost breaking it off its hinges in my haste to get inside and save Sally.

43

The corridor inside was neat, with nothing to impede my progress as I ran down it and towards the rooms at the back where the only three doors were clustered. The middle one was slightly ajar, so I took that first, kicking it open and covering the room with the pistol that I had drawn as soon as I was out of public view. It was a bedroom, and quite empty, other than a bed and a canvas wardrobe that was stuffed full of clothes.

As I came back out, I hesitated for a second and then kicked the one to the right open to reveal a kitchen that was smaller than my bathroom at home, but just as neat. Either this guy rarely stayed here or he had OCD.

That left the final door, along with the problem that I had made so much noise going in that they had to know I was there and would be waiting for me. At least I knew they couldn't have got out the back way though, as the flat was in the basement and there would be no other exit.

I stood in front of the door for a moment, trying to listen around my heavy breathing but couldn't hear anything, so I very carefully flicked the handle down and pushed the door open with my toe, standing well to one side. I was glad that I had, as a samurai sword, probably a replica but still looking more than dangerous enough, was thrust through the space that I had recently been occupying.

It was followed by an arm clad in black leather, and I swung around the frame and into the room to see the hulking form of Lek at the other end of the arm, wearing his trademark black leather thigh-length coat and a calm, businesslike expression on his battered face. I wrapped my left arm around the one holding the sword and pulled backwards sharply, trying to snap the elbow. He dropped the sword, however, and that gave him enough leverage to grab me with his other hand and pull me into the room which contained a small sofa where Davey was holding on to a terrified-looking Sally, who was handcuffed and had black gaffer tape over her mouth.

I didn't have time for more than a glance before Lek threw me up against the wall, the plasterboard groaning under the impact. I shouted in pain, my vision suddenly exploding into a riot of colours as I struggled grimly to bring my pistol up to point at his face in an effort to stop the fight before he won. He saw the movement and let go of me with his left hand long enough to savagely chop at my wrist, making my fingers spasm and release the gun. It fell to the floor with a thud, and he punched me hard in the face, almost making me pass out as I heard Davey's laugh in the background, clearly enjoying the spectacle.

The laugh brought me back from the edge, and I lifted my right hand, fingers hooked like claws as I dug them hard into Lek's left eye. He screamed but I kept the pressure up, driving him backwards across the room as he made a grab for my fingers with both hands. I brought my knees up one at a time, over and over, driving them hard into his unprotected groin and stomach and he sagged against the wall, yelling with every strike that thumped into him. As a finisher, I chopped my elbow into his jaw, satisfied as I saw his eyes roll up into his head.

He hadn't even hit the floor when I was turning, heading back for the weapon, but Davey already stood there, pistol held in his fist and an evil grin lighting up his face. 'Clever chap, you managed to find me. Shame you couldn't stop me though, as I'm gonna have a bit of fun with your bird. Hope she likes it up the arse, cos if she doesn't she's in for a bit of an eye-opener!'

I growled low in my throat and moved towards him. The pistol went off and the sound alone was enough to deafen me. It was a few moments before the pain in the top of my left arm registered, and I looked down in shock to see a spreading crimson stain on my sleeve. At the same moment my knees gave out and I sank to the floor, my head suddenly light and woozy. I could faintly hear Sally screaming behind her gag, but my entire focus was on Davey.

He was advancing across the floor with the pistol held out in front of him, still smoking slightly and wafting the scent of cordite around. 'Hah,' Davey chuckled, 'I never shot anyone before, I like it. Not as much as cutting, but it's not bad.'

I looked up at him, trying to muster my strength for one last heroic effort, but it had gone and I just stared at him, trying to work out how not to die. I wasn't coming up with many ideas. He stopped a few feet away and brought the pistol down so that it was pointing right at my eye. And it may have been my imagination but I thought I could see the bullet with my name on it glinting in the darkness of the barrel.

'Anything you want to tell me before I pull the trigger?' he asked, rubbing his groin with his left hand as if he was getting off on the power.

'Yeah, now I know why they call you Cunting Davey,' I growled, using the nickname that no one ever called him to his face. I was too weak to do anything useful and my only hope was that I would make him mad enough to kill me before he made me watch what he was going to do to Sally.

A look of anger crossed his face, and he jabbed the barrel of the pistol into my forehead. 'No one calls me that, you piece of shit, no one!'

I feebly batted at his hand but he kicked me in the chest and I fell over backwards on top of Lek, who was still out for the count. I looked up at Davey again, seeing his face red and his eyes bulging. At any other time I would have laughed to see him so angry, but hilarity was the last thing on my mind as I prepared to meet up with Tate in the hell they reserve for coppers.

Davey took a deep breath, calming himself with more self-control than I'd given him credit for, before he leaned in close again. 'I just want you to know, before you go, that this is all your fault. Just a little reminder that everything I do to Goldilocks over there, every little squirm and whimper, is down to you. Just think about that.'

He raised the pistol, pointing it at my face. I saw his finger whiten as it pressed on the trigger. I squeezed my eyes shut, unable to watch as he killed me, and I jerked as the gun went off, followed by an *oof!* and a thud as Davey fell into me.

My eyes flew open and I saw Sally lying on Davey's legs, still bound and gagged. She had managed to get off the sofa while he was distracted and trip him as he fired. Her determination gave me new strength and I grabbed Davey by the throat as he struggled to point the pistol at me.

I grabbed his gun hand with my left and forced him onto his back, the pistol held tight against the floor as I choked the life out of him with my free hand, fingers digging into the soft flesh and hooking together behind the trachea.

His face went red and his eyes bulged as he struggled for breath, and he kept trying to raise the pistol but I kept squeezing, putting all my anger and frustration into the grip as his feet began to drum against the floor. With a final roar, I pushed down with all my weight and heard a crack from his throat as something small but vital broke. With a last cough, he died, the light fading from his eyes as I watched.

I rolled off him, removing the pistol from his still twitching fingers just in case, and then pulled the tape from Sally's mouth, somehow numb to the fact that I had just taken another human life. It was as though I had placed my feelings in a box somewhere and hidden that box away, to be dealt with later when the pain wasn't demanding so much of my attention.

'Oh God, Gareth, he shot you, he was going to rape me, oh shit, oh shit, you're bleeding, you need help!' she blurted as she sat there shaking.

I managed to get my warrant card out and find my spare handcuff key, fumbling a few times as feeling began to leach from my injured arm. I got the cuffs off of her, then I lay back and let the pain wash over me, gritting my teeth so that I didn't cry out.

Sally gently began to check me for injuries and I roared in pain as her hand hit the bullet wound that burned in my left bicep. She immediately grabbed a tablecloth, pushing it firmly against the wound to stem the bleeding. She pulled my right hand across and clamped it over the cloth to hold it in place as she searched for her bag, found it and pulled out her phone, still sobbing quietly as I just stared at her. I wanted to say something, to take her in my arms and reassure her, but it was all I could do to stay awake. I only vaguely remember all of this, as repeated beatings and blood loss were taking their toll, and by the time the cavalry arrived I was fast heading towards unconsciousness, unable to feel anything other than relief as paramedics placed an oxygen mask over my face and eased me onto a stretcher while I slipped into the welcome darkness.

44

I came round in a private hospital room, with the bulldog features of Steve Barnett hovering over me. 'Are you awake, Gareth?' he asked, and I ignored him while I did a mental checklist.

My arm still hurt like hell and my head was throbbing but, other than that, I felt remarkably unharmed. I tried to turn my head to look at Barnett but found myself restricted by a neck collar. 'What?' I managed, before coughing hard enough to make me want to pass out again.

Barnett leaned over me with a look of concern on his face. 'Look, Gareth, I'm really sorry I have to do this to you.'

My addled brain was confused. *Surely this man hated me, why was he being nice all of a sudden?* 'Do what?'

He took a deep breath. 'Tell you that you're under arrest for the murders of Simon Tate and Quentin Davey. You don't have to say anything, but it may harm your defence if you do not mention, when questioned, something which you later rely on in court. Anything you do say may be given in evidence.' He sat back, looking more than a little uncomfortable. 'I'm sorry. I know it's the last thing you need right now but I got told to arrest you as soon as you were awake enough to understand.'

'How's Jimmy?' I asked, unable to care about anything else.

Another voice, this one deep and gruff, cut across the room

and made Barnett curse under his breath. 'Jimmy's fine; they're treating him now and they think he'll make a full recovery. DC Barnett, can you do me a favour and piss off before I kick you out myself?'

I turned my head to see Derek Pearson standing in the doorway with a bunch of flowers in his hand and a stern look on his face. Barnett nodded and reached out as if to take my hand for a moment, then pulled his hand away and left the room.

Pearson took his place next to the bed. 'How are you feeling?' he asked, putting the flowers somewhere above my field of vision.

'Like I got beaten shitless and shot. How's Sally?'

'Waiting outside. It was her that called me and told me that Barnett was here. He's been your scene guard since you arrived.'

I hadn't the energy to be surprised, I hurt too much. Instead I asked the question that was preying most on my mind once I knew everyone was safe. 'How much shit am I in?'

Pearson leaned back so that he could make eye contact without me having to crane my neck. 'Some, but not as much as you could be. I just want you to know that I think you did a good job out there, Gareth; all of us think so. Get some rest and we'll speak again soon.'

He smiled as he stood but I could see the lines that recent stress had worn in his face.

'Do you think I'll keep my job?' I asked, needing to know but dreading the answer.

He paused in the doorway, looking back for a moment as if carefully considering the question. 'We'll see,' he said, and the door swung closed.

Epilogue

I woke up groggily from a dream where I had been trying to kick open a door with Jimmy stuck on the other side, bleeding to death, while the wood resisted my frantic efforts. Gradually the banging of my kicks resolved itself into the sound of someone thumping on the door downstairs. Swinging my legs out of bed, I threw on a pair of jeans and staggered down the stairs.

'All right, hang on,' I yelled, fumbling with the lock.

When I eventually got it open Jimmy stood there grinning, looking pale but healthy. I gawped for a moment, surprised to see him. During my two-month suspension and investigation into the Davey case we had been forbidden any contact, as it was felt that we may collude on our evidence to keep each other out of trouble.

'Should you be here?' I asked, glancing up and down the street to make sure no one was watching.

His grin got wider. 'Probably not. You make terrible coffee, but I'm prepared to take the risk. You gonna let me in or just stand there staring at me all morning?'

I stepped back and gestured him inside. I followed him through to the kitchen and began to fiddle with the coffee machine. 'To what do I owe this pleasure then?'

Jimmy perched on the edge of the table and watched me critically. 'How's the arm?'

I flexed it, looking down at the puckered round hole where the bullet had entered. 'Fine most days. I know when it's going to rain though.'

He laughed. 'We live in England, Gareth; it rains every day.'

I passed him a steaming mug and leaned back against the counter. 'So come on. How come you're here?'

He was clearly enjoying my unease but finally relented. 'Good news, fella. You've been cleared of all charges and, pending a medical, you'll be back at work on Monday. Pearson thought you might like to hear it from me.'

I almost dropped my coffee. In the last two months they'd systematically torn apart my life, looking for anything in my story that could point to what had really happened. I'd honestly been convinced that I'd either be out of the job, in prison, or both by the end of summer. I'd been interviewed half a dozen times and had the house searched no fewer than three times. I'd been forbidden contact with anyone from work other than Sally, and only her thanks to the Human Rights Act.

'Really?' I managed.

'Yeah, really. I don't know all the details but Tate's murder has been put down to Davey, and *his* death has been put down to self-defence. He was trying to kill you after all.'

I shook my head in wonder. I'd told the truth about everything except the drugs and the moment in the farmhouse kitchen with Tate, despite the fact that I knew that I was setting myself up for a fall. Somehow I'd managed to slide out from underneath all the charges and come up smelling of roses. I almost pinched myself to make sure that I wasn't still dreaming.

Jimmy caught my eye again, this time looking slightly uncomfortable. 'One thing though, mate, I have to ask. When they had me tied up in that room, I swear I heard them talking about some drugs you'd nicked off the Budds. I wasn't exactly what you'd call with it at the time, so I assumed that I'd misheard.' He left the sentence hanging, not quite a question.

I thought about the drugs hidden in next door's garden. As far as I was concerned they could stay there until they rotted away; I wanted no further part of them in my life. Had I not taken them in the first place, Jimmy would never have been kidnapped, nor would Sally, and I wouldn't have had two months of being slowly torn apart by the investigation.

'Gareth?'

I blinked. 'I'm sorry, mate, I was miles away. You must have misheard them.'

He knew me well enough to know that I was hiding something, but he didn't press me. 'Come on, I owe you a beer.' Jimmy set down his coffee mug and headed towards the front door.

With a final glance out of the window towards where the drugs were hidden, I followed, putting them out of my mind with a final promise to myself that, no matter what happened, I would never step outside the law again.

KILLER READS

DISCOVER THE BEST
IN CRIME AND THRILLER

Follow us on social media to
get to know the team behind
the books, enter exclusive
giveaways, learn about the
latest competitions, hear from
our authors, and lots more:

/KillerReads 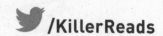 /KillerReads